CW00829683

After Melissa

Also by Judith Jones

Baby Talk (1998)

AFTER MELISSA

Judith Jones

Constable · London

First published in Great Britain 1999
by Constable & Company Limited
3 The Lanchesters, 162 Fulham Palace Road
London W6 9ER
Copyright © Judith Jones 1999
The right of Judith Jones to be
identified as the author of this work
has been asserted by her in accordance
with the Copyright, Designs and Patents Act 1988

ISBN 0 094 79650 5

Set in Palatino 10 pt by
SetSystems Ltd, Saffron Walden, Essex
Printed and bound in Great Britain
by MPG Books Ltd, Bodmin, Cornwall

A CIP catalogue record for this book
is available from the British Library

1

Kerry Lake was an expert, her special area babies and, above all, baby talk. So, she could regard it as a requirement of the job to stand still and do nothing at all when this baby was taken into his car by Titch Raybould and slowly driven away.

Of course she had doubts and almost rushed downstairs to stop it. That would certainly have been possible. Fear for the child seemed to make her legs shaky – feeble in the ankles and knees – but not useless. Kerry might only need to appear, not even say very much. Titch would probably bow out fast. Titch was famed for slipping away from trouble. Titch was non-confrontational.

She convinced herself that to interfere would be a mistake, though, a weakness. Instead, she watched the Saab move off and tried to regard the taking of the child as progress, an investment. If you were the expert in babies and baby talk you grew used to risking babies' lives. You grew used to looking for the brighter side of things, and quite often there was one, and even more than one. Oh, more than quite often.

This would never mean, though, that she could shut off all anxiety, all tenderness, all responsibility. She felt painfully bound to the child and knew the child felt bound to her. This bit, the second bit, was the worst, the bit that reached her strongest. They could not have depended more on each other, she and this child. Kerry had worked to build the relationship. One of her flairs. To hang on now, nicely concealed, as the Saab drew clear – was it a betrayal? Sudden breathlessness and the trembling in her legs, arms and hands said *Yes*, while her brain silently screamed *No, no, no*. You listened to the brain, didn't you, not to the damned ungovernable, sentimental body?

Did you? She wanted to get to her own car and follow the Saab. She had the training, knew how to stay in touch unobserved, close, not too close, ready for sudden accelerations or turn-offs, prepared to jump the lights, and stuff the road ragers.

But there was other training, too. It said, *Stay put*. It said, *Think positive*. It said, *Stop playing momma*. In any case, the Saab would be out of sight and among late afternoon traffic on the main drag by the time she reached her own vehicle. Kerry would not be able to get anywhere near, perhaps not even six or seven behind it. And, suppose she did try to follow . . . Oh, she had the training, but it was still hard to stay unnoticed when car-trailing. If you could see *them* they could see *you*. Raybould was not some sleepy driver on mild terms with the world. He knew what the world could do and that the mirror could help stop it doing it to *him*. Once she was spotted, the whole project might be ruined, would be. So, swallow the risk. She worked to kill the miserable breathlessness and will her way out of the shakes. And, talking of mirrors, thank God there was not one in this room. She knew what her face would look like – like a montage of fish innards. This was not the first time she'd had to lie low and watch and hope.

Her doubts and agonies were natural. The young did depend. Look at animals. How the world restocked itself. It could also be said, though, that adults depended on children. Children offered them one or other of those unmatchable, creative, *positive* roles – fatherhood, motherhood. One day, Kerry might get to know about motherhood.

However, she was not this child's mother, and its baby talk was not infant-to-parent but informant-to-detective. *Stop playing momma*. The baby who talked to her was thirteen years and seven months old with the beginnings of breasts, her name Melissa. In just over two years she'd be at GCSEs. Afternoon wear was a black school skirt, a white school blouse and black school shoes. Her brown-to-auburn hair had been frizzed but was losing it, and hung to just above her shoulders, flayed cardboard style, obscuring half her face while she talked to Raybould in the street and then moved towards his car. Just the same, Kerry had seen she was nervy but smiling, the barmy, arrogant little cow, or skilled, brilliantly brave little trouper. Perhaps she didn't know Kerry was watching. Melissa did glance about a lot, as if expecting to spot someone.

All child informants were known by Kerry and her police workmates as babes or babies, and what they provided as baby talk. There was some affection in the terms, some protective-ness, and some cynicism. Listening to baby talk, sieving it, testing it and recommending whether to act on it was Kerry's corner, not much envied by anyone else. Oh, come on – galloped away from by everyone else. She had never lost a child. In fact, no child run by Kerry had ever even been beaten up that she knew of, and she *would* know. The word would be around. What point in hammering someone as a warning if people did not hear about it?

Kerry's peachy record, plus colleagues' contempt for kid grasses, made the job hers for ever. Other detectives despised them because, although almost all informants lied and doctored and decked their stuff for sale, children by nature lied much more – lied and doctored and decked their stuff as routine and without always seeming to know they did it. Like most kids, informant kids lived a lot of make-believe. They wanted the world to be the way they said it was, and could convince themselves it was, whether or not they were on a high.

'Yes, all right, maybe I can get you info,' Melissa had said on their fifth or sixth meeting. It must have been well on in their acquaintanceship because at first she had loathed the whole notion of grassing. 'You're never going to see no info like this except from me,' she promised at this later get-together. As to GCSEs, she would not sail through the English paper. Or maybe she talked rough because it was the thing to do among her crew. Grammar was for headstones. 'I'm in touch.'

'Oh, yes? Who with, Melissa?'

'Your mates are on my back again. Get them off and I can bring you what you want. That's your special job, yeah? Everybody knows that.'

'I don't want you putting yourself into danger.'

'You care?'

'Of course I do.'

'I can get a meeting.'

'Who with, Melissa?'

'Titch Raybould himself, most likely.'

'Titch doesn't push at schools.'

'Of course he don't, not *personal*. I know that. He got to stay sweet as lavender. He got others to do it for him. But he wants to know the scene – for planning. He wants to know who'll buy. He wants to know which kids' parents might be smart and notice things and start making trouble if they find their kid is on something. Or which kid might go blabbing to the teacher. Titch don't want no tangles like that. He wants to find who to send his dealers to, no bother. This is business.'

'How do you know, Melissa? You've met him before?'

'I know him. One to one, me and Titch.'

'How?'

'This will cost you, mind. Not just getting your mates off of my back, but that as well. Cash. Twenties in a rubber band.'

'We'll see what you come up with.'

'What I come up with.' She repeated the phrase sing-song, as though it was funny, or as though it insulted her and had to be mocked.

'If what you get is any use to us.'

'Cash.'

'Melissa, I don't supply cash so you can spend it on more substance.'

'Substance.' Again that tone, half giggle, half snarl.

'Speed. E. Brown. Whatever.'

'I've told you I'm off it all. Gone natural.'

'I know you've told me.'

'And it's right.'

'OK, it's right.' Kerry had given it back flat, straight, no giggle, no snarl. 'So, you'll let me know when you're going to see him.'

'Why? You want to check I do?'

Absolutely she did. 'No, no. Just to know when I might start getting material from you.'

'Material?'

'Information.'

'So you can draw the cash ready?'

'I'll see what you come up with.'

'You said.'

And this afternoon Kerry secretly watched Melissa to discover whether what she might come up with was better than bullshit, stouter than make-believe. Kerry knew now that it probably was. Melissa could get to him, one to one, as she said.

Would Melissa stay safe, though, and able to tell her more? Always this job's big, obvious agony and terror was that if a kid turned out genuine and talked real insights the kid had to be in peril. You could say the same of all informants. With kids things were worse. They found it hard to think non-stop about danger, or at all. Their carelessness would enrage Kerry sometimes, and was another reason her colleagues left it all to her. They had absorbed that medicine bottle warning, *Keep away from children.*

From the first-floor window Kerry had the back of the Saab in sight until it reached the junction and turned left to join mainstream traffic. As she lost sight of it, she felt more agonisingly than ever that she had abandoned the child. Stupid. Any treachery had happened when Kerry failed to stop Melissa disappearing smug-faced and eager into the Saab, the job written all over her.

2

It had taken a while to recruit Melissa. It took a while to recruit most child informants. There was an art. You went slowly. You had to start from the presumption that this child – any child – would hate the notion of grassing, would probably hate the police, might hate you personally, hair-do to corn plaster. With Melissa it had been all three. Of course you did not use the word grassing, or any of its creepy equivalents such as touting, snouting, narking or even informing. Perhaps *informing* was the worst, in fact. That had the pains of exactitude about it and the starkness of official lingo. The kid herself, himself, might use any one of them, or the lot, insisting, as kids did, on brutal clarity. But you ignored this, kept talking nice wide and worthy generalities, at these early stages. Looking at the possible recruit you had to think you could be looking at a corpse. You were asking a child to volunteer for that. You were levering a child into that.

'I don't know what you think, Melissa, about someone who lives rich and safe by getting young kids hooked, I mean kids down to eleven, ten, even on brown.'

'I don't know kids like that, eleven, ten, who are what you call hooked.'

'I could show you. Do you think people who do that to kids should get away with it, Melissa?'

'Whick kids?'

'Kids like you.'

'I'm not ten or eleven. I'm not hooked.'

'You shoplift. Why? You steal to sell to buy. I'd say that's being hooked.'

'*You'd* say.'

'How much is it costing you? Free fix first time, but not after.'

'It isn't costing me a thing because I don't do it.'

'How much *was* it costing you?'

A standard recruiting dodge, this edgy chat. It allowed a bit of pressure. It was more or less safe. Some kid might be picked up for attempted breaking and entering or shoplifting and the usual thing would be a warning and a word to the parents and the school. Now and then, though, if Kerry was lucky, Harry Bell would agree to let her talk to the child, and for this time he would forget about telling the parents and the school. For this time only. That's where the pressure came from.

Kerry could use the suite at the nick designed for interviews with alleged rape victims, unless they had an alleged rape victim. It was homely and soothing – armchairs, easy-on-the-eye wallpaper not blank cream paint like other interview rooms, watercolours and thick beige carpet. Melissa looked around at it, her face bright with suspicion and resistance when Kerry first showed her in. You could see the child was thinking *Here beginneth the soft soap. Watch thyself.* Perhaps she guessed what the suite's main function was. She might know girls who had been brought here after an attack and who had described the suite for her. She sat upright all the time in one of the easy chairs, eyes sharp, shoulders stiff, no relaxing. In a rape suite she was not going to get herself seduced. That is, seduced into finkdom, although another reason some detectives, male and female, wanted no contact with child grasses was the sexual perils of such intimacy – false accusations, true accusations, interdependence, temptation, canteen gossip, bonding perceived as gone beyond, or gone beyond.

'My home telephone number is in the book. K. Lake.'

'So?'

'It's not something I'd want you to have on you written down.'

'I haven't said I'll do it.'

'Coming to the nick this time is all right – if you were spotted by anyone, I mean. That could be to do only with the shoplifting. But best you don't show up here again.'

'There won't be no again.'

'I'll be doing a talk at your school on drugs. No need to show you know me.'

'I don't. And *you* don't know *me*.'

'If anyone saw you come in and asks what happened, just say a warning from Mr Quinn. I don't figure.'

'You're only the grasses department, are you?'

'Mr Quinn's our expert at warnings.'

'What are you an expert at?'

3

To get a view of the afternoon meeting between Melissa and Titch Raybould Kerry took a spot on the first floor above a small delicatessen – in its store room and general junk den, whose curtained windows overlooked the street. The contents of the room scorched themselves into her mind with the urgent, daft clarity that meaningless things did when Kerry felt nervy. Christ, *nervy*, what a fart-arsing feeble word. Was she sending Melissa up the street to death?

In the watchtower room there were a few rolls of carpet, an

old freezer, a lopsided leather armchair, an unconnected bidet with three grey-covered box files in it, an electric lawnmower – its flex a tangled mess on a hook in the wall, a purple hat box and what looked like two clay pigeon launchers. These things unsettled her, made her suspect she was into disorder. More stupidity. In fact, the room allowed her to keep very efficient surveillance on the area immediately below, and this area was all she needed. She had been able to stand concealed at the edge of the curtains as she watched Melissa and Titch and felt pretty sure she was not spotted by either. Obviously, it would have been catastrophic if Raybould saw her. But also Melissa. Kerry had told her and told her again that she would not be there. You had to convince these children you trusted them, regarded them as equals, and workmates. Most young inform- ants loved status at least as much as money. Even those like Melissa who started hostile all through could finally start dreaming they were detectives. It would not help Melissa's fantasies if she found Kerry doubted her, spied on her, chaper- oned her.

Now, Kerry went downstairs and looked around the rear door into the shop briefly to say thanks and goodbye. The store room was a very useful spot, especially as arrangements had needed to be made so quickly. It was a very useful spot except that a room above a shop required permission from the shop- keeper. He and his wife were obliging and affable in the finest tradition of British shopkeepers, and no doubt chatted to cus- tomers about this and that, and about the plain-clothes cop who used a first-floor room to keep an eye on something in the street – a fascinating mystery and rather disturbing, all things considered.

Ultimately Kerry did drive after the Saab, but ultimately was ultimately and nothing more than a terrified gesture. She failed to see it and expected to fail to see it. This action took a shaving off her sense of guilt for a minute and a half.

4

When she first heard Melissa's body had been found and what had happened to her, it was awkward guilt as much as anything that kept Kerry buttoned, silent. Awkward? God, another milk-and-water word! This was a child dead. Guilt paralysed her. Shame ravaged her. She wanted to weep, came close, but, no, she couldn't here. She would weep later, when she was alone, and off the premises.

It was Vic Othen who told her about Melissa in the corridor to the CID room at headquarters. And he told her gently, as gently as something like that *could* be told. Vic always looked after Kerry. Perhaps he knew there had been the connection between her and Melissa. Vic tended to know more or less everything. Kerry could not be sure whether it was an accident that they met in the corridor like this, or if Vic had been waiting around there until she arrived at work, so he could be the one who broke it to her and show her some support and tenderness, if they were needed. Yes, he always looked after her. She did not speak, or nothing beyond what anyone might have said: 'Oh, God.' He would probably be able to read everything that needed to be read, though, in her face. She did not give him anything more in words, and could not have given him anything more in words. Confusion, horror and the guilt and shame dazed her and took her voice. She walked past Vic, went into the CID room and sat at her desk. She pulled some papers to her. Vic had followed but did not join her. Perhaps he was hurt. Perhaps he saw that she had to be by herself. Not long afterwards, Harry Bell walked through the room, looking appalled and enraged. She should have gone to him then and said what she knew, but she still could not force herself to speak. What was it – selfishness, self-disgust, feebleness, cowardice? Perhaps all of them.

And, because she did not immediately say what she had seen from the window, she found herself unable to speak of it at all.

How would she explain away a hesitation which swiftly grew from those few minutes of crippling, overwhelming shock to an hour, then to half a day, then to all day and a night? At the end of the hour she had almost decided she must spill everything to Harry and the murder squad people – the child's planned rendezvous with Titch, her school clothes, her relieved smile, real or put on, the climb into the Saab, the stately, hearsey move off – yes, that, *hearsey, hearsey*, hindsight hearsey – the left turn into concealment. But Kerry still did not tell any of this.

Obviously, it was brilliant, crucial information. Obviously, it was more or less criminal to hold back. But she felt that if she spoke it would be to state her responsibility for what had happened, a kind of confession. The idea terrified her. Just the same, in the evening and next morning, she drew very near to disclosure again, and again chose silence. Chose? It was hardly anything as rational as that. Her silence was in charge of her. She had wept by now, wept at home, but in secret. That resolved nothing for her.

After twenty-four hours it became unthinkable to speak of Melissa and the Saab to Harry Bell. There could be no pardonable explanation for having stayed quiet that long. She watched the investigation get nowhere. They were already talking DNA. For DNA you needed some kind of shortlist, though. You could not DNA every man in a city. They would probably focus on the area near where the body had lain. That struck her as despair, not logic. Most likely, Melissa was killed somewhere else then dropped there. Now and then Kerry would get a vision of all of it, start to finish. This came unasked for, tearing at her mind, and she struggled to block it out. She managed that, but only after a foul minute or two.

5

Schools were another one of Kerry's skills – talking to them, preaching to them, fraternising – and she had been up to

Melissa's comprehensive soon after that first meeting at the nick, long before her death. In many of these schools, you could, of course, feel the hatred, mostly from staff but some from the kids, too. New generations of teachers took over like a relay baton all the anti-police tics from their predecessors in the sixties and seventies, the way teachers used to take over decent grammar and love of a school and its traditions. Less than ten years ago Kerry had been in the same sort of comp herself. It had the identical architecture – tat with windows – and the same sort of woozy, pinko staff who'd say, 'I see you more as a social worker,' when she told them she might go into the police. You saw wrong, my mentors, and not just on that. Part of the skill in Kerry's job now was to pretend you did not spot the contempt, of course, and to chat on sweetly and robustly as if you were all allied against drugs and had met only to decide how they should be fought.

She wore trousers. Legs were a mistake. Even so, a few older boys in the audience would always signal up secretly but convivially to the platform that they would like to get their head between her thighs and/or shag her. They did it by closing their eyes in delight and letting their rolled tongue emerge slowly through wet lips, or by crafty, simulated wank movements with one hand, sometimes two. It could have been a police canteen or Harrow. She kept plonkingly talking and working her flip charts. Never so far had any of the pupils actually got a dick out, or not as far as she could see. The training – yes, there was public address training, too – the training said you should by eye contact and other techniques seek rapport with your listeners. She thought she had some of that. Now and then one of these boys would answer the open invitation and stay behind for a private conversation. She would have to decide then whether he might really do some- thing as an informant or was only interested in telling the neighbourhood he had fucked a cop. This would probably rate even higher than fucking a teacher, though lower than a member of the governing board or inspectorate.

The anti-drugs spiel she gave only concealed the real point of her visit. She was no drugs specialist, but mugged up the stuff as cover. She made a big thing of explaining that all the playful slang names for products – jellies, Harry, herb, mushies, Lucy, poppers – all these comfy words were thought up by traders to disguise the evil of their business. A school had to be the right place for a bit of language analysis.

But she was there mainly to recruit, and had her own ways of spotting children who might turn out helpful. It had to be done with laborious tact and secrecy. Many teachers resented the presence of a police officer in the assembly hall for whatever reason. Narually they saw it as interference by heavies. They would have been outraged to discover that Kerry's real purpose was to trawl for assistants. She could sympathise, half sympathise. It was not what schools and education were meant for. But they were not meant as sales targets for firms like Titch Raybould's either. How else did you stop them? Kerry did not believe that any kind of chinwagging from a platform would keep kids off drugs. The only way to do it was to hit the supplies, and for that there must be informant help. So Kerry would keep a smile on and a nice tone of voice as she talked and mingled, and, when she sensed opposition, think to herself, Up yours, Madam Blackboard, And yours, Mr Marxist-Remnant. Did these guardians of learning's holy flame want classrooms and the future full of thieving dying young junkies? *Brown is down*, as the phrase went, meaning heroin could be bought at a fiver a fix, or less. A bit of tarting, a bit of mugging, a bit of shop clearance and any pupil could turn herself, himself, into a steady customer, steady meaning helpless.

So, this job required Kerry to be diplomat, sex object, sex tease, spy master, turner of the other facial cheek, scholar. She loved the range of it.

'I've been reading, you know, *Model Behaviour*?'

'Oh, yes,' Kerry replied.

'Jay McInerney, you know?'

'Oh, yes,' Kerry replied.

This was question time. The girl would be Sixth Form and on her way to university, most probably. She looked like Media Studies or possibly Languages. In her undergraduate pre-police days, Kerry had shared half a house at Oxford with a girl who resembled this one: tall, thinnish, long-faced, beautiful if you liked a forceful nose, somnolent-seeming, but not.

'Giving what you could call the *positive* aspect of heroin?' the girl said with dogged gentleness. She might have been put up to this by a teacher with a habit.

'Oh, yes?'

Melissa was sitting behind the older girl and a bit to the left, head slumped forward, her face mostly obscured by hair style. Perhaps she was dozing, or just crushed by boredom.

'McInerney's narrator in *Model Behaviour* says he didn't try to dissuade one of his friends from taking heroin by telling him it was dangerous because that was the whole point of taking it – "the authenticating virtue" I think he calls it. Does it ever strike people like you – well-intentioned, devoted people, nobody doubts that – but does it ever strike you that when you give these warnings they might do the reverse of what's intended? Perhaps the affectionate, cheery nicknames for drugs are not needed, anyway, because people long for dark risk.'

So right. Cow smart-arse. Kerry smiled encouragingly, desperate to look unfazed. 'You mean what someone called "heroin chic"?'

'It was Clinton – the grass smoker who didn't inhale, ho-ho. But chic is not bad to be, is it? I mean, they call Parisian women chic, don't they – what a lot of other women want to be? And then there's *Trainspotting* and *A White Merc With Fins*. Perhaps they try to give the plus side of the drugs scene. These are popular books, popular with the young. Why? Do you think about that at all, I wonder.'

'You consider getting your hand down the worst public lav in Scotland to retrieve your fix is positive, as in *Trainspotting*?' Kerry replied.

The headmaster, on the platform with Kerry, stirred a little in his chair. After the questions came informal chatting, and Melissa either left or stayed very clear, as had been agreed. Kerry did not think she was going to find any other likelies.

6

Melissa had *really* liked it when the lady cop came up the
school and did her chat about drugs, the usual old dandruff.
What Melissa liked the best was this cop never looked at her,
like Melissa could *feel* her not looking at her, it was strange.
The cop could see her, that was sure, because Melissa was
sitting in the middle of the second row right up the front in the
Assembly Hall, nearly close enough to get a bit more of Poison
Breath's poison breath but not quite. He sat there by the cop
looking really holy when she was going on about how bad
drugs was, he had to – his job. Being a headmaster you got to
be against drugs, that's obvious. You could not have a headmaster coke snorting or mainlining, although he got a private
loo to do it in by the side of his study. But then when he come
out all trippy and his eyes with clouds on and his tongue all
dozy in his mouth there might be parents to see him or a kid
to be told off for setting fire to another kid's hair and he would
not be great at it.

Melissa liked the way the lady cop did not look at her, not
even once, and not a smile, because this showed they had a
secret. Melissa thought it was great and exciting to have secrets.
If there was someone looking at the lady cop and then looking
at Melissa they would not of been able to tell that these two
knew each other and had been having a private talk not very
long ago. This was like them old spy films when spies had a
talk out of the side of their mouths on a park seat but they
pretended they had never even seen each other before and after
the talk one of them would go one way and the other the other
way and not even saying goodbye. So, when all the other kids
and Poison Breath was listening to the cop or asking questions
Melissa could have a good laugh inside because there was a
situation with this lady cop and her that nobody in this Assembly Hall knew about, and it was more important than all the

listening the kids did and Poison Breath and more important than them big-mouth questions from Jessica Frome, the long string of noise, who liked to be called Daisy, not Jessica, because she thought Jessica was too posh. Her mother and father must of thought it was really great to know kids was calling her Daisy when they spent all that time picking Jessica for her, but not Poison Breath, he had to call her Jessica, because that was what was on the school register, not Daisy, which could be the name of a cow not a sixth-form prefect. She was not mainlining, Daisy – her arms was clean, Melissa had got a good look at them once when there was netball. But she might be snorting. She lived in a big house by the lake. Her dad had some money and they were the sort who would call a kid Jessica.

Melissa thought the lady cop did not *really* know drugs, not *really* know the way them Drug Squad police knew them, their job. This lady cop could say it all because she had learned about it, the way you could tell some teachers did not *really* know about something they was telling you, they had just *learned* it the night before so they could come in and spout it because the headmaster had told them they had to. Melissa thought that maybe this cop only did drugs talks in schools so she could be *in* the school and find kids who would grass to her, the way she wanted Melissa to grass. They could be *so* clever, police. They was not clever the way Daisy Frome was clever, books and big words and the loud voice, but police was clever in other ways. They would do things that seemed to be one thing but was really something else, to hide it, like plain clothes. Melissa felt a bit ratty about this. She wanted it to be a secret just for her and the cop, she did not like the idea that the cop could be finding other grasses. Maybe there was all sorts of kids in this Assembly Hall that the cop did not look at, the way she did not look at Melissa, because they was her grasses, or she wanted them to be one day soon. Melissa had looked about now and then in the hall to see if there was any other kids who she could tell the cop did not look at, but it was hard because you could not *really* tell if she was not looking at them because she was *trying* not to look at them because she knew them or because she was just not looking at them because she

19

did not notice them. There was a lot of kids here that somebody from outside would not notice, because they was so ordinary, real life's-a-bastard faces.

When Melissa looked around to see if there was any kids the cop was not looking at she saw some of the boys doing all that dirty stuff to the cop, the way they always did when there was a woman from outside on the platform, looking up their skirt if they was playing the cello in one of them groups that did the stringy music from way back that came sometimes, and making all the dirty signs with their mouth and hands.

The cop saw it but she pretended she did not and just went on talking the way the cello woman would go on playing the cello even though boys was getting down on the floor to squint up her skirt when her legs was open around the cello. The cop was good at pretending she did not see things, the way she pretended she did not see Melissa, and maybe others. After the talk she waited around with Poison Breath near the platform to talk to any kids who wanted to talk to her by theirselves, and this might of been when she was being clever – that police way of being clever. So, when a kid started talking to her about maybe having a little problem lately with E, or even H, some of them, the cop could say to herself this might be a kid who would be all right for grassing to me, unless she could see the kid was so bad on substance she or he would go rabbiting to the world about grassing and getting everything wrong because their head was done in by substance. A grass who would rabbit was the worst grass, and worse than not having a grass at all.

This Daisy asked the lady cop all sorts about books. That was the way Daisy was clever – reading. She really knew about libraries. The police way of being clever is not books. One of them books was pretty good, *Trainspotting*, Melissa had read it, it was funny but also sad. Her friends thought it was funny but sad also. Her friends were Avril and Florence. They bought *Trainspotting* between them because they heard about it and they wanted to read it. Florence was not really a main friend but nice. Avril was Melissa's main friend but she went to live in Portugal now. Her father said move to Portugal because of his job and so on. But Melissa had e-mail going with Av. She

20

would tell her about this cop at the school. They had a code for the e-mail. It was really great. In the code you did not write every word backwards but you did write some important words backwards and if you said ecilop it was police and if you said sgurd it was drugs. In e-mail Melissa would say this cop was in the ecilop and she came to the school to talk about sgurd. This code was so nobody could know the message such as parents getting into your e-mail letter box. Often parents was nosy.

The cop did not know about all these books that Daisy asked about only some, you could tell it, you could tell it the way you could tell it sometimes when you asked the teachers a question and they would just say anything because they did not know the real answer, but because they was teachers they had to say *something* and keep on talking or someone might have a chance to ask another question they could not answer. Teachers was taught how to do this in the college they went to to learn how to be teachers, just keep talking so everyone else had to shut up. Most likely the people who taught the teachers to keep talking kept talking themselves when they was teaching the teachers to keep talking, so the teachers would not have a chance to ask any questions about how to teach. That's how it seemed, because they did not know how to teach, only how to keep talking. Melissa felt a bit sorry for the cop when Daisy started with them books. Daisy was the sort who would get these questions ready the night before because she had to show she was clever enough for college and if you had a face and a nose like Daisy it was *really* important to show you was clever because what else did you have? In the college she might meet a boy who had a face like hers and a nose and then they would both mention books and they would understand each other and the next thing they would be shacked up, books every-where. Most likely Daisy did not like police because she liked books but Melissa thought some police might be all right, and somebody had to make sure there was not too many drugs and get after old shaggers who liked kids, girls or boys. There had to be *some* drugs, yes, but if there was too many they just did people's heads in for ever and this was no good at all. Who would drive the buses then or be able to stay awake long

21

enough to do lion taming in the circus? Melissa agreed with quite a few things the lady cop said. She might be all right in a way. The other way she was clever was wearing trousers.

7

Harry Bell ran morning meetings for all Melissa inquiry detectives. Pictures of her had been pinned to a cork board on the incident room wall. Some were portraits and other shots picked up from her parents and the school. Each officer had copies for putting before the public in a sightings trawl. They had also been issued to the media. These photographs showed Melissa in school clothes or sports gear or leisure outfits and at various ages. Mostly she posed and smiled for the camera, but once or twice might have been unaware. There was an Assembly Hall picture with her face circled in blue crayon among a lot of other seated children, all about her own age, taken before the day that Kerry spoke there.

In these photographs, Melissa could look happy, sometimes pretty, sometimes distrustful or sullen. On the whole Kerry felt more comfortable with the unposed shots. It was unnerving now to meet Melissa's eyes. Kerry, trap still shut on what she knew, could read an accusation into them, saw sadness even when the child was laughing. Crap. But although Kerry knew her reaction was sloppy and false, it still hit her.

Displayed on the board as well, and *not* for public viewing, were two 10″ × 12″ police photographs of Melissa as found, face up, no clothes, one taken from directly above, one from her left side. These death pictures told nothing that was not already well known to everyone in the room. Perhaps they were exhibited to keep people angry and working. To their right Harry had fixed an enlarged section of street map covering the city centre and with Melissa's school near the edge, circled in yellow.

At the second briefing, Bell said: 'We're still in the dark about her movements after she left the classroom. We know she skipped the last lesson and did not turn up for the school bus. That means we have a gap from about 2.50 p.m. Nobody saw her leave the building. Mr Quinn and I have been up to the school ourselves, talking around – staff, kids, neighbours. It's a long time since I've done that kind of work, and probably some of you would have handled it better. I felt I had to look and probe a bit for myself on this one. And so did Doug Quinn.' Bell went closer to the board and pointed at the circle. 'It's possible she did not exit via the main gates, here, but through the playing fields on this side, which would bring her to the edge of the Page estate. Kids do go that way, apparently, if they want to dodge off, especially as it's a short cut to the centre. I think the centre of town is where we should be working hardest at this stage and I've asked Hilary and George to show the Melissa identification pictures in main street shops. Nothing yet, though.'

'We concentrated first on the department stores and sports-wear and fashion shops, sir,' Hilary Melville replied. 'We'll widen it now.'

'It wasn't in character, not in character lately, that is – not in character for her to miss school or lessons,' Bell said. 'The head tells us she'd become a conscientious kid now, although she was erratic and might have been into substances a while back – no certain proof. So, did she leave early because of some crisis, not just for a drift around the shops? Perhaps to meet someone? I gather her pals say there's no boyfriend.'

'None recently,' Jane Hill replied.

'None they're aware of,' Bell said.

'We're still questioning,' Hill said. 'As we know, the doctors say she was not a virgin at the time of the attack. So, there'd been someone.'

At both these first two incident room briefings grief and self-contempt still gripped Kerry like chest pains. Would a man have suffered like this? Maybe. Possibly her feelings would have been less powerful if she knew all she had to do was confront and nail Titch Raybould. But she could not believe Titch did it. She longed to. So simple. Impossible. Her notion of the Saab as hearse-like was only that, an overheated flashback notion. Although Titch would be capable of killing a grass, even a child grass, rape and sodomy were beyond. Titch had values. Titch

23

had professionalism. He would annihilate a grass because such a murder to ensure silence was traditional and hallowed. Sex rated no place, not even as a warning to other informants, and definitely not degraded sex against a child. The trip in the Saab had been some kind of work trip, no abduction. There was something subsequent to the car and Titch.

Just the same, at that second meeting, George Ince said: 'I agree it looks like sex and only sex, sir, but do we still rule out an informant angle – silencing her, punishing her? Fortune School does a lot of drugs. Famed for it. Has she been grassing about the trade there?'

Bell half sighed, half hissed. Everything to do with informants, adult or child, he loathed, despised, tried to ignore, even though as head of CID he would know detection did not exist without them, and even though he had to make it possible now and then for Kerry to try some recruiting. Nominally, Harry Bell oversaw the whole informant network, but he would have liked to stay at a distance. He continuously expected these secret whisperers to bring catastrophe. For Harry, the horrible death of Melissa might seem the disaster he always dreaded. He feared the outcry if the public learned he ran a department that exposed child informants to such perils. Bell knew about the child informants, of course he did, but liked to pretend to ignorance; or, more than that, he liked to pretend sometimes that there weren't any. He did not try that now, but half shut his eyes to the situation, all the same. 'Kerry would be aware if she was informing,' he told Ince. 'And Doug, as Controller, would have listed the girl. As Registrar, I'd even have heard of her myself.' Bell remained a great detective, systematic and intuitive. He longed for things to be done without the use of grasses, that was all. A dreamer, even at his age.

'Just that if she's now such a good pupil, not into drugs herself any longer, she might want to fuck up the business,' Ince replied. 'Brownie points. A salary. And the secret *gloire*. Kids love that.'

It was not a bad guess. George needed watching, and perhaps a bag over his cage.

'Kerry?' Bell called.

'As you say, sir, not officially known,' she said. It was true.

24

Melissa had never been registered as an established informant. She did not produce that kind of quantity of stuff and had received no payments from the grass fund. Contacts between her and Kerry stayed unofficial and confidential. They had merely been possible run-ins for a proper relationship later, after all the checks and tests – like that check and test from the store room window. Nobody had a full idea of Kerry's connection with Melissa, except, conceivably, Titch Raybould. She swore to Kerry her parents had not been told, and Kerry more or less accepted this.

It struck Kerry now that she could do some individual work on the child's murder, using private material. She wouldn't say she *owed* this to Melissa, nor to the Slaters. Owed was melodrama. Nothing was owed to anyone, and she did not believe in the cop as avenger. She still considered she had acted more or less right by the child in a hazardous game. But it would also be acting right to bring in whoever had done what had been done to her. If Kerry could get a conviction some of her grief at the violation and slaughter might slide away. And some of that foolish self-contempt.

Ince kept on: 'What does that mean, though, "not officially known"?'

'Not one of our babies, George,' Bell replied. 'Not registered. No code name. You know the drill.'

'But don't some people run informants on the quiet?' Ince asked. 'Drug Squad people, for instance, using confiscated substance as payment.'

'There's a procedure,' Bell said. It was spoken like a recorded answer, a set piece, itself a procedure. 'We insist people follow this. The Home Office insist people follow it. People who don't are in trouble.'

'Well, I know, sir, but aren't there ways round that? Some officers are selfish, career mad. They don't like handing over a good grass for general use.'

Yes, there were ways around it: there was no disclosure. Listening, Kerry felt trussed up by her silence, but could not really regret this. Melissa's death questioned her judgement, and her judgement had always been sharp and acknowledged – on the accelerated promotion course after Oxford, and regularly in her personal assessments. She found she could not do anything now that might make people judge her at fault. A career could be shattered, and she had a duty to her career. Was that egomaniac? Hard? Well, possibly. She had better recognise it, did recognise it and always had.

'At this stage we focus on sex, George,' Bell said. 'Sex, sex and sex. There's enough evidence, for heaven's sake. We're doing the paedophile list, of course, but are unfortunately running against first-class alibis. So far.'

'Unbreakable, sir,' Viki Chancellor said. 'Genuine.'

'Sex, death,' Bell replied.

Yes, sex, death. And if Kerry had spoken when she should Titch would be inside now and accused of sex, death. She was horrified to think of her bosses or Mark or the media or Melissa's parents – Christ, them above all – horrified to imagine all these people asking why she allowed a compromised kid like Melissa Slater to step unguarded into such peril. And naturally they *would* ask and go on asking. There were certainly good answers. Hadn't they been enough to let Kerry watch Melissa into the Saab? But they would not have been enough now to stop or turn aside the condemnation by others. She might have answered that she did not realise the child *was* compromised, had no cause to think Raybould or anyone else knew Melissa talked in secret to the police. Informants, and even apprentice informants, needed to get close to their targets or they'd have nothing to inform with. Seen like that, the Saab ride was required by the job and, in fact, a triumph. Oh, God.

The Slaters would not have swallowed this, and it was their sorrow and their reasonable, spitting disgust Kerry most feared. Nor would those nosy, pious, tough, official groups endlessly monitoring police work with children accept her argument – the Home Office Select Committee, the National Association of Youth Justice, the National Association for the Care and Resettlement of Offenders. Such bodies understood how hard it was to collect high-grade knowledge on big style villains, and they did sympathise. But they did not always sympathise unconditionally, and particularly not when children were the providers. The watchdog folk would say she had actually encouraged Melissa to get with Titch. This was fair. To bring informant and villain together constituted Kerry's trade, her appointed and prized role. Entrepreneurial. If you did not do it, could not do it, you would net no villains.

'I'd like you and Kerry to speak to some more people at her school, children and staff,' Bell said. 'Kerry, you know the scene at Fortune. I'm going to see the parents again. I interviewed them immediately after discovery of the body, of course, and twelve hours later. They talked, were really remarkably coherent but still a bit disorientated. Some things could have been clearer. They'll have recovered a little by now, perhaps. The father has his strangenesses, but perhaps that was only shock and grief. I'll be looking for anything extra on her friends, her habits, her anxieties, trying to find whether there've been changes in behaviour lately – anything similar to cutting school. You do the same at Fortune. See what she's been talking about. We have to define her new pattern. I gather her main friend has gone to live in Portugal because of her father's job. Did Melissa find a replacement pal? That kind of thing.'

The incident room meeting dispersed. Bell called Kerry back. 'She's not, is she, Kerry?' He was slim, grey-haired, big-voiced, wonderfully benign-looking, devious, flinty, immeasurably experienced, devastatingly sharp. 'She's not someone unregistered who talks? I noted George's point about the career mad. This child was in for shoplifting not long ago, wasn't she? Did you do some of your charm on her?'

'I –'

'But would you tell me?'

She was going to protest but then suddenly decided he might have jumped in, cut her off, like that because he did not *want* her to tell him. Yes, immeasurably experienced, immeasurably devious. Perhaps Harry preferred Kerry to push on, using whatever she had, whatever she kept to herself, as long as she got someone into the dock without troubling him, or implicating him, at least till the end. He knew about Melissa and Kerry but did *not* know about Melissa and Kerry. Clean hands looked increasingly desirable as retirement came nearer. She said: 'Rumbled grasses don't get raped and sodomised, sir.'

'Good girl. Why didn't I say that just now?'

'Tough words to use about a child.'

27

He gave that sigh-hiss again. 'I'm a detective superintendent, Kerry, and quite used to tough words and tougher sights.' He glanced up at the body pix of Melissa on the board. 'But I wouldn't like to be responsible for that, however remotely. And I will not be.'

Harry would be scared of the media. It was reasonable. She felt afraid herself. Like the watchdogs and Melissa's parents, journalists would dismiss her excuses. Didn't newspaper people and broadcasters thrill to expose what they decided were wrongs? Didn't they *live* to expose what they decided were wrongs? Hiring vulnerable kids as spies could easily be written up to look abusive, especially if what the doctors said had happened to Melissa reached reporters. Things like that *did* reach reporters. Informing was a smelly word, anyway, and the notion of finking by children always made even some pro-police folk retch. They might only be pro-police because they did not understand what policing was, or what detecting was, at any rate. Of course, Kerry knew she herself had not thought Melissa entirely safe. If she had, why act stricken as the Saab bore this schoolgirl baby out of sight? Why goofily tag along much too late in its track, looking for her, or looking for consolation, mocking up care?

8

Melissa had hated Avril's dad for taking her and the family to live in Portugal just because of some stinking tales and his new stinking job. That was what happened to kids. You did not have no rights. You just followed.

To: Avril Grant
From: Melissa Slater
Subject: Everything

Saturday

Yes yes Avril there is e-mail for you for you personal and alone from your still dearest friend Melissa. I do not believe them mucky tales. Honestly I do not. I do not think I would want to be still your dearest friend and do e-mail to you if I did.

How are things out there in the foraine sun Av? Here things are pretty much like as always but I am still nearly right off all that stuff just a bit of something now and then.

Plus I got a new friend well sort of friend not really a friend at all more like a shadow really but someone I been talking to a bit. She is too old to be a friend but she might be all right I dont know. Her name is Kerry. Now get ready get ready ready ready because here comes a word in that code we made up for e-mails before you went. You know how it works. I do not want to say because of keeping secrets but if it was cat it would be tac. Well Kerry is a detective in the ecilop. There will be some other words in code so you better start thinking. When you send me e-mail send it Saturdays. My dad does not look at the e-mail much on Saturday or Sunday because he is not working then. So I will read it and wipe it off when you send something. But we better have the code as well. I will send you the e-mails on Saturday as well because I esspect your dad is the same. I esspect they have Saturday and Sunday there just like here.

Kerry was up the school this week to give a big jaw jaw about sgurd. That is more code did you notice???? She knew all the names and she said it was a pity some of the names was funny such as jellies because sgurd are not funny. All the usual old chatter. How stupid it is and bad for the skin and girls only 12 or 13 going with men to get money to buy sgurd plus getting beat up by their pimp if they did not get enough money from men.

But the first thing was before this they had me down the ecilop station because they said I been in Marks and Sparks to get items to sell to buy stuff. It was such a lie but she comes into the room full of talk and all that kindness. You know how they do it. I did not say nothing. I mean nothing what she wanted me to say. Course not. Then I gets a big jawing from this higher one you know how they do it all kindness and like being on your side this time. Well I act sort of dum with both of them that is always best. What they expect from kids.

So anyway when she comes up the school another day she gets trouble from this big skinny kid called Daisy in the Sixth a lot of brain and hooter if you can rember. Her real name is Jessica a voice all plonking like the hoofs of a horse and a prefect and going to Oxford or Cambridge or somewhere like that. She starts asking Kerry about sgrud in books such as that great book Trainspotting that we was reading just before you went and in the cinema???? It is the one in Scotland. Well this was real funny because Kerry did not have no clue how to answer it she was not esspecting this but she said about that grotty Scotch toilet in Trainspotting which I expect you rember it is such a laugh and he dives into it in the moovy of Trainspotting which is not in the book but a moovy is more arty and he is trying to get his packet of stuff back dropped down the filthy toilet. This is the moovy we saw with them two syob who were really nem. I liked yours best his hair and not so noisy as mine.

Old Poison Breath did not like the talk about the mucky Scotch toilet he was on the platform with Kerry and you could see him frowning and moving about on his chair like really shocked. You would think he never heard of a toilet.

Will you be there for ever? I wish my dad would have a factory for computer stuff over there so I could live out there in the sun too and no Poison Breath. What are the syob like? What is the English school like such as GCSEs?

I might be able to get extra cash because this friend Kerry wants me to help her. I dont know if I will. This is by turning into a ssarg for her about sgurd at school and so on. That is what all the talking was really about I knew it. Av would you let yourself turn into a ssarg??? People hate a ssarg if you are found out. They are creepy. She says it is to stop evil that is all so I should. She knows I could help her because I know that one we both knew if you rember called hctiT. But I dont know it is a dirty thing to do and it is dangerous. I have heard of a ssrag who was killed. They just shot her. So I might not. Mum and dad would be very cross if they knew because it is so dangerous.

Well thats enough code Avril. I bet you got a pool and vine plants and everything it must be great. Well Avril e-mail me soon soon soon. I know you are lazy. But soon yes and tell me all about the syob over there. Sorry more code!!!! I expect they all got dark hair like in Spain when we went on holiday and quite romantic its their way I like it and plenty of deodurant because of all the purspiring. If you do not understand their langwage you will not know if they are saying something real nice to you about your hair or trainers but I expect they will because your trainers were from Britain if you have still got the same ones. I dont suppose you even know what the word for a ring is yet over there. But you will have time to learn this.

With lots of love from your good old friend,
Melissa Slater

9

At the end of that first meeting with Melissa at the nick, Kerry had said: 'Now, Melissa, you've got to go up and see Mr Quinn. He'll have a little talk with you.'

'I thought like this was instead. You know, like – '

'It's best you really do see him, so if people ask about what happened here you can tell them and it will sound right. In case anyone checks on you. Some people might want you to tell them what Mr Quinn looks like and about his voice and his room, trying to catch you.'

'How do you mean *catch* me? What are they going to catch me at?'

'Just have a good look around so you can describe him and the layout of his room. Some of these people know what he's like and his room. The word will be out that you've been brought in from Marks and Spencer for pinching and they might wonder why you're released, no charge.'

'So I say because I didn't do no pinching, that's why.'

'They'll wonder what happened in here. You say only the

warning from Mr Quinn this time and return of the merchandise. You'll be all right then.'

'Who's going to check on me?'

'Folk get to hear who's brought into the nick.'

'Whick folk?'

'Not your parents, or the school. Don't get anxious about that. But folk who could be dangerous.'

Kerry went up alone first to Doug Quinn's room. 'This going to be one of your deals, Kerry?'

'It might be, sir. I can't tell yet whether she'll bite.' And it was true then. In any case, Kerry always tried to delay handing an informant over to the system. All detectives were like that. They wanted exclusiveness. They wanted to *own* their best grasses, not share them with colleagues, as the rules ordered. Detectives disliked the bureaucracy – all that rigmarole of Handler, Controller, Registrar. The informants loathed it, too. They preferred one to one, saw it as more like a friendship, personal, and safer – nothing on paper or disc. But, of course, this secretiveness soon became impossible, especially if the informant expected to be paid. Most did. The cash came from bureaucracy.

'Decent, middle-class family, I gather,' Quinn said.

'She talks slob. Dad's some sort of planning consultant, working mainly from home. Detached house, two cars, on the Internet. Mum works part time for British Telecom.'

'So, what happened to the kid?'

'It does happen, doesn't it, sir?'

'What kind of information can she bring if she should move our way?' Quinn asked.

'Organisational. I think she might know Titch. His network.'

'Buying from him? Pushing for him?'

'She says she's clean now. I doubt it. She's probably doing something, if only E.'

'Or why is she thieving?'

'Right.'

'What kind of things?'

'T-shirts, blouses – easily into a bag.'

'Do we know where she sells it?' Quinn was good at warning talks – looked manufactured for the role. There was something

benign and something inflexible in his face. He sounded considerate and not foolable. He was bald, and his scalp glowed pink
and cream and disarming.

'Market stalls, I should think,' Kerry replied.

'Should we look at that?'

'Not yet, if you don't mind, sir. I don't want to disturb the
scene.'

'She'd get ripped off?'

'Maybe they'd give her a fifth of face value. Some labour
involved – they'd take the M and S labels off.'

Quinn was in shirt-sleeves but put his uniform tunic on now
for gravity. Kerry went down for Melissa.

10

*I ought to tell them what I know, I ought to tell them what I know, I
ought to tell them what I know. I ought to tell them about Melissa in
the Saab. Stuff it. Not yet.* Which meant probably never.

Kerry went ahead and fixed up another visit to the school for
tomorrow. This time Viki Chancellor would come with her.
And this time it would be for a trawl, not a lecture. They would
look for information about Melissa's last hours, while Kerry sat
immovably on information about Melissa's last hours because
she thought she could do better for Melissa that way. This was
what she wanted above all, wasn't it? Wasn't it? True, it would
be better for herself, too. The interests of a detective and a grass
almost always coalesced beautifully. They coalesced even when
the grass was dead, and perhaps especially then.

The evening before the trip to the school, one of the children
who had been whispering things to Kerry for much longer than
Melissa and *was* registered and salaried came to visit her at
home. Of course. Kerry had expected this. There would probably be others. The kids were scared now. They all had her
address and telephone number, because they must not be seen
around the nick. She tried to put on reassurance and hide her
distress.

33

Mark resented the kids' entitlement to turn up at the flat. *Are we Barnardo's, for God's sake?* Kerry would still attempt to explain to him now and then why it was necessary, but also now and then felt like giving up.

Lois Fauld, cover name Cheryl, was still definitely a user off and on, probably nothing more than weed, though. Sometimes she had that nice, over-sweet, friendly, hay-loft smell about her. She could be erratic, forgetful, moody, excitable, a bit clinging, but Kerry did not complain about that, the clinging. Quite a lot of these children needed some support. *Are we Barnardo's, for God's sake?*

Lois was older than Melissa, probably brighter and more thoughtful, and, so, much less happy with herself. She spoke in slow, loud, agonised bursts which she might have picked up from some TV or movie actress, though Kerry could not identify her. 'My mother is reading out to me from the news-papers all the time about the dead girl.' Lois gave her left foot a few blows with the other. 'Mum tells me that if I'm ever tempted to go into this scene – that's what she calls it, this *scene*, like a play – she picks up words from newspapers – she wants to think she talks youth – *so* sad – you know how they can be, Kerry – anyway, this *scene* . . . well, saying if I'm ever tempted, just make sure I think about this girl.' She stopped and when she started again brought her voice down momen-tarily to not much more than a string of gasps, less than whispers. 'I mean, Kerry, there was extra to being killed, wasn't there? Bad things done to her pre death. I mean, *really* bad, my mother said. And the word on the street says so, anyway. *Vile* things. Do you know what I mean? Yes, you do because it's in the reports, isn't it? I know you're upset about it. You look older. Not old, but really older. You knew this kid, I can tell. You cop the blame? Cop!' The joke seemed to restore her and she spoke full out again. 'She was on the list, was she? Of course she was. That's what the word on the street is. That list – it's a peril, Kerry.'

'What word on the street?'

'I told you – that she was working for the police.'

'Who?' Kerry asked.

'What?'

'Who says this?'

'On the street, you know.'

'Gossip.'

'*Did* you know her, Kerry? Like you know me, I mean, I expect there are a lot. Professional. I think you're in charge of all that. Kid grasses. I'm not ashamed of it – grassing. I hate these bigsters and their BMWs and Saabs done on junkie cash. My mother says a scourge, infecting everything. They could be.'

'Lois, there's always going to be gossip and silly rumour when something like this happens.'

'I think you've been crying about it. That's what makes you look old. Older. But crying a lot – that's for the old. All they've got is the past and the past is nearly always so rotten, or so good but gone. Sometimes my mother cries about my father and then her face gets all straggly and old. You know? Over on one side and like dragged down and lumpy and pink, like meat on a slab. I don't mean your face is straggly, no, no, but older. It's because of my dad that my mum keeps reading things out to me about this girl – because she's by herself and she thinks she must do everything to look after the family. Sends me to further ed. college, not to a job. It's called "single parent", you've heard of that, Kerry? There's more of it than ever these days. Also called "breakdown of the family unit" which will be a real item of the millennium.'

'We think a sex crime.'

Grey-blue, sharp, her eyes flickered a bit as she focused her mind on this. 'There *was* sex, yes. Not just ordinary sex. That's what I mean, vile. My mother read it out. It didn't say it straight out, but you could tell what they meant. My mother said pervy. Have you ever had sex like that, Kerry? I suppose I shouldn't ask, but you're older and you're in a relationship. It's called *experienced*. I mean, do men want that a lot – the other way? I knew some men wanted it like that with other men, obviously, no choice, I suppose. But, God, us? My mother said this was done to the girl as like a warning because she messed with someone of power in the scene. That's what she said, "of power in the scene".' Lois did a heavy pulpit sort of voice. 'She didn't get those words from the Press, she made them up. They sound weird, yes, but they're not too bad, are they? "Of power" is right for some of them, all sorts of power, power over all sorts, not just kids, power over all kinds of people, people in big jobs, maybe with uniforms even. So, my mother said make sure I heard this warning if I didn't want to end up similar. She was pretty, wasn't she? I saw pictures in the newspaper and on TV and she looked a bit pretty. Someone pretty like that should be even more careful, the silly little cow. But it doesn't matter, it could happen to anyone. Men don't care as long as they can get . . . Well, that's what my mother said.'

Lois was not pretty. Her mother had been cruel to tell her, though. Kerry did not know much about mothering, but it seemed obvious that a mother shouldn't do a child down, a child who was clever enough and sensitive enough to feel what was being said. And so that sudden bitterness. And so something close to envy, regardless of what her prettiness had done for Melissa. Lois was big and lumpy in the face and body. Her shoulders drooped a little. Her features showed real liveliness now and then, but almost always the liveliness of dread. She smoked occasionally for the same reason everyone else smoked, or snorted or mainlined. They wanted to be somebody else and perhaps some*where* else, and they wanted the transformation fast. They longed to escape what had been dished out to them, and this was the way. Kerry understood these feelings. You could even argue it was narrow-minded and arrogant to be satisfied with yourself as you were. Kerry did alcohol from time to time in the search for a bit of transformation. And Mark. And most of their friends.

Lois had on navy trousers, held up by a wide black leather belt, and a red 'Football, the lovely game' T-shirt. She wished to be in a team she could tell people about, not the one she *was* in, the informant team. Kerry made them both some coffee and brought the biscuit tin.

'Plus also on the street that she knew Titch Raybould. Is that right, Kerry? Is that why she was on the list? I mean, *Titch* – he's top level.'

'I don't believe she was on any list.'

'The sort of list I'm on.'

'I don't believe she was on any list.'

'You didn't know? It's wrong what they say on the street – that she was working for the police sometimes?'

'I wouldn't be allowed to see such a list. Nobody would be, except the officer in charge.'

'Ah, Mr Controller. Now, he'd never tell about it, would he, Kerry?'

The tone of this – one part sarcasm, the other a plea for confirmation. Kerry could not make out which was stronger, but probably the sarcasm. You often ran into such terror in the children – a conviction that an agreement existed at the top between people like Titch and the police, so that no real secrecy and no real safety existed despite all the show of precautions and confidentiality. These were kids who had learned a long time ago to be untrusting, unchildlike. They knew they were not the only ones who could talk.

'*Seen* with Titch, in his car,' Lois said. 'On the day it happened.'

'Who says this?'

'On the street.'

'More rumour,' Kerry replied.

'I heard it twice. Two different people.'

'They saw her themselves?' Kerry asked.

'They know someone who saw her.'

'That's how rumour works. Like a chain letter. Then you get it from two different people or ten different people, but it all starts with one person making it up.'

'They said a Saab, and Titch does have a Saab. Sitting in the front in school gear and laughing and talking and him laughing and talking, like . . . like very friendly. Do you know what I mean?' It was a taste of hers to say things between the lines. Lois must have come to believe this was adult.

'Everyone knows he runs a Saab, Lois. Who saw it?'

'Not someone who would go to the police ever.'

'It's gossip – make-believe. Or someone wanting to get Titch Raybould and putting the tale around.'

'*You* want to get Titch Raybould, don't you, Kerry? Don't you?'

The question was real. It reeked of confusion.

'Definitely. But for things he's done. The trade network.'

'He didn't do Melissa Slater?'

'We'll bring him in eventually, and it will be because of good information we get from people like you, Lois. We fit it all together and then one day we're ready. When we've got something that will work in court.'

'"Fit it all together." Is that what they mean when they say "fit someone up"? How many people are there like me? I didn't realise – it must be a lot.'

'You're important,' Kerry replied.

'Was *she* important? Is it dangerous to be important? If you're important there'll always be someone who thinks you're important because you're a menace to him.'

That was a pretty good summary. Kerry said: 'I meant, because you're important we look after you.'

'Was Melissa important?'

'Different.'

'My mother would go spare, really spare, if she knew what I do. The money – I can't go buying with it, or she'd see. Savings.'

'But your mother would want us to catch people like Titch, wouldn't she, so they can't get at kids.'

'How do you mean "get at"? Like with Melissa Slater?'

'I mean get at – sell them stuff, hook them, put them on the game.'

'My mother? She would want you to catch them, yes. But she would not want me in it. She wants me into a lot more education.'

'Policing can't operate without the help of good people,' Kerry said. Lord, some chewy pronouncement. She heard Mark come in from work and go into the kitchen. She had the door to the sitting-room shut and he would catch the voices and know that he must not open it and look in. Kids did not like that. Kerry did not like it, on their behalf. These meetings were one to one, no witnesses. Lois glanced towards the sounds Mark made. If he did appear perhaps she would give him the once-over, wondering whether he seemed the sort who would expect a girl to do it that other way which intrigued her so much. She might even ask him, as she tried to get an idea of what the future had for her. Kerry could have told her no, nothing like that. She wouldn't have minded if there had been – anything to show an all-round, intemperate interest in her by Mark.

'Could you really arrest Titch?' Lois asked. She was sitting in an easy chair but not easy, her body hunched forward and clenched tight. Her eyes were hard on Kerry now and empty of faith in her.

'What you've told me isn't enough, you see, Lois. It's helpful, but not enough. This is only someone telling you that someone else saw her in the car. I need things you've seen direct. You, your own eyes.'

'You could ask him – was she in the car?'

'What do I do when he says no?'

'You tell him you've got information.'

'I haven't.'

'You have. I've told you.'

'Not information. It's what we call "hearsay". Wool.'

Lois drank her tea and leaned forward a bit further. 'Don't you *want* to get him, Kerry?'

'Absolutely. But look, you mustn't go around talking like that about Titch. It might be hazardous.'

'It's only hazardous if she really was in the car, isn't it? He wouldn't be bothered if he could prove it was rubbish.'

'People who are scared and angry are not always logical,' Kerry replied.

'I could get killed, you mean, and all the rest of it pre? But if you worry like that it shows you think Titch did her, doesn't it?'

'We wait to see what the investigation finds.'

'I always think you know more than you say, Kerry. But that's police, isn't it?'

When Lois had gone Kerry went into the kitchen. Mark was sitting at the breakfast bar reading the *Independent*. She kissed him on top of the head. 'Sorry, a crisis,' she said.

'Grave?'

'To do with the girl who was killed.'

'Oh? One of yours?'

'It's upset a lot of the kids.'

39

'Meaning *your* lot. I expect it would. Is that what you've been troubled about yourself, Kerry? Did you know her, then?'

'That sort of death disturbs everyone, poor mite.'

11

Eventually there had been a reply from Portugal to Melissa's e-mail.

To: Melissa Slater
From: Avril Grant
Subject: Avril on the Continent of course

Sábado – meaning Saturday to you, kid.

I was going to write sooner, Mel, but busy, busy, busy – the new house and new school, everything upside down. I miss everything over there. My dad might come back for a buisness trip to London but I can't go with him because of school. It is one of the British schools in Oporto so nearly all the syob are British or American. One or two are all right, but mostly so ORDINARY, telling you about their crummy CDs or how they can jump the deepest kerb on their skateboard. Really INTERESTING.

Portugal's kerbs are very deep. You would think they are scared the road will get to be the Duoro any day. That's a river, ignoramus. Of course I see Portugues syob in the street and shopping and some are not too bad, but mostly ordinary. The CLOTHES – well you wouldn't believe, right back to Unity One. Pathetic. I saw a Portuguese boy in a Fair Isle pullover. How could he be romantic in a Fair Isle pullover? The TV is terrible – soccer all the time and really old old movies with Jane Fonda. Have they stopped teaching you a bit of grammar at school????? Plus spelling!!!!! God!!!! Or doG if you want him in the silly code – get it?????? People would have to be REALLY stupid if they could not see through this code. Make sure the letters are wiped off the screen as soon as you have read them.

40

Sometimes I think you talk and write rough just so people will not think you are trying to be smart, like that girl who did not want to be Jessica but Daisy. But I know you are REALLY smart really.

When you say about going to see that movie Trainspotting with those two we met, it would be best to be a bit careful if you see them again in town. They were not really syob, you know. They were nem and both were more than twenty I think. You said you liked the one I was with, but – well, I got a bit scared. Well, you know that. That crazy little window and the washbasin!!!! I think he could be rough and nasty. I mean REALLY. He could be a efink person. I mean it. He was getting rough and nasty. People sitting near us told him to keep still and they asked me if I was all right. I said I was and he knew he had to behave after that. If you see him again I think he's too old, although nice looking and paying at Trainspotting. But you never know what they want when they pay. Yes you bloody do. Was yours nice, even if you liked mine more?

I don't know about being a ssarg. How much pay? There was a girl near where I lived who they said was a ssarg called Lois. People were not supposed to talk about it – supposed to be so secret, but they did. Ugly fat-arse kid but money in the Post Office. People knew about it, that's the thing, Mel. Some people hate all sessarg and they would say good riddance. They say it's dirty. But I also think it's dirty if dirty crooks with their fat cars and greasy gold medallions etc. get kids so they don't know what they are doing and will do anything for a xif. The thing is the ecilop don't seem to be able to get them, so maybe they need all the sessarg they can get. In Portugal there does not seem to be a lot of sgurd. I do not even know where I could get some if I wanted to. Mostly I don't. This is a Catholic country and the Pope is against all that. He is against nearly everything except kissing the ground. I wonder if he gives it a French kiss when he is in France??????

So be careful, Me. I am glad you said you do not believe all that rubbish. If you get extra money e-mail me to say what clothes you buy and so on.

Love from your special friend,
Avril

To: Avril
From: Melissa
Subject: Worry

Saturday

Well at last I got your answer today. The thing is Av I haven't got nobody else I can tell about problems here and I been feeling quite a bit lonely so when your e-mail came it was REALLY great. I bet you are not telling me everything about the syob in that school. I esspect they are all after you and saying about love. Over here on TV is Teen Spirit all about REALLY young girls having love and a baby because the syob will not wear anything. One girl said she had big boobs when she was only 15 so she went to be a model, lucky kipper.

I do not know how much money yet if I start to ssarg proper. I been meeting Kerry a few more times and she is defnately doing a lean on me but I am still not sure. She says she cannot say nothing about money yet because she does not know what I can give her and her bosses will want to know that before they say OK to money. They are in charge. She knows I know hctiT and he is the one she is after. I can tell she wants to know how he pays for things such as the Saab and his suits and the house and clothes for his lady real great clothes. I seen her a couple of times they could be Versace. Her name is Joyce. Well of course Kerry knows how he pays for them but she wants me to find out how his firm works and all the people in it.

And hctiT is leaning on me himself. He wants to know everything about the school. I think he is trying to find out about every school and I am just the one for our school. He wants to know who will buy. That is staff and kids and who it is safe to ask. He is making lists for every school I know it.

You ARE a clever boots. How did you know? I did meet them two we went to the moovy with and they were up by the school maybe looking for us I do not know how they knew the school. It really makes me laugh when I think about that wash-basin in the Regis. Your one with the black curly hair asked about you and I said gone gone gone. He was upset a bit. He said why did you go. I did not say anything about my d. I just decided he should be in the code but it is no good putting him in the code because it is the same both ways so I will just call him my d.

But I wouldn't go with them two. I just talked. Your one said he could always come that way again by the school if he felt like it. I do not think they live around here. I did not say anything. I did not want to because to me he was still yours though you are not here now. My one did not say very much. I never liked him. A fatty.

If I knew about the money I mean if I knew I would get some and how much I think I would be able to make my mind up. Of course they are saying they have been good to me. This is about something they say happened in Marks and Sparks but I say it is a lie. I know it is the way they do things them ecilop.

I hope the weather is good in Portugal and that you do not fall over a steep kerb.

Your dear friend
Melissa.

12

If it came to a bet, I'd pick this headmaster as more likely than Titch.
Disgraceful, slanderous, sick thought.

He said: 'Sergeant Lake – Kerry – is that all right? – I feel we know each other reasonably well by now, don't you? – and I'm Gerald – perhaps you could tell me in more detail – '

'This is Detective Constable Chancellor – Viki Chancellor,' Kerry replied. They all sat down in his room, Gerald Rose behind the desk.

'Fine. Now perhaps you could tell me in more detail than was possible on the phone what you'd like to do here in my school.' He was middle height, slightly built but athletic-looking, his face narrow, small-mouthed, intent, a face that was searching for something, she thought. It might be fulfilment or well-earned prestige or well-earned devotion. His breath seemed a bit off. He said: 'As you asked, I've made certain arrangements, but – Kerry, Viki, you'll understand, I know, that I have to be a little careful about allowing people from outside to interview our children, even the police.' He chuckled with good wryness. 'In fact I'm afraid some parents might say *especially* the police! It pains me that it should be so – but, well, sadly, it's the direction things are going. I have an obligation to the children and to the parents, of course. At the same time, I naturally wish to co-operate with you and your colleagues in all possible ways, believe me. This is an appalling crime and you have your duties. A vivacious, affectionate child destroyed just as she had begun to move towards lovely womanhood. Appalling, yes. A child who had come through a difficult time – drugs involved, yes – had fought her own way out of it. All of us – parents, staff, children, myself – all of us know that this monster might attack again, Melissa Slater now, another child tomorrow. And we will certainly do all we can to prevent this happening.'

'Thanks, Gerald,' Kerry replied.

'But, much as he would wish to help, Gerald Rose is not sovereign in these matters,' Gerald Rose said. 'There have to be certain procedures, procedures to safeguard the interests of us all, yourselves included. I'm sure you would wish everything to be carried out in such a way that there can be no recriminations.'

'Like what – the safeguards?' Viki Chancellor said.

He smiled behind the desk and waved his hands, and Kerry thought the signal said reasonableness. 'I do need to know first how you wish to run things.'

'Just talk to people,' Viki replied. 'Gerald.'

'People, of course. Which people?'

'Children, mainly. Yourself,' Viki said. 'That's already happening. Other staff.'

'Yes, that's what I assumed,' the head replied. 'Which children? Mainly her classmates, I imagine.'

'Right,' Viki replied. 'Whoever comes.'

'If that seems all right to you, Gerald,' Kerry said.

He nodded, half nodded. 'These are quite young children.

44

One or more members of staff would have to be present at all conversations. And should a child become distressed – '

'We would close the interview, obviously,' Kerry said.

'Kids are often a lot tougher than we think,' Viki said. 'Gerald.'

'Are they, are they?' he replied.

Probably he felt he should not be told his trade by a detective. Kerry could sympathise. Viki did not do tact, could never play soft cop.

'Now, School,' Gerald Rose said, 'I have called this special assembly today to introduce you to these two ladies on the platform with me. Well, one of them you may recognise. She was with us not very long ago to speak about the dangers of drugs. This is Detective Sergeant Kerry Lake.'

She got up for a moment and offered the full hall a grin. Senior pupils stood at the back and Kerry looked for the tall girl who had given her a hard time on the bright literary credentials of drugging up, but did not spot her.

'And her colleague is Detective Constable Viki Chancellor.'

Viki rose from her chair and managed a short smile, *Do right by me and I'll do right by you.* They were both in trousers. Kerry had warned her. Boys in the hall would be delirious all the same – double police pussy.

But when he addressed the children as 'School', Rose was able to put a lot of team spirit and pride into the call, and the pupils seemed to rally to it, perhaps even the boys. Kerry could not see any face-making or hand-jerking now. 'School, these two officers are here today because of the death of our young friend Melissa Slater. The officers are part of the police drive to find and arrest whoever did those things to the girl we all knew and liked, now so regrettably taken from us. Kerry and Viki would like to talk to some of you about Melissa, and perhaps to some of the staff. They want to ask what she might have been doing in the hours just before her death. They would also like to know if she spoke of having met any new people lately, any strangers. I expect you have seen on television how

45

detectives work when there has been a crime, as in *The Bill* and *NYPD Blue,* if you're allowed up that late! They have to search for the truth, and all kinds of people help them by recounting what they have seen or heard. But I want to say that, whenever Kerry or Viki talks to any pupil on his or her own, myself or some other member of the staff will be present. I also wish to say that only children who wish to meet the officers will do so. No child *has* to take part. When you are telling your parents about what happened here today I would like you to make these points very clear to them, please. Any child or any member of staff who *does* wish to talk privately to Kerry and Viki should come to room Ground 11 between 2 p.m. and 4 p.m.

'Now, School, are there any questions?'

Kerry saw that same tall girl edge herself forward a little from out of a group at the far end of the hall. Her voice sped the distance to the platform like a rat up a gangplank. 'Will a record be kept of what is said by any pupil to these police officers? If so, will such record be made available to the interviewee or, in the case of younger pupils, to the interviewee's parents or parent?'

'These are informal conversations,' Viki replied, 'that's all. No notes or record.'

'What does "informal" mean in this context?' the girl asked with nice demureness.

'Informal,' Viki replied.

'Plus, I am interested in the *status* of the member of staff who will be present at these interviews,' the girl said. 'Will this presence be a participating presence, an observing presence or an, as it were, umpiring presence?'

'Oh, certainly entitled to intervene, Jessica, should it be deemed necessary,' the headmaster replied.

'Will the member of staff be present as, as it were, the pupil's *friend* – in the sense that the accused at a court martial has a *friend* to make the defence – or will the member of staff be there merely to facilitate matters for the police officers by putting the pupil at ease and possibly encouraging the pupil to find answers to the questions?'

46

'Sort of fair play, Jessica,' Rose replied. 'To ensure that all is above board, properly regulated, civilised.'

'Properly regulated according to which provisions? Civilised on whose terms?'

'I'm quite sure Kerry and Viki will not apply the third degree, Jessica,' Rose said, beyond a chuckle now and into solid merriment.

'It's the parameters that I'm uncertain of,' Jessica replied.

At once Rose discarded jokiness. 'School – *parameters*, a word from Latin and Greek made up of *para*, meaning near or beside, and *meter*, from the Greek word *metron*, to measure, as in gas meter. And so Jessica's word *parameters* is not to be mistaken for *perimeters* but means the qualities in a thing or situation that enable us to measure it. Jessica wants to know, you see, what are the limits, what are the rules, if you like, of these meetings.'

Viki snarled: 'School, some people don't have rules or limits. They kill and defile kids.'

Rose might be a creep, but Kerry admired him for the spontaneous session on that word – the quickness with which he saw he must interpret for the younger and/or dimmer children. Her Latin was shaky and Greek absent but she thought he might even have the definition right. He had probably been a very good teacher and was now perhaps a very good headteacher. His wholesome chuckles and laughter would be excellent for neutralising a crisis, among pupils or staff.

He gave them a classroom off the Assembly Hall and said he would sit in on the first interviews himself together with Mrs Ferguson, the Religious Education teacher. At first, no children came. Gerald Rose did not seem too troubled about this.

'They're terrified,' Viki said.

'Like, I imagine, any school, School has a tradition against what they call, I believe, "finking",' the headmaster said. 'That means talking to the police, I think.'

'I think it does,' Viki replied. 'It's too open here.'

'Open?'

'Any child coming to this room can be observed coming. The word spreads,' Viki said. 'I don't mean just spreads in *School*. Outside. Some of these kids live on a battlefield. Now and then they die on a battlefield.'

'Outside?' he asked.

'It's what they're afraid of,' Viki said. 'That apprentice lawyer who asked the questions in the hall – she's scared them. Made it sound like a charge room.'

'Jessica?' he replied. 'Why, Jessica is one of my very best pupils – intellectually mature and rigorous, certainly, but we try to inculcate that. Yes, doing Law, as you said.'

'She more or less told them to use the right to silence. Who does she run with outside?' Viki asked.

'Outside?' he said. 'Run with?'

'Contacts outside *School*,' Viki replied.

'Oh, I don't really see that as my business or – '

'What did you, personally, make of Melissa?' Viki asked. 'Gerald.'

'Make of?' he replied.

'Strike you. How did she strike you? How does a thirteen-year-old get into a situation where she's double raped and killed?' Viki said.

'Get into a situation?' he replied. 'I don't understand. Are you saying her way of life brought this upon her? How? I don't see it like that. I see her as preyed on by some force of evil.'

'That, too,' Viki said.

'And it is the task of all of us to track down this force and put it where it can do no more terrible damage, and, of course, your task above all,' Rose said.

'Why we're here,' Viki replied.

'Could this be our opening client?' Kerry asked.

FIRST SCHOOL INTERVIEW: LESTER

A boy of about fourteen approached. He looked hesitant but determined, his face anxious, drawn, guilty. As he walked he stared all the time at Rose, as if the Religious Education teacher and Kerry and Viki had no role. The headmaster took a couple of steps towards him in welcome and said: 'Lester, you have something to say?' He pointed the boy towards the empty classroom. All of them went in. Lester was tall, dark-haired, long-nosed, thin, his face very pale, eyes bright and wary. Kerry was reminded of pictures she had seen lately with a newspaper article on a doomed matador. Gerald closed and locked the door. They sat at a pupils' table in the centre of the classroom, Lester at the head, Viki and Kerry on one side, Rose opposite.

'I can tell you one thing, that's all,' Lester said. His voice was feeble, frightened. 'Maybe it's nothing, anyway. What I saw, though.'

'That's all we want,' Kerry said.

'This is not grassing, not *real* grassing, because I wouldn't do it, but he messed me about, tried to mess me about. You know?'

'We don't even call it grassing,' Viki said. 'We regard it as acting like a witness.'

'Yes, but you're police.'

'And without witnesses the law could not work,' Viki replied.

'There's truth in that, Lester,' Mrs Ferguson said.

'Only that she knew Titch Raybould,' the boy replied.

'A. R. W. Raybould?' Viki asked.

'We call him Titch,' Lester said.

'Why are you sure of this?' Kerry asked.

'Yes, sure,' he said.

'You've seen them together?' Kerry asked.

'In a way,' Lester replied. 'But I'm sure.'

The headmaster said: 'Raybould is . . .?'

'He deals drugs, sir,' the boy replied.

'Yes,' Rose said.

'Or he doesn't deal drugs himself, not himself, actually,' the boy said, 'he's too big, but he's got all sorts. They deal *for* him.'

'Yes, we know about him,' Viki replied.

Rose said: 'We do see something of the problem here. I often wonder why, if you know about him, you don't – '

'He's so big they can't,' Lester replied.

49

'We will,' Viki said.

'So you're the pigs who might fly,' Lester said. 'Titch wants the school.'

'Wants it?' Mrs Ferguson asked.

'Monopoly trading here,' Viki said.

'I've seen him up at the school,' Lester said.

'Titch himself?' Viki asked.

'Outside. In his car. It's a Saab. You know that, do you? You watch him sometimes.'

'A Saab, yes,' Kerry replied.

'Looking at the school as at an objective, do you mean?' the headmaster asked.

'Objective?' Lester asked.

'A target, Lester,' Mrs Ferguson said.

'They're all doing it,' Viki said. 'All the major dealers. Schools, colleges, it's obvious.'

'This Titch and Melissa spoke?' Rose asked Lester.

'Titch stayed in the car,' Lester replied. 'He always stays in the car. He sent Gaston.'

'Gaston Devereux?' Viki said.

'Once, at a rave, Gaston tried to touch me up – all that,' Lester replied. 'He's like that. He got real unfriendly when I wouldn't.'

'Ah, I see. Why you are talking to us now?' Kerry said.

'A kicking when I was on the floor. I'm against him and any firm he works for.'

'What did the two of them do when they waited near the school?'

'The Saab's parked out of sight but near. Always. Gaston talks to kids he knows as they're coming out, or wants to know. He's building the trade. His job.'

'Talks to Melissa?' Viki asked.

'No, not Melissa. Gaston's just a low-life pusher. Melissa doesn't talk to nobodies like Gaston. But I've seen him watching her a lot, really watching her.'

'But why?' Mrs Ferguson asked.

'You mean why if he's gay?' Lester replied.

'Yes,' Mrs Ferguson said, 'that's what I mean.' She seemed to put on the bluntness for a moment to show a Religious Education teacher could discuss such things without embarrassment. After all, there was worse in the Bible.

Lester said: 'He might go both ways. A lot of girls fancy him. His foreign name.'

'Did she speak to Raybould on the occasion we're talking about, Lester?' Rose asked.

'Not speak.'

'Did she get into the car with him?' Viki asked.

'She wouldn't do that. Not right near the school. He wouldn't allow that,' Lester replied. 'They had a smile to each other.'

'That's all?' Rose asked.

'A real smile,' Lester said.

'What does that mean, Lester?' the headmaster asked.

'This was a smile saying something,' Lester replied.

'That's all?' Rose asked.

'Then she walked on,' Lester said, 'and Titch waited for Gaston in the Saab. This was a smile that meant they already knew each other but they didn't want to show it then.'

'Are you sure of this, Lester?' Rose asked. 'I don't know what Kerry and Viki make of what you say, but – '

'This is fine,' Kerry replied. 'Thank you, Lester.'

The headmaster left with him. Mrs Ferguson remained for the next two interviews. Both were with pupils. No staff came.

SECOND SCHOOL INTERVIEW: LIZ

'Once a man called Gaston – nearly everybody in school knows Gaston – he was up at the school – well, not *in* the school – *near* the school, like always – he said he had some H and it was free. He wanted to give me this H, it was in his hand. He said just take it.'

Liz was fourteen, small, bony, red-haired, dull-eyed, her voice an edgy monotone.

'Melissa saw him and came over, came running over, screaming at him to leave me alone and saying I wasn't one for that because I never did drugs and she hit at his hand with her hand and knocked the heroin packet down to the ground, it was raining. I did not even know Melissa then, not really, or her friend, Avril, except in the playground once I heard them call ...' She glanced at Mrs Ferguson. 'I heard them call someone ... like someone we know, but I won't say ... they call him Poison Breath, and it made me really laugh, I didn't know how they could have been so close to him. Gaston was really ratty about that when she made him drop the H, you could see how cross he was when he bent down to pick it up, saying things to himself, saucy things, which I'd say but Mrs Ferguson's here. And Melissa was telling me all the time to go straight away before he was ready again and never to speak to him again, even when she was not there, just go and maybe go out some other way from the school on other days. So, I do, and I've never seen Gaston again, I don't want to.'

'You mean they called Gaston Poison Breath?' Viki asked.

'No, not Gaston.'

'Who then, Liz?' Viki asked.

'No, not Gaston. Melissa said that afterwards Gaston used to come up to the school and even around her house just staring at her.'

'Stalking?' Viki asked.

'Just staring. He didn't *do* anything. Staring. Ratty. Like to scare her. Maybe he was scared to *do* anything because she knew Titch. That was what other kids said.'

THIRD SCHOOL INTERVIEW: FLORENCE

'I wasn't like her *main* friend, not her *best* friend.'

'But a friend?' Kerry replied.

'Her *main* friend was called Avril but she's gone now.'

Mrs Ferguson said: 'Avril Grant moved to Portugal with her father's job.'

'But I would go out with Melissa sometimes, and sometimes with both of them,' Florence said. 'They were like older?'

'No, I don't think so, Florence,' Mrs Ferguson replied. 'If my memory is right, they were both a little *younger* than you.'

'But I mean *like* older,' Florence said.

'They behaved older?' Kerry asked.

'When we were out sometimes. Not when we were in school,

but when we were out sometimes. If you met them and you did not know them you would think more than thirteen.'

'Both confident children, yes,' Mrs Ferguson replied. 'Avril very clever, very articulate. A little forward, perhaps, but this is forgivable I always think in a bright child, even natural.'

'And Melissa, did she tell you things about herself?' Kerry asked. 'Did she talk to you more after Avril went? Perhaps you became her main friend then.'

'E-mail,' Florence replied. 'They're both on the Net. I'm on the Net at home, too, but I wouldn't send to Avril because I wasn't a *main* friend, not to her or Melissa. That's what I mean, like older.'

'When you did go out with them perhaps you met people,' Kerry said.

'Once we did.'

'Yes?'

Mrs Ferguson twitched a bit and Kerry wanted to stare her into stillness, but kept looking at Florence.

'It was *they* met them, really.'

'But you were there?'

'At first I was there.'

'Where?'

'This was to see *Trainspotting*.'

'The cinema?' Kerry said. 'But you'd all be too young for that, wouldn't you?'

'That's what I mean, they were like older.'

'They could bluff their way in, but not you?'

'They met two boys. Well, not boys, really. Like men. Lots of talk, like, you know. Like men. And Avril talking, sort of grown up. I didn't hear it all. I was like . . .' Her face tightened, grew sad.

'They were a foursome?' Viki asked. 'You were on the edge?'

Florence wondered about those words. 'Yes, like on the edge. Sometimes before when I went out with them, like on the edge if they met boys.'

'They had arranged to meet these two?' Viki asked.

'No, just met them – while we were looking at the times board, wondering if we could go in. I don't mean Avril and Mel were slaggy. Of course kids say things about Avril but I

53

don't believe it. Not just picking up boys. They just started talking about the picture, that's all. We all wanted to see *Trainspotting* because of reading the book. There is a book as well as the film, you see.'

'And these boys came over and began chatting you up, did they?' Viki asked.

'Men, really. They were as old as my brother. He's twenty. Saying were we going to see *Trainspotting*?'

'But only two of them and three of you,' Kerry said.

'But Melissa and Avril did not want me to go home,' she said. The humiliation of it was in her round pale childish face. 'They were my friends. Not my *main* friends, but they would not send me away because of . . .'

'Because of the foursome,' Kerry said.

'I didn't like them, anyway,' she replied.

'You were very, very wise, Florence,' Mrs Ferguson said.

'I wanted to see *Trainspotting*, though.'

'Better without,' Mrs Ferguson. 'The film isn't at all about trainspotting, you know, Florence.'

'I read the book.'

'Why didn't you like them?' Kerry asked.

'I don't know. I didn't think they were nice.'

'They didn't want you there?'

'Sort of selfish. They didn't care.' She looked as if she might begin to cry.

Mrs Ferguson said: 'Perhaps that's enough now, sergeant.'

'Could you describe them?' Kerry asked. 'Each about twenty. What else?'

'Or more than twenty,' Florence replied.

'Tall? Fat? Thin?' Viki asked.

'No, not very tall. One was thin and with dark hair, a lot. Curly.'

'Nice looking?' Kerry asked.

'But like hard. I was scared of him.'

'You did well not to accompany them, Florence,' Mrs Ferguson said.

'Scared why?' Viki asked.

'All that curly hair – like crazy?' Florence said. 'And his eyes.' It was as though she wanted to say more but something stopped her. Perhaps the presence of Mrs Ferguson. Perhaps the presence of Viki and Kerry themselves.

'What about his eyes?' Viki asked.

'I don't know – not nice. You could see he was thinking. I didn't know what he was thinking. He was with Avril – I think he was with Avril, because they started the talking, but I think he wanted to be with Mel. He was looking at her a lot. The other one fatter, skinhead cut, brown hair, a bit sort of dozy. I think he had the haircut to make him seem hard. Melissa was with him.'

'Any names?' Viki asked.

'I was like on the edge,' Florence replied. 'Like you said. I didn't hear everything. But the dark one, the curly one, I think he said Colin. He said from Ireland.'

'Did he have an accent?' Kerry asked.

'His *name* was from Ireland, not him. I think that's what he said. I didn't hear the other one's name. I was by the popcorn counter, and people were asking for popcorn there, talking, and the till going so I couldn't hear.'

'You returned home by yourself and the four of them went into the cinema?' Kerry asked.

Florence paused: 'They said sorry next day, Melissa and Avril.'

'They were all right?'

'All right? Of course.'

'Did they say what had happened?'

Mrs Ferguson stood up.

'They said about the film,' Florence replied. 'They told me about the film, because I didn't see it.'

13

When she asked Mark what she should do about Melissa's death and the investigation Kerry knew what he would reply, and she wondered afterwards if the only reason she *had* asked was to get him actually to say it. His answer became more than just an answer. She turned it into a symbol. Had she *wanted* him to act to pattern – to miserable, honourable pattern – and so free her? Poor Mark, was he being set up? She listened properly, nodded a couple of times and thanked him at the end. She said she was looking for every point of view before making up her mind, and then decided, with a logic she recognised as shaky, egomaniac and maybe no logic at all, that she could now go to bed with Vic Othen, if Vic Othen would go to bed with *her*.

This was not a hasty or whorish thing though, was it? Was it? Not a bit. She and Vic had been near fucking at least once before. At the time, she was upset about something in the job and wanted consolation. That all? He had thought so, the decent, patronising bastard. She had not. She could recall the conversation, could recall Vic getting damn scrupulous:

No, Kerry, I don't think so, you're stressed for the moment – not thinking well. A need for comforting's poor reason to start a love affair. I wouldn't want to be just a medicine.

For a while Kerry had mulled this. *No, you're probably right. For now.*

Yes, for now. I'll go home. For now.

For then. That was a while ago. At breakfast today with Mark she said: 'I've put myself in a dodgy spot. Tell me how this looks to you.'

It was almost 8.30 a.m. and Mark would have to leave for work very soon. She needed him to talk about things, but not talk very much. Everyone said he had a terrific analytical mind. He could sometimes settle down on a subject, really dismantle it, given time. So, don't give him the time. 'The death of this child – in the papers and on TV,' she said.

'The girl?' He had his second cup of breakfast coffee on the table before him. The routine was he would drink this slowly reading a newspaper or chatting – say, seven or eight minutes – then put his own and her crockery and cutlery into the machine, nip to the bathroom to clean his teeth, and leave. He liked to be out of the flat by 8.40. She did not despise routines. Everybody needed some. Mark had a lot, though, and he really stuck to them, like a Borstal timetable.

Kerry said: 'I'd watched her get into a car with a man just

56

before she was killed and felt so bad about it – guilty, I mean – that for a moment I couldn't tell anyone when I heard she was dead. Abused and dead.'

'For a moment? That's all right, surely. Quite understandable.' He gazed at her across the table with a question in his face, as if he sensed she had done some serious editing. He knew her.

'More than a moment. I was sort of dazed. And then, of course, it became too late to tell anyone.'

'You haven't said anything even now?'

'I can't.'

'And the man?'

'He's not likely to say anything, is he, even if he didn't do it. He'd have to prove himself in the clear.'

Mark swallowed a mouthful. 'Christ, Kerry.'

'I know.'

He stayed quiet for a while and put his cup down. 'Darling, this will sound – oh, I don't know, it's bound to sound pat, I suppose, but you must tell them at once, even so late. Surely.'

'I can't.'

'You know who killed her?'

'I know she was in the car just before.'

'You know the man?'

'Oh, yes,' she replied.

'Madness not to say. I mean, it's criminal, isn't it?'

'I can't believe he did it.'

He considered that for a time. Then, his voice grew very tender. He would know he was kicking her special skill, but he meant to kick it, temperately. 'I've an idea this is to do with the damned informant game. Is it?'

'Yes, the damned informant game.'

'Shadowy areas, Kerry. I know, I know, darling, you'll say this is how nine-tenths of police detection gets done. Just the same, I wish you could . . . Oh, I do wish you could move into some other kind of work.' He finished the coffee. His voice toughened for a second. 'The thing is, how can any organisation operate if its own members hold back crucial information?' His lightened tone again immediately. 'Is this you looking for some career advantage, love?' He tried to make it sound like a minor

57

reproof for an outbreak of ambition, but could not completely get rid of the weight.

'A bit of that, maybe,' she said. 'Detective's stockpile. But mainly what I said – guilt, shame.'

He began to gather the breakfast things for the dishwasher. 'You *have* to tell them. Look, I understand the wish to push ahead of other people. Of course I do. What a career *is*. But the personal aspect has to be set against, and subordinated to, the needs of the whole organisation or . . . Do I sound all-knowing, pompous? Just the same, things have to be like that, or, my God, it's chaos. An organisation must be able to forecast and rely on the behaviour of its components. You must see this, Kerry. And especially when the organisation is a police force investigating a terrible murder. Maverick behaviour is . . . well, frankly, inexcusable. You say you're sure the man in the car could not commit that act. But is it really for you to decide? Sorry, but I've got to ask. Your expertise is the children. A pity, I think, but that's how it is. You're not in charge of these murder inquiries, are you? Couldn't you be in appalling trouble for withholding evidence?'

'What I meant – a dodgy spot,' she replied.

He closed the machine and was going to make for the bathroom but delayed. 'Look, would you like to talk to one of our lawyers? Bernard's done quite a bit on the criminal side. And he's entirely discreet. I'm sure he'd be able to assess things, suggest a way out.'

It was kindly and very practical. 'Thanks, Mark. Not yet.'

'The longer the worse. We don't have to be lawyers to see that.'

'Not yet. Mark, you'll be late.'

At the nick she looked for Vic Othen but could not find him at once. Nobody knew where he might be. Although Vic stayed a detective constable he had seniority back to the Bow Street Runners and ran his own schedule. He and Kerry were not a team, but she had worked with him once or twice and come to admire him, despite the cigarettes. Well, obviously more than admired – dim, heartless, sexless term. Kerry was getting good at anaemic words. Perhaps she was scared of the livelier ones, and where they might take her. She was intrigued by Vic, had been for months, or longer.

The contradictions in him fascinated her, drew her. He seemed careless about rank and advancement, yet had a brilliant competence that everyone recognised, including himself. Oh, yes, there was something which came close to arrogance in Vic. Well, she had some of that herself. But Kerry's fast-track progress and fast-track ambitions seemed hardly to register with him, except as cause for genial mockery. This shook her and attracted her. And yet he did have some respect for show. He kept himself gorgeously dressed and elegantly coiffured: his hair was grey, but sleek, gleaming grey, not defunct grey.

Possibly Kerry was finding the bad side of fast-trackery. She had become so used to adulation that if it was denied by someone she had to win him over, or the whole mystique of her success might begin to look shaky. Her thinking sounded calculated. It was not. It was panicky.

While she waited for Vic now, Kerry wrote up from memory the meeting with Gerald Rose and the three schoolchildren. The notes looked weak. Lester had guessed from a smile that Melissa knew Titch. This was clever of him but told Kerry nothing new. Did the episode when Melissa intervened between Liz and Gaston add up to much, or the cinema meeting with the men-boys described by Florence? As far as she could remember it, she wrote down Gerald Rose's description of Melissa: *moving towards lovely womanhood, vivacious, affectionate.* They were probably terms any headmaster might use of a thirteen-year-old girl, weren't they? Anyway, was she remembering right? Did he really say 'lovely womanhood'? She would have to check with Viki.

Just before lunch, she saw Othen come in and sit at his desk. At once she went over and pulled a chair up close alongside him. 'Vic, I've put myself in a dodgy spot. Tell me how it looks to you.'

'Dodgy how? The peril from outside or in?

'In.'

'The worst.'

'I know. Melissa Slater – I watched her get into a car just

59

before she was killed and felt so bad about it – guilty, I mean – that for a moment when I heard of her death and so on I couldn't tell anyone.'

'You mean for lots of moments?'

'I was sort of dazed.'

'It became impossible?' he said. Vic was too old a hand to let the horror at what she was telling him appear in his face, or even in the way he held his body. He sat smiling a little and relaxed as before, but somehow she knew he was enormously troubled by what she said, possibly even more than Mark. Vic would see all the perils instantly and know in detail their seriousness. After all, he was one of the trade. Perhaps it was the pauses in his conversation now that signalled to Kerry how alarmed for her he was. After half a minute or so he said: 'It *is* too late to tell them, is it? Perhaps Harry would ... He likes you, Kerry. He might understand.'

'He'd understand. He wouldn't forgive.' She found she was snarling. Christ, she came to Vic for help and he tried to help and she treated him like this. 'Harry *shouldn't* forgive,' she said.

Vic gazed at nothing for a while. 'Right,' he said eventually.

'So, no way out of it.' She took care to make that sound like a statement, not a question. She had no right to ask him for solutions when she had decided there weren't any. Yet it *was* a question, really. She wanted Vic to bring some magic from his store. Why else had she searched for him today? He was someone who looked after her. *So, look after me, now, Vic. Please.* Kerry did not say this, but Vic would sense it, wouldn't he?

'I've landed myself in that sort of situation myself,' he said.

She stared. 'Is that right, Vic?'

'Which detective hasn't?'

'It's a murder, for God's sake. Hoarding evidence on a murder. Are you trying to pump up my morale – only that?' He would do this, had done it in previous cases. It annoyed her and sustained her. She needed it. She wanted him because he understood her and hardly ever tried to change her. Stand by your girl. She could rely on him for that and for this she loved him. That was the non-anaemic word she required, and slightly feared.

'Yes, a murder,' he replied. 'It's only worth doing at all on a big case.'

'Vic, this is a pep talk, isn't it? Lies, fictions?'

'Whose car? Gaston's or Titch Raybould's himself?'

'You knew that? How?'

'Titch's?'

'Knew it how, you sod?'

'He's been targeting the kid's school, I hear. Targeting a lot of schools. Putting Gaston in. You were using her? Probationer grass? Smart work to get her into Titch's Saab.'

'Yes, wasn't it. Brilliant. "Take a death trip for me, Melissa, would you, dear?" '

'Bollocks, Kerry.' The hesitancy was gone. He had taken over her troubles. 'Drop the self-pity,' he said. 'It's not you. Titch wouldn't do that to her. He might kill a grass, even a kid grass, but not the rest of it.'

'What I thought.'

'You did well not to say anything. It would have sent things in the wrong direction.'

'What I thought.'

'We work on this by ourselves, quietly,' Othen said. Suddenly, he had transformed the disaster into a starting point.

'We?'

'Of course. Don't you want the help? But perhaps you'd like to corner all the praise?' It was a genuine, unsarcastic question.

'What praise, for God's sake, Vic?'

'When we catch him, the right one. When *you* catch him. That's how you see it?'

'I need the help.'

'Good. What we have to do is build ourselves a portrait of her recent life.'

'Harry Bell and Doug Quinn want that, too.'

'We'll have our own.'

'I know a bit – from talking to her, obviously, and from interviewing kids and the head up at the school.'

'That's the kind of thing.'

'But Viki was with me at the school. This is not private information.'

61

'Never mind. We can add it to what you *do* know privately,' Vic said.

'What the schoolkids and the head could tell us was pretty thin.'

'We take that information and imagine our way forward from it.'

'Imagine?'

'Build,' he said. 'We need to talk to Titch – see where he put the child down, if he did.'

'If he knows I saw her get into his car he'll realise I should have disclosed that – he'll see I've started playing some shady game, and he'll use that against me.'

He switched. 'So we don't tell him you saw Melissa in his car.'

'Why else would we be talking to him?' she asked.

'I'll work on that one. Then we take the incidents you heard about at the school and try to plump them out from what we – you – know of her, which is more than anyone else knows of her. That's what I call detection.'

'God, I wish I'd talked deeper with her.'

'We've all been in that spot, Kerry. Useless regret. But, now, she can't tell us for herself what happened, so we help her out. Yes, build. You and I must have a proper pow-wow.' He glanced about the crowded room. 'Not here.'

'No.'

'Pub?'

'As bad as this,' she replied. 'Your place?'

He frowned minutely. Vic kept his scruples fresh. It was a pain.

'Where do we get privacy otherwise?' she said. 'There's nobody else in residence with you at present, is there?'

He did not answer that, as if it did not require an answer. 'OK,' he said, 'my place, this evening.'

'I'll bring some wine.'

'This has to be a very clear-headed creative session and policy discussion.'

'Of course, of course,' she said.

'And you'll have to drive home afterwards.'

'Understood. I'll bring some wine.'

14

There had been a time at school and in her life altogether when Melissa Slater decided that the thing about being nearly fourteen was it was *really* great. It was like the beginning of being grown up. She could feel it, like a real buzz. This was not just because old Poison Breath told her she was *moving towards lovely womanhood*, this was what he said, *moving towards lovely womanhood* and really close when he said it, so she got the full poison as well as the words, *really* close, that way of his, and moving even closer towards someone who was moving towards lovely womanhood. She had had to dodge out. She nearly had a giggle when he said it but she did not want to breathe in too much. He said the same thing, the same words, to Avril, she told Melissa, *moving towards lovely womanhood*. His voice could get like a tremble in it when he said this or similar. You could wonder if he had a come in his pants. Some people could get off on words, it was well known. He had thought up them words so he wanted to give them a real go, saying them to two girls not just one, but not when the two girls was together, or maybe more than two. If you was a headmaster keeping an eye on everything in the school in that way of his you might notice quite a few girls *moving towards lovely womanhood*, and if you was a headmaster you could move towards them and tell them about it, that was all right for a headmaster, like telling them they better do better at spelling, gasping a bit and tonguing his own lips, *real* juiciness.

But Melissa could feel it, anyway, the growing up, without Poison Breath to tell her and getting trembly. Avril said she was the same, they did not need the message from him. It was not just periods and boobs, but everything. In some countries you could be married when you was fourteen and have babies, this was well known in geography. You could see them in magazines holding a baby in South America or Africa and their husband near. Usually the husband was older with a double necklace of teeth from pigs, and a small black beard on the end of his chin. In the paper not long ago it said maybe soon in Britain there would be sex when kids was fourteen. Well, there was *already* sex when kids was fourteen and lower, that was obvious, but the paper said this would soon be all right, not just something kids had regular without saying. Fourteen, not lower, not yet. The law would say this was all right, not too young.

The law. Kerry was the law and she already made Melissa feel grown up. Them talks with her – like talks grown-ups would have. These was important talks, business talks, not talks for a kid. Melissa liked them. She did not tell Kerry everything, not yet. She told her a lot but not everything, not everything about Gaston or Titch or that night at the pictures with Avril et cetera and that *really* crazy washbasin. Lucky, Avril went to Portugal not long after that washbasin.

This was grown up, also – to keep some stuff private, even from Kerry. All grown-ups had private sides, they did not blab the lot, not all at once, maybe a bit at a time. Melissa thought she was growing up very fast, and she loved that.

But some kids, girls, when they was nearly fourteen was not at all grown up and not *moving into lovely womanhood* a bit. This was not because they was not lovely. They might be, but not moving into womanhood yet. They were still just like kids. They did not seem to be moving at all, just stuck where they had always been, nice but only baby nice. Sometimes you had to look after kids like that, such as Liz Quant and Florence Cass. This was what Melissa thought. She had got *really* ratty that day when she saw that Gaston try to load some H on Liz Quant. This was H for sure, not just grass or poppers. Well, Liz was just a kid, she did not know a thing – nice, but she did not know a thing.

The thing about Titch himself is he would not try to get someone like Liz on to H, never. He would see what kind of kid she was, just a baby kid. But Gaston – he would try anyone. All he wanted was, get them hooked and it was easiest to get them hooked early. So he would give them H, give them the first lot and maybe even another one. Up the school, hanging about and then, *Hello, there, kid, here's a nice little presie for you,*

and plenty more where that came from. You will really fly with this.
Like your friends. Melissa had heard it. But then after that they
would have to have it and he would say they had to pay for it
now and they would have to go thieving from the shops or
their parents or bunking off school to go street tarting, many
car punters liking young ones, thinking they were first or
nearly. Gaston would have them himself first, especially girls
but not always.

A girl like Liz she would of just taken it, she did not know
how to say no. Melissa used to be like that, so she started
screaming at Gaston and knocked the stuff out of his hand and
told Liz to get away. So when she was gone Gaston starts, of
course he did, saying don't think she could come on his ground
fucking things up just because she was shagging Titch Raybould, Mr Fucking Supremo. This was the way he talked
always, but not when he was trying to get some young kid to
take the H. Then he would be all creepy and nice. It was not
true, what he said about Titch. Gaston *would* think that, someone like him, because he was dirty right through, and he said
to watch out cowbitch because he would not forget about that
H being hit to the ground and made a fool of like that in front
of a kid by some kid slag, it was not true. He was in jail so
much, Gaston, he did not know what ordinary things outside
was like or an ordinary kid like Liz. But Melissa did not get
scared of Gaston, it was all noise most probably. He would be
scared himself in case she told Titch everything. That was being
sarcastic when Gaston said Mr Fucking Supremo, but that is
what Titch was, Mr Supremo, without the fucking or without
the fucking of her. This was the kind of thing she would never
tell Kerry about because it would be terrible to tell her Gaston
thought she was like that with Titch, it made her ashamed. She
got really all hot and shaky when she thought about that. You
could never tell what police would believe, even if you told
them it was not true. Police were a bit like Gaston – they saw
dirtiness everywhere. It was because they had to spend so
much time talking to bits of rubbish like Gaston, and because
they was trained to think dirt, anyway, most likely.

15

When Melissa had that row with Gaston up by the school about Liz Quant, Titch was not there but sometimes he would come up with Gaston and Melissa would see him sitting in the Saab and just watching Gaston giving out stuff or selling it, but Titch would not get out of the car himself, he did not do that kind of work, not now, although maybe he did once before he became so mighty. He would be listening to music on the car radio or a cassette, Titch liked a really great yelling number called *The Messiah*, which is a famous Jewish word about many holy matters, and Randy Crawford numbers such as *One Day I'll Fly Away*. When he was sitting in the car you could see why he was called Titch, and when he was not sitting in the car.

The thing about days when Titch used to come up to the school in the Saab with Gaston or one of the other workers was she would never speak to him or show she knew him. This was a bit like when Kerry came up the school. It was a secret matter. She might look at him once, or how would she know he was there if she did not look once? But no wave, and no talk. There would be a lot of kids about because Titch would come up at the end of the day for the school, so Gaston or one of the other workers could catch the kids when they was going home. There was kids like a kid called Lester who had eyes bigger than yo-yos, he would be watching, watching. He was not a bad kid and brainy, he could see what was what if he had a chance, so he had better not have a chance. You could not tell which kid might be a big mouth, even brainy kids. It really gave Melissa a giggle inside herself when she thought even a brainy kid like Lester could never guess she knew Titch, just like she had a giggle because nobody could tell she knew Kerry.

Daisy or Jessica was brainy, too, and she might see things but she would never big-mouth because she said all kids must be able to do what they wanted to do, she thought kids should be *really* free, especially when it was a new millennium. It was

66

rubbish. Avril said if Daisy was like that she should not be a prefect, telling kids not to run in the corridors and going spare because some kid stuck gum in a library book, only that droner Geoffrey Chaucer or something like that. Melissa could not tell if Daisy was doing any stuff, she never seemed to be off of her face, and not even brainy ones could hide that. She might of looked better if she was off of her face.

16

Yes, they had met two boys in the Regis. This was when they was pretending they was trying to decide which film they wanted to see, but they knew. It was *Trainspotting*, not some Disney drool. They was talking in the foyer about who would go for the tickets, because it was an 18. Not Florence. Avril said it better be her because she could do a *real* voice, a voice *really* greasy it was so grown up. *Three, please, and what time does the picture actually come on screen, not the ads and trailers, the picture its very self? Trailers – so noisy.* She practised this and they was laughing. She could sound like a true grown-up woman. That was why some kids said them filthy tales about her and why her father said they had to go to Portugal. Melissa did not believe it. Most probably she would never ask her dad about something like that. It was horrible.

And then one of the boys must of heard Avril practising and said: 'You're dead right – in trailers it's always buildings blown up in flames or cars crashing off a bridge or the police commander shouting at the detective to give up his badge and gun, he's *off the case*. I'm Colm.'

'Colm?' Avril replied.

'It's Irish. It means something over there.'

'What?' Avril said.

'Something in the landscape. Maybe a hill. Or a wood.'

'I believe there are a lot of woods in Ireland,' Avril replied, 'such as "By Killarney's Lakes and Dells", which is in my piano book, and a dell is a wood.'

Avril knew all sorts of things and the thing was she didn't only know them, she knew how to get them out and talk about them at the right time. It was a good idea not to listen to her playing the piano but it was great to listen to her talking when she wanted to.

Avril, Florence and Melissa had all *really* wanted to see *Trainspotting*. Jessica who was Daisy had told them about it. Melissa used to think that maybe Daisy knew how dim it was for her to talk to young kids about freedom like she did when she was a prefect and bossing them. This was why Daisy would mention books like *Trainspotting* sometimes when she was looking after Melissa's class. The book was about kids doing what they wanted to do, mostly boys who was nearly men, but a girl from a school was in it, also, having it off with one of the boys. The boy was *really* surprised when he found out this girl was only a schoolkid and he was scared in case of her parents and the police, although the girl wanted it and it was not her first. Daisy wanted to show she was not *really* someone who liked to boss kids around, but she did boss the kids around but she pretended she did not like to boss the kids around and so she told them about this book about kids doing whatever they liked. This was brain. Most likely she would be great at college, ideas coming out of her everywhere like rain from a cloud.

That book was *really* great. Then they wanted to see the film which Daisy said was also great and she called it 'utterly faithful to the work', meaning they copied the book, *really* copied it. Three of them read that book, Melissa, Avril and Florence Cass, so they only had to pay £2.33 each for it and taking it in turns, Florence first. She was a bit like Liz, she was very nice, but a kid kid and nearly titless so far and not moving towards lovely womanhood, so maybe she did not really understand all the book. But she knew it was not about trainspotting. She hated the part where he messed the bed, but this might be only natural after a lot of drinking and drugging, they could upset you all ends. Florence wanted to come to see the film, and that was all right, she was a friend and nice. Melissa and Avril did a bit with make-up and padded their bras to look older but Florence could not do anything like that, she was just as usual, her blouse flat as a bath mat and hair like soccer refs on *Match of the Day*. The thing was you had to be careful if you padded your bra if you met boys because they would want to be topping at skin level of course if you had done it nice and then they would find out and they might say falsies to everyone after.

Melissa had thought it was great to be talking to boys in that spot, where you could smell the frankfurter stall and popcorn and hear the ticket machines. Melissa thought it was really like living, with the thick blue carpet with like a black pattern of arrows or spears on it and the people serving the popcorn and frankfurters wearing white uniforms with pink stripes and great hats, like a chef's hat, very clean. The lights were *really* bright so you could nearly count all the whiskers in people's eyebrows.

'And here's Jake,' Colm said.

'Jake?' Avril replied.

'His name's Maurice, but he doesn't like it,' Colm said.

'Jake's a terrific name,' Avril replied. 'It's like wild, like the prairies.'

'A bit,' Jake said.

'More wild than Maurice,' Avril replied. 'Maurice sounds like a day at Skegness. I'm Avril.'

'Terrific,' Colm said.

'It's French.'

'That right?' Colm replied.

'Meaning April,' Avril said. 'They have all sorts of different names for the months over there, and most probably in Germany and other countries such as India. In France March is M-a-r-s, but they don't say the s on the end like a z, so they won't mix March up with a Mars bar, which are international.'

'April's my favourite month,' Jake said. 'This is the spring, and primroses.'

'You a poet or something?' Avril replied. 'And this is Florence and Melissa.'

'Melissa?' Colm said. He was standing by Avril, because that was how the talk had started and because she was a big talker, but Melissa thought he would like to be near to *her* really. 'That's from abroad, isn't it?'

'Could be,' Melissa replied. 'Maybe from Jamaica or Peru,

somewhere like that. Like tropical.' Avril was not the only one with foreign countries just because she was called Avril. 'My father read it in the Marriages column of a paper when they were waiting for me. If I had been a boy, I don't know what.'

'Someone getting married, someone, such as you, getting born at nearly the same time,' Jake said. 'This is how life is.'

'You *are* a poet, are you?' Avril asked.

'He gets thoughts,' Colm said. 'Which picture are you going to see?'

'*Trainspotting*,' Florence replied.

'We were wondering about *Trainspotting*, yes,' Avril said. 'But I heard parts of it are *coarse*. It's been around before hasn't it?'

'Yes, I saw it a couple of years ago,' Colm said.

'Oh?' Avril replied. 'Well, maybe we – '

'But we want to see it again,' Colm said. 'It's so great.'

'My, it *must* be good,' Avril replied.

'We could go together, the four of us,' Jake said.

Melissa did a count, pointing at all of them and making it really strong when she pointed at Florence: 'Five.'

'Oh,' Jake said. 'Yes.'

'Florence loves that book, *Trainspotting*,' Melissa replied. 'She *really* wants to see the picture, don't you, Flor?'

'Oh,' Jake said.

'It starts in five minutes,' Colm said.

Melissa thought he was having a good look at her although he was still talking most to Avril. Melissa thought it might be Jake for her. He was all right. His name was wild but he did not *look* wild he looked a bit dozy. Sometimes they were safer like that, a sort of old baby. Colm did not look safe, he looked like he could be a bit rough and perilous if things did not go right, she did not mind that, it might just be he was more sparky than Jake. They were not really boys. She thought they were both twenty or even twenty-two, especially Colm. He had dark hair, curly and a lot, she liked that. He was not too tall and he was thin, but not too thin, and nice hands, thin hands with long fingers, you could think of him serving necklaces in a top shop, nothing cheap and cheerful, putting necklaces around necks in front of the mirror and the women *really* liking it, their skin and his fingers. Jake was fatter and his hair was brownish and cut right down short, so he would look hard and not like a Maurice but a Jake. Most likely his mother *really* worried about him, she might be a single parent, he looked so dreamy, what Avril called a poet. But it might just be scared of the world if you only had a mother. It did not leave much room for mistakes. Melissa knew a lot like that, girls and boys.

'One thing I hate, it's standing in a ticket queue,' Avril said. 'You get the tickets, Colm?' She was making sure it was her and him, she *really* liked him, anyone could see. She could be like that, pushy, her little teeth all shiny and fierce. There was no probs for him to buy the tickets, being old. 'It's not much of a queue,' Jake said, 'because it's been here before.'

'Even a small queue, I hate it,' Avril replied, 'I've got our money.' She held it out towards Colm.

'For three?' he said.

'Of course,' Melissa replied.

'Right,' Colm said, but it did not sound like he liked it.

'No, I think I'll go home,' Florence said. She was a kid but she was not a stupid kid and Melissa saw she could tell Colm and Jake did not want her, this was a foursome. Nobody ever heard of a fivesome. When she was older she might become a girl who was not always spare.

'No,' Melissa said, 'you *really* wanted to see this film, Florence.'

'I think I'll go home,' Florence replied. She was all stiff and upset and her face like an old wreath.

'You can come with us, *really*, Florence,' Avril said.

When she said 'us' like that it made it sound like this foursome was the thing but they would not mind if she came as well, like just coming along with the foursome because the foursome wanted to be kind.

'I think I'll go home,' Florence said. She was nearly crying but she was a good kid and did not cry properly.

'You could see the film another time,' Jake told her.

'It will be starting,' Colm said. He said he would pay the lot.

'Oh, no, really,' Avril cried.

But he did. Inside when they sat down, it was him then Avril then Jake then Melissa. Avril leaned forward in her seat so she could talk to Melissa just before *Trainspotting* started: 'If we get separarted when it's over, see you in the place tomorrow, Mel.'

'Right,' Melissa said.

That meant Avril wanted to go somewhere with Colm by theirselves after. Avril said 'the place', she would not say school, because she did not want Colm to know she was just a schoolkid after bra padding and talking old about Mars bars known to all nations. Most likely she would be all right, she could keep him talking about Killarney's lakes and colms. Colm leaned forward in his seat also and looked down the row to Melissa and gave her a smile in the darkness but he did not say anything because even if he fancied Melissa she was with his friend now and Colm was with *her* friend and you had to behave right, except Melissa thought none of them behaved right about Florence, that was *so* sad.

17

'Luckily, Titch was able to get here as soon as I called him,' Vic Othen said, silver hair, silver moustache, gleaming under the plastic chandelier. 'I've been stressing this is unofficial, Kerry, and now he can see it it – you arrive bearing claret!'

'Unofficial? I don't know what it means,' Raybould replied. To Kerry, his voice sounded mild and vastly untrustable, full of West Country cream-tea fatness. 'All I know is I'm talking to two police officers and I've no lawyer with me. Am I mad suddenly, Vic?' He struck his forehead playfully with the ball of his right hand.

'You know me, Titch,' Othen replied.

'Yes, I know you, Vic, and I still haven't got a lawyer with me.'

'And you know Kerry,' Othen said.

'A bit. I've met her. So, I'm on my own in a police officer's flat with two detectives, one of them older than history and with all the tricks, and the other much younger, but already a sergeant and fast-tracking it, so she must know all the tricks, too.'

'Unofficial meaning it's not at the nick, Titch, and nobody at the nick knows about this meeting or will know about it, or not from us, anyway,' Othen replied.

'Am I going to tell them?' Raybould said. 'Do I have regular chats with Harry Bell and Doug Quinn?'

'I'm sure they'd like to be fans. As I said on the phone, we hear some information that could be damaging to you and we'd like to dispose of it here in private discussion. We felt a duty to try to contain things before they slipped out of control, a duty to help you.'

'Oh, Christ,' Raybould replied, 'where's that fucking lawyer?' It was odd to hear swearing in his soothing, lay preacher's purr.

'Kerry especially,' Othen said. 'She was really strong on this. Hence the urgency and privacy.'

She had come here tonight with some urgency, yes, and expecting privacy, yes, privacy for just herself and Vic. But he had summoned Titch. Was Vic scared of her, repelled by her? She did not believe it, yet for a few seconds felt so hurt and disappointed she could have blurted something at him and left. He was . . . he was what – fifty years old? More? She was half that. Did he have to send out for protection from her, a chaperon?

'"Damaging information,"' Raybould said. 'The old-style mystery, the old-style interrogation suite double-talk. "We only want to help you." Oh, absolutely. There can't be damaging information about me, Victor.'

'But you came,' Othen replied. 'Now, why, I wonder? I'm going to pull the cork and pour.' He crossed the room to Kerry and took the wine, then went out into the kitchen.

'Excuse me, but something on between you two?' Raybould asked her.

'On?'

'You know.' He was in a fine brown three-piece suit and suede shoes with patterned toe caps. The high-buttoned waist-coat gave him something close to winsomeness. Titch knew how to use style. Looking at him, you could believe he began as a carer, but had perhaps met snubs or ingratitude, and so turned to greed and viciousness instead. Occasionally, these would appear in his small round face more strongly than the traces of sympathy.

'We work together sometimes,' Kerry said.

'But I heard you were in a long-term thing, a relationship – some catering businessman, doing all right,' Raybould said. 'Cohabitation.' He brought out a small leather notebook and consulted a page. 'Mark Taber? On Stephen Comble's board no less? But now it's you and Vic? Sharing secrets – only there aren't any. A hot link joins you? This is murky, if I may say.' He put the notebook away.

Vic came back with three wine glasses and the opened bottle on a round tin tray. It was decorated with a picture of men and horses doing medieval battle. He poured out carefully and handed the glasses around. They sat down, Kerry in an easy chair, Titch and Vic on a long stout-armed beige settee. Titch stretched out his little legs and seemed relaxed. In his face was a genial curiosity about why he had been invited, eyes alert, a semi-smile in place, no evidence of worry.

'About the dead child, Melissa Slater,' Othen said.

'A bad do,' Raybould replied.

'We don't see much progress,' Othen said.

'These kids, some of them – very shadowy lives,' Raybould replied, 'taking God knows what risks. Seemingly so much older than their birth certificates say, and yet still children, with all the weaknesses. I shudder.' He did, hunching his shoulders up and closing both eyes for a second. Titch believed in gesture. 'Just the same, no kid deserves that.'

'Did you know her, Titch?' Othen asked.

Raybould gave a yell of ripe laughter and then turned to Kerry: 'Subtle laddie, isn't he, our Victor? You like that? What's going on, I wonder.'

'This is a kid who did some drugs not long ago, now clean,' Othen replied. 'We wondered if you knew her.'

' "Did some drugs"? What's that to me?' Raybould said.

Vic suddenly stood up, walked quickly to the far side of the room and lifted three framed pictures away from the wall in turn – or prints, not pictures, gentle sailing boat scenes. It was an invitation to Raybould to look behind them. 'We're not bugged here. Would Vic Othen do that to you?' he said. Raybould ignored the show. Bugging could be a bit more sophisticated than that, and he would know it. Vic sat down again. 'So, you don't have to talk like you've never dealt a cellophane packet in your life, Titch, or run a string of pushers, nor pretend your income's not about fifty times what you tell the Revenue. That's what I meant, unofficial. No need to deny your soul and profession to us. We all have to work.'

'I was asking her when you were out in the kitchen, Vic – something heartfelt and hormonal between you two, even at your tired age?'

'So you could have come into contact with the girl when she was experimenting,' Vic replied. 'You like to help youngsters along, don't you? Have you seen pictures of her on TV or in the Press? Recognise her, Titch?'

'It's my view Kerry didn't even know I'd be here tonight,' Raybould said. 'She came for a little love tryst – wine and eyes bright. There *is* a fashion for the older man, I hear. Think of Clinton. But even when the older man's only an eternal DC. Look at her face now. You're miserable to have me present, aren't you, sergeant? That's all right. I'm not hurt.'

Yes, she was miserable. Yes, she felt humiliated. It had been a big move for her to come tonight, away from the usualness and comfort of Mark, a big move to give him lies. She had told Mark it was work, but at the nick, not Vic's place, naturally. Well, no question it *was* work. For Kerry it had been a huge change to decide at last that perhaps she needed two kinds of loving, Mark's intelligent, considerate, long-term, often passionate kind, and Vic's kind, if he would let it turn into loving – that easy, thorough understanding of her and the readiness to ally himself no matter what she had been up to. Perhaps it was a job thing, a colleague thing, yet more than this, too, wasn't it? Was it?

'*Did* you know the girl?' Kerry said.

'What "dangerous information"?' Raybould replied. 'It doesn't exist. I know I do nothing that could make me dangerous to *anyone*.'

75

'We get a murmur about the girl being seen in your car on the day she was killed, Titch,' Vic said.

Raybould laughed aloud again. His face remained untroubled, his voice serene. 'What murmur would that be, Vic?'

'This comes to us privately,' Othen replied. 'That's your good luck.'

'But what kind of murmur?' Raybould asked.

'A witness.' Vic left that hanging and gazed about the flat. The pause was meant to unsettle Titch. Kerry gazed about, too. She liked the place. It looked what it should be for Vic – clean or cleanish, with no one style of furniture or décor or pictures, in fact, no style at all, but comfortable enough. Comfortable enough for someone who did not intend to stay in much. His settee was the smartest piece. He must have turned spendthrift briefly. Or a partner had persuaded him. Where was she now? Kerry ought to have found out more about Vic's home life. It couldn't all be Titch.

The place stank of cigarettes and would have even if he wasn't smoking one now. Probably he did forty to fifty a day. Although she disliked thinking about his lungs, she did not mind visualising the rest of him in quite a bit of detail, despite his age. Neither she nor Titch smoked. Perhaps someone had told Titch smoking stunted your growth, but not told him soon enough. 'So who says all this?' he said.

'A member of the public, obviously,' Vic replied. 'We've been asking around, showing pix. This person thinks she saw a girl resembling Melissa Slater in a car with a man she did not recognise but who seemed to the witness rather low in the driving seat – a shortish man, then – with fair hair and a plump but "not unhandsome face". That was her phrase, "not unhandsome". When Kerry and I heard this, especially the last bit, Titch, we both said, *This has to be A. R. W. Raybould*. We did not say it aloud, naturally, audible to the witness, but in our hearts, Titch. When we compared reactions later we realised that this had been our common instantaneous response. Plus we both felt, independently, that you were sensible enough, modest enough, not to be offended by the grudging description.'

'Who?' Raybould replied.

'Come on now, Titch,' Othen said, 'do we finger someone who talks to us? Witnesses who'll say something and live are scarce.'

'Just an ordinary, well-intentioned Josephine Bloggs,' Kerry said.

'It's shit,' Raybould replied. Kerry felt again the jarring wrongness of bad language in his mellow mouth.

Othen nodded. 'Kerry and I said to each other as soon as we could discuss such dangerous information privately, *This doesn't seem like Titch and could be total shit.* As you remarked. I mean, the *sex* didn't seem like you, although the portrait *did*. It's no slander, for instance, to say you're short, Titch.'

'Shortish,' Kerry said.

'Wrong identities twice,' Raybould said. 'The girl. Me.'

'Is your car black?' Othen replied. 'Our witness said a black car, probably a Saab.'

'Oh, Jesus, that's sensational,' Raybould said. 'A black car! Not many of those around are there, Vic, Kerry?'

Raybould had not drunk any of the wine but began to lift it to his mouth now. He stopped, though, and put the glass back on the carpet near his feet, his hand totally without shakes. 'This is someone trying to fuck me up, yes?' he said. 'This is someone trying to get Adrian Raybould out of the scene.'

'A Josephine Bloggs,' Kerry said.

'Arseholes,' Raybould replied.

'You're saying the girl was not in your car?' Vic Othen asked.

'I get a lot of envy, a lot of rivalry, a lot of sick hate,' Raybould said. 'It would be easy for one of them to give you a whisper like that, wouldn't it? Not themselves, personally. You'd smell the scheme. But some patsy.'

'This would be a black car, quite a size, which is one reason the driver looked small, driving up towards the Clocktower mid-to-late afternoon on the day,' Othen said. 'The girl smiling and chatting away, apparently. She was that kind of kid, I gather, very open.'

'If they can get me nailed for something like this my company's finished and they move in and collect the bits,' Raybould replied. 'Asset-stripping made easy.'

'What does your company do these days, Titch?' Vic asked.

'Miscellaneous trading.'

'As ever,' Kerry said.

'Some property development, some general contracting,' Raybould replied.

'We need to know where you put the child down and at what time, Titch, that's all,' Vic said.

'Which child?'

'The one seen with you in your car,' Othen said.

'The one seen in this so distinctive black car?' Raybould asked. 'Not my car. Mistake – suppose the witness exists at all.'

The witness existed but could not disclose herself to Titch, any more than she could to Harry Bell. If Titch realised she had been hiding something so crucial from her superiors he would have an exquisite hold on her. Kerry said: 'Once we know where she left you, and when, we can –'

'Or another much rougher idea comes to me,' Raybould replied. His face took on pain now, looking appalled, betrayed. 'Forgive. But you're operating with one of the other firms, are you – taking a subsidy? You smash Adrian Raybould for them – for, say, Ivo Kyle or, say, Bright Raymond – and you're on an income. Vic, I'll admit you're not famed for taking – the opposite. But have things changed? You're looking around for funds in a rush because you two will set up together? Is Kerry losing her junior tycoon? So *understandable* you should be searching for cash. As you said, Vic, we all have to work. I know you'd be a good provider. You'd adjust your priorities, the way we all have to sometimes.'

How sweetly the suggestions were made, she thought, and the questions put, despite that sudden tightening of his face. How gently, insultingly, chattily.

'I expect you've read in the Press, Titch, there's a gap of more than seven hours between the last sighting of Melissa and the finding of the body,' Othen replied. 'That is, between a sighting near the school and the discovery. But the sighting Kerry and I speak of brings her down into the town and near the Clock-tower, and is about two hours later than when she was seen near the school. This is valuable information, exclusive information, so far. You can appreciate why we'd like to close that ignorance gap even more by finding from you how long she was in the car and where you took her to.'

'Alternatively, you might be able to tell us you were some-where else at the time our witness thinks she saw you, Titch, and prove it,' Kerry said. 'In that case we'd obviously have to accept – misidentification.'

'How long can we keep this material private, that's the real tough one, Titch,' Othen said.

'Which material?' Raybould replied.

'If our witness should come to think we're not using properly the tip she gave she might decide to go official with it, you see. That's what we want to save you from, Titch, because however bad things might look we're convinced, Kerry and I, that you're not the kind of lad who'd abuse a kid.'

'*Can* you prove you were somewhere else, Titch?' Kerry asked.

'So which of them are you two working for?' Raybould replied. 'I'd say Ivo Kyle. It's Ivo? Bright Raymond wouldn't have the brain to set up something like this, nor the all-out evil. Ivo? Well, Ivo is Ivo, as we all know. Ivo craves monopoly. Ivo will follow his star – and you two will follow Ivo, for a stipend? It's neat. And can Ivo pay enough?'

'If you were using this kid to list pupils who'd be interested in a substance it was natural for you to be with her occasionally, Titch,' Vic answered. 'This would be a standard business meet-ing, whether it took place in your Saab or anywhere else. We can accept that. You've always liked to conduct an orderly trade. Oh, all right, it's true you've got pushers like Gaston on your staff who'll barge in on anyone for the sake of a sale, even very unsuitable kids, but that's Gaston – a bit of a maverick. He doesn't always follow your policy. *Your* thinking involves decent, systematic research, and with that in mind you'd keep in touch with an ex-user like Melissa, who could give you guidance. In a way it's admirable, Titch. Our dread is, though, that someone like Doug Quinn or Bell, or a jury for that matter, would not see it so. They hear of a little girl destroyed and they hear of her being seen in your car a matter of hours before. This could look conclusive, Titch. You need people who under-stand you – Kerry and myself.'

'It's a treat to watch your work, Vic,' Raybould replied. He stood up. 'Well, I'll leave you two to your intimacies now, shall I? I'm afraid I've intruded for too long. Sorry. Yes, I'll do what you suggest, sergeant.'

'What?'

'Prove I was elsewhere at the time.'

'Fine,' she replied.

'This will upset your earnings plan?' Raybould asked. 'I don't want you left bereft.'

'Our only object is to eliminate you from the line-up, Titch,' Othen said.

'I'll need to provide one or two folk to tell you I couldn't have been driving the Saab near the Clocktower that day because I was somewhere else – which I was, and provably was, I'm glad to say.'

'Fine, Titch,' Kerry replied.

'So, how do you square it with Ivo when you have to drop this rubbish, Vic?' Raybould asked. 'Or Bright Raymond? You've botched an assignment. I'm still around and will go on being around. You know what Ivo can be like about what he sees as failure.'

'We long to get you out of a pit, Titch, that's all,' Othen replied, 'because we know and respect you.'

When Raybould had gone, Kerry said: 'Was he making us an offer?'

'How?'

'He wants to buy us from Ivo Kyle, or Bright Raymond.'

Othen looked amazed. 'Christ, I didn't pick that up. But you might be right. Sharp, Kerry.'

Was he humouring her?

'He knows he can't get a solid alibi,' she said. 'He *was* in the car with Melissa and he believes we have a witness. Of course he does. How else would we know? He probably didn't destroy Melissa, but sees he could so easily be lined up for it because of the car journey. A delectable little trap. Police work like that. Did Ivo or Raymond do her to frame him – with our help, as

Titch thinks? He's right, isn't he, that people want him annihilated and his empire shared out?'

'That comes with the job. But Titch *will* produce an alibi. Gaston and a few other teamsters will swear they were playing hunt the slipper with their boss at the time. It's standard.'

'Of course. That's where the offer comes in. He's telling us, Don't blast the alibi, don't even test it – because it's bound to be false. He'll raise whatever he thinks Ivo or Bright Raymond are paying us, and then he expects us to say "Ta, very much, Titch," and forget about him. Remember his words, "And can Ivo pay enough?" "I don't want you left bereft." He sees a conspiracy to wipe him out, Vic, and he fights it in one of the only ways he knows – a better bid.'

'Am I getting dull, Kerry?'

'Vic, you saw it, didn't you? You're being kind. Again.'

'Time I quit,' he replied.

'You saw it, didn't you? You did hear the clink of coin? He thinks you've finally gone rotten. He'd expect it. People like Titch don't believe anyone can stay pure for ever. It's to justify themselves. They consider they simply went dirty earlier, being smarter.'

She felt as she recalled feeling sometimes as a young, inexperienced girl. There would be a conversation with a man which seemed to be about a neutral, maybe professional topic, and yet you were listening all the time for a word, a joke, a bit of attitude, an omission that would reveal the sexual message, something that said what the talk was really to do with. Which was the Woody Allen film where he and Diane Keaton talk banalities while captions show their true, mating-game thoughts? *Annie Hall*? Something like it could be happening here now. And she wanted it to happen. Oh, yes, yes, she did want that. The talk had turned personal. It was about *her* skills as against *his*. It was about his allegedly faded reactions as against her allegedly young, fast-track understanding. The fact that he might be playing dumb out of consideration for her and her rank did not matter, or not much. The essential was that it set up a relationship, one to one – *You're* like this, Kerry, and *I'm* like this. We reveal ourselves to each other, expose

81

ourselves, you might say. Of course, it was still only in police things, professional things. Or was it? They could lead on. Titch had sensed there might be more.

'He's right,' she said. 'I was hurt you'd asked him here tonight.'

'We had to talk to him, Kerry.'

'But tonight?'

There was some wine left and he poured for both of them, then lit himself another cigarette from the last one.

'You're still scared I'll get into something I'll regret, aren't you?' she said. 'The something I'll regret getting into being your bed.'

'Like that, yes. Possible loss of a junior tycoon for you, as Titch said. Someone your own age, someone with a gorgeous future.'

'It needn't happen,' she replied.

'It might. In exchange for what? Pardon the self-contempt, but a retirement-age smoker. I see you wince like a doctor when I light up.'

'Relight up. Vic, I think you make out I'm brighter than you so you can tell yourself you're not seducing some kid nincompoop.'

'Only brighter than I am *now*,' he said, 'age having slowed the wheels a bit.'

'I don't believe it.'

'Don't you think it's half-witted of someone like me to refuse a girl like you?' he asked.

'You wouldn't take advantage. You're known as a gent, Vic, a lovely gent. But not a stupid gent. You *haven't* refused me. You postpone things until you think they're right. You build me up to lay me down. It's delightful of you.' She was still sitting in the easy chair, her glass of wine in her hand.

'I don't know how I did it,' he said.

'What?'

'Postponed things.' He stood and crossed the room to her from the settee. Bending down alongside the chair he briefly kissed her. She had put her mouth up to him. It would have been hurtful if he had ignored this. He was a gent and couldn't do it. She had counted on that. It seemed wrong to be sitting, as if she were receiving tribute. 'Is it bad, the smoke breath?' he said.

'Bad, not impossible,' she replied. 'But I think you could put the one in your hand out – for the duration, don't you?'

He took another long pull at the cigarette, though, before throwing it into the fireplace. She saw a scatter of other butts there. He drew her up from the chair and held her to him as they kissed again, held her gently, both his hands palm down lightly on her shoulder blades. She held him, too. He felt wiry and solid and hers, for now, anyway. He was not much taller than Kerry, perhaps only just up to police height for men. She liked this. It was part of that ease and suitability between them. They were made for each other, but there had been a mess-up in the dates of manufacture.

His bedroom seemed all right. Christ, she had wanted to get in here for long enough, so it *should* be all right, no quibbling now. Kerry found herself momentarily looking for traces of another woman, other women. What was she expecting to spot – a pair of high heels under the bed? There had been a partner, perhaps even a wife, she knew that, though not when. So? She would be going home to Mark, wouldn't she?

The bed was a double. Perhaps this had shoved her into thoughts about his past. There was a built-in wardrobe, a pine dressing table, print pictures as dull as the ones in his living-room. She prayed one of the women had chosen these and that he left them in place through indolence, not sentiment. She would hate to feel he had picked such trite stuff himself.

A friend had told her that grey hair on a man's chest was the biggest turn-off ever, but she found she didn't mind it. Stripped, Vic looked fit, nimble, too pale. She waited for him to take her clothes off, but he didn't do that, let her undress herself and she felt disappointed. Perhaps he needed yet another sign he was not pressurising, only having her, this gifted younger woman, because she wanted him to. God the politesse, the older-man restraint. How did you smash them? Possibly when a man, older or younger, was into a rape case, and especially *this* rape case, he grew even more delicate with a lover.

Not how it should be, not how it should be, not how it

should be. There was Melissa dead; and there was her and Vic alive and on the edge of happy sex, maybe love. Melissa must not be allowed to overwhelm them. Kerry became calculating, self-aware, when she would have wanted to be just carried along. For half of half a second she actually thought about proclaiming their temporary freedom from the Melissa horrors by telling Vic she wanted it up the bottom. But she didn't – tell him or particularly want that. What she wanted, apart from having him, was to let Vic know life and its quirks and demands kept going, despite the agonies all round. God, wasn't he old enough to know this? How did she get to be teaching him? She was a fast-track cop, not a fast-track sex therapist. When she was naked and before he had touched her properly she took his cock in her hands and gave it some affection and a bit of reverence. That ought to let him know he would not be violating her. Yes, tactics. More calculation. But it would not always be like this.

'Love me, Vic,' she said, 'Titch expects it.' Even jokes seemed useful.

'Why I asked him here. For his blessing.'

'Right,' she said, 'I guessed there must be a purpose.'

In bed he lay for a moment with his left ear on her right breast. 'I've thought about your tits for at least weeks,' he said.

'*Only* my tits.'

'*Starting* with your tits.'

'That's OK then,' she said. All the same he spent a while with them. Mark was fond of her breasts, too, and she thought it was wonderful to get this extra endorsement through Vic's cupping with his fingers, and sucking, and sighing. It would be weird to have nipples that smelled of Marlboros. She did not check.

Then he said something like what she had thought he might: 'You'll ask yourself what it means, you and me only getting to bed at last because of Melissa Slater's rape and death.'

'No, it doesn't mean anything. Why would I ask myself that?'

'Because you're a thinker, Kerry. I bet it says on your documents you're a thinker.'

'Well, documents aren't everything. For instance, it doesn't say on them I'm a wild and committed fucker,' she answered, 'but I am, with the right bloke. You, for instance.'

'Yes,' he replied, eventually, 'you are, aren't you?'

'This is just a lovely, loving time for us, and there'll be others. Melissa's still dead and torn. Things don't have to be all tied into a pattern.'

'There, I knew you were a thinker as well,' he said.

She found she expected him to have body scars – he had been around so long and in so many big and violent cases, some years before her time, but part of folk memory at the nick and passed on. He was unmarked, front and back, though. This also disappointed her. She had wanted to comfort and restore a damaged, stressed hero, bring him the juicy balm of youth, comparative youth. She wanted to displace his woebegone antique need to comfort himself with smoke. This was to have been lovemaking as therapy. It had turned out to be love-making as lovemaking.

He lit up again now. An older man might be deeper into his weaknesses than she had realised. There was going to be a learning side to getting loved by Vic and fucking him.

18

After the day that Melissa hit the packet of H out of Gaston Devereux's hand when he was trying to give it to Liz Quant, he started coming up the school or even being in Melissa's street sometimes when she went to school or came home, and he would just look at her.

One thing Melissa had known was Gaston Devereux had to have what they called *respect*. People like him were always on about it. If they did not get this *respect* they could turn angry and rough. Melissa knew he would think he was not getting respect that day. This was a businessman messed about in the street by a kid. That was what he thought he was, a business-man, and in a way, all right, it might be true. He never wore

85

jeans, always a suit and a white shirt with a tie, shoes not trainers, and no pony-tail.

There was some other kids about, going home from school, and he would really be ratty about that, them seeing. This was bad for what was known as his *image*. People like Gaston had to have *respect* so their *image* would be all right. He was ratty when it happened but she knew he would go home and think about it and get *more* ratty. He would think he looked stupid – him having to get down and pick up the H from by Liz's shoes like some tramp with cigarette ends although he had a suit on.

Now and then when Gaston was doing this staring he would say something to her. Sometimes it was not anything too bad, just cheeky, really, when she thought about it. He did not always say she was shagging Titch. 'And how is the anti-drug squad this afternoon?' he asked her once. But that really scared her at first because she thought he knew about the talks with Kerry. He might think Kerry was in the Drug Squad. That would be bad, bad, bad, and not even Titch would look after her. But then she thought Gaston was just being cheeky and sarcastic. He meant Melissa herself on her own was the anti-drug squad because she had knocked the H down. So perhaps it was just a joke. It might mean he was not so ratty now, just joky, and he would stop coming after her. So she did not say anything back to him, just had a little smile but one he could see, sort of friendly, so he would know she knew it was only a joke. You had to worry what someone like Gaston was thinking. There was a lot of tales about him.

The name Gaston Devereux sounded a bit like noblemen in the olden days in tales about Arthur and the Round Table, and so if you had a name like that you needed even more respect. It was different for someone like Titch Raybould. He would want respect as well, yes, but if you were called Titch this was a bit ordinary, really, so Titch might not need so much respect. In any case, Titch was up there, yes, Mr Supremo, so he nearly always had respect, he did not need to worry about it very much. If somebody did do some *behaviour* against him he could put heavy people to see to them and this was a fast way to get respect – they would find out they better show it, and they *would* show it if they had bad injuries from the heavies, because

86

injuries like that made people give respect not to the ones who did the injuries but to who sent them. Often people with their arm in plaster or teeth gone could be the most respectful you would ever meet.

Of course, Gaston was scared of Titch and injuries. Even if Gaston was ratty Melissa knew he would not do anything *really* bad against her out in the open because she knew Titch. Even when he said she was shagging Titch that could be bad for him if she told Titch but she was too ashamed to tell Titch.

But Gaston had to do something, he was so ratty – it was *really* childish, this staring. He thought it was the way to get respect back. He thought he could frighten her by doing a gaze like that. She had heard of it, it was what was called in the papers, stalking. Sometimes he would be in his car just staring or sometimes he would be standing there just staring. It was not just because she had stopped him selling stuff that he was ratty. It was deep. It was because kids saw him like that in the street and would talk about it. He had plenty of other people he could sell to. This was not the only school, and he sold to a lot of grown-ups, anyway. Titch and his firm did not sell much to schools at all, it was just that he thought about the future, which is important in business, he told her that. He said great businessmen always thought of times about three or four years in the future, not just next week, like Marks and Sparks wondering what the clothes would be like in, say, the year 2002 so they could get them ready. So, he sent Gaston to get a few kids at the schools, that was all, so when they grew up a bit they would have a true habit and need it regular. They wanted bright kids so they would have good jobs when they grew up and there would be plenty of money for crack and H.

The next time Gaston came up the school he said: 'You *really* think you can stop it, you, you little sadness.' He was really hissing it.

'Leave me alone.'

'*How* could you stop it? *How* – some nothing kid? This is a fucking *industry*.'

They did not give a shit about swearing even in front of a young girl, people like Gaston. It was not long before Avril went to Portugal and she was waiting for Melissa in the queue

87

for the school bus. She could not hear what Gaston said but she saw him talk to her. 'Was he trying to push stuff? He knows you're clean, doesn't he?'

'He's a pest, that's all.'

'Oh. Does he fancy you? Hanging about?'

'He's rubbish.'

'A lot of them like him – lovely brown eyes and his suits. I heard Daisy likes him, but with a nose like hers?'

It had worried Melissa, the way he kept saying *How? How?* sort of hammering that word at her. It made her think again he might wonder if she was talking on the quiet to a police officer. The way he said *How?* did not sound joky at all.

19

In a black mini-skirt, black shoes, white blouse under a black long-sleeved sweater, and carrying a full school bag by a strap from her shoulder, Kerry walked from the school, into its yard and across the playing fields, towards the short-cut streets on the Page estate which they thought Melissa took on the day she died. Three television crews with hand-held cameras followed her. *Were her legs and behind all right these days in a mini?* Gerald Rose, the headmaster, watched her go, an absorbed, unflinching stare. Probably he was thinking about the differences between someone who had moved into womanhood, but was dressed as a child, and someone who had had womanhood ahead, or should have had. This was a big and depressing day for the school.

Superintendent Harry Bell believed in the power of re-enactments to get people's memory going. You staged the run-up moments to a crime and hoped to bring out recollections from witnesses' subconscious, things they might not realise they had seen. Kerry did not go much on re-enactments, and especially not this one. She always feared they signalled despair, meant an investigation was stuck. But all detection was about uncertain, faltering visits to the past, and you did it sometimes like this, with costume and a show. Television loved costume and a show, and would give you big coverage. *Were her legs and behind all right these days in a mini?*

Harry was here this afternoon to watch and speak his appeal for witnesses of Melissa's last walk. Perhaps a re-enactment had brought him success on other cases, and detectives, like villains, preferred to act to pattern. He would do his piece to onlookers along the way and to the cameras and radio recorders. Harry was good with the public, face to face or through the media. He came over as benign, uncrafty and honest, and some people might want to help him.

Kerry found it unnerving and yet a comfort to mimic the dead child. She felt a kind of merging with her. Mad, though possibly it was what some actors managed occasionally when taken over by the character they played. Yet this went beyond that superficiality, became spiritual. Kerry knew things that Melissa had known, and which none of these others did. It was as if Kerry and the dead girl had a precious, secret alliance. Perhaps, then, Kerry was more like a medium than an actor. She knew, and Melissa would have known, that this re-enactment was even more useless than most of them – in the wrong place and about an hour too early in the day. Melissa might have come this way at 2.50 that afternoon, she might not. It was more or less irrelevant because she was seen later, at 3.45, unhurt, even smiling. Kerry's walk now would stop on the Page housing estate because this was as far as Harry Bell thought guesswork could go. Yet Melissa's afternoon had hardly begun when she crossed the estate. It began when she stepped into Titch's car down close to the centre. Where it ended was a mystery, but at least Kerry knew the start, and Melissa would have known it, too.

Kerry walked fast, despite the school bag. The theory, after all, was that Melissa acted out of pattern dodging off school – out of recent pattern, anyway – because she was excited and had to hurry to meet someone in the town. And, of course, that bit of the theory was right. Kerry could have told them, and naturally did not. Should she try to walk like a thirteen-year-old urgently on her way to a rendezvous? Could she remember how a het-up thirteen-year-old walked? Probably it was another crazy element in the whole crazy procedure that Kerry should pretend to be this doomed teenager. Kerry had her fair to mousy colouring and slim to middling build, but not many twenty-five-year-olds could make themselves look thirteen and a half. And Kerry's face and features were rounder, less angular than Melissa's, perhaps less beautiful, more run-of-the-mill.

Harry had considered asking one of the child's school mates to do the re-enactment, but then grew anxious about the politics – all those worthy, hindsight, watchdog committees ready to bite if something went wrong. Harry feared setting up endless trauma in a child asked to represent this stroll to imminent violation and death. Or he feared being accused of that. Watchdog committees were hot on children's trauma. Harry decided Kerry knew enough about the roughnesses of life not to slip into that state, and ordered her to get her hair something like Melissa's and find the right kind of clothes. Bell wanted the theatre of a re-enactment, but not painful realism, and not recriminations.

Kerry felt ashamed about pretending to endorse his rigmarole. Only a little ashamed, though. Above all she was conscious of the bond with Melissa, something spooky and elusive, something greater even than the famous, forbidden, complex soul bond between a detective and her/his informant. Melissa had never quite been a full informant for Kerry, but it did not matter. The overlap of identities was present now and oddly powerful – much more than what came from the mock-up school uniform. As she and the troupe passed through the playing fields, Kerry found herself talking to the child, talking in the smallest of whispers, so the television people should not hear, but talking all the same. 'You and me – we're in the know. We'll nail whoever did those things to you, Melissa. Nobody else can.' Mystical, almost. Lunatic, almost. Arrogant, totally.

Some older boys were on a soccer training session and stopped to watch as Kerry and the procession went by. There were a couple of long wolf whistles. In the midst of death we are in life and lust. So, her legs and behind might be all right in a mini, then. She did not want to pull schoolboys – wasn't she into older men, or an older man? But it was a cheer-up to know youth could fancy her still, on the school platform or off it. She stayed apparently remote and indifferent, though, and did not look towards the boys. She was Melissa this afternoon and senior pupils would never have bothered to wolf-whistle a thirteen-year-old, would they? God, sex was such a puzzle. Who knew what *anyone* would do?

They left the fields and entered the Page estate. She made her way through the four interconnecting streets which might have taken Melissa to the edge of the town centre. There had been announcements in the local media that the re-enactment would take place and a few people stood at their front doors or in groups on the pavement to look, mostly women. This was all right. It would be mostly women who were around the estate mid-afternoon when Melissa did the trip. But they would not have been on the doorstep gazing out for her then. That was the problem with re-enactments, one of the problems. You wanted people to watch and you wanted to prompt their recollections, but you could only do it by setting up conditions different from what they were on the day. The phoneyness of these exercises always seemed to Kerry crippling. She kept going, meeting no eyes. For as long as she could she aimed to preserve a warm, imagined, private confederacy between herself and the child.

Of course, if Harry ever found out what she knew when she did this insane performance he would annihilate her. That would be only reasonable, unless she'd done what she'd just told Melissa she'd do and nailed the killer by then. In detective work, as in most trades, an outright and lasting success generally disposed of quibbles about method. And if the success did not come? Mark might be right and Harry would have her charged for withholding evidence. He would be enraged that she had made an idiot of him this afternoon. Oh, hell. She made an effort, got rid of this dread and focused instead on the merger of personalities with Melissa. Vic's assurance that all detectives now and then went in for concealment from their superiors and trickery did console her, though the assurance might be only a comforting lie. There was real goodness to Vic, not necessarily rule book goodness. Rule books were for rulers and he would never be one of those. He knew how to be kind.

At the end of the last street she stopped and put the school bag down. One of the cameras was on her face at once and a reporter said: 'Sergeant Lake, if this produces nothing what do you do next?' Perhaps he had seen re-enactments before and knew they were not much more than a publicity invitation to his outfit and others like it – the police getting co-operative because it suited them. So, the reporter would reclaim independence through tough questions.

Kerry said: 'We're confident it *will* produce something, either via interviews with the residents now, or after your programme has been screened.'

'What were your feelings?'

'Great sadness, of course. Great determination that the killer must be caught.'

'Was it eerie, presumptuous, indeed, to assume the personality of a dead child you did not even know?'

Arsehole, I did *know her*. But she said: ' "Assume the personality"? I wouldn't put it like that. I covered the same ground, that's all.'

'But the clothes, the bag?'

'Just reminders.'

'Do the police believe this killer might strike again?'

'We shall do all possible to prevent that.'

'Have you a message for other girl pupils at the school?'

Yes. If you're going for a ride in Titch Raybould's Saab, stick with him. Titch wouldn't rape and bugger. He was nicely brought up. Admittedly, he might kill. But she said: 'Stay in groups. Look after one another. Report anything unusual, especially approaches from men unknown to you.' She sounded like a government health warning.

The reporter went to interview Harry Bell. Kerry could see Viki, George Ince and three or four other detectives talking to people who had watched. There was some head-shaking. The detectives had clipboards, but none of them wrote anything. Kerry strolled over and listened to the end of Bell's filmed talk to the camera. It was the usual promise of confidentiality to anyone who came forward with information. Harry could sound as though he believed there were at least half a dozen people viewing who might be able to bring crucial help, and who would. It was one of his flairs. If likeability made good coppers Harry would have been unstoppable. When he had finished, he said to Kerry: 'People will at least see we haven't gone to sleep. Could you do it again, please? We might pick up a few who missed the first show.'

Kerry went back to the school and came down once more through the fields and into the estate. This time, she was by herself. Television, radio and the Press had left to prepare their material. The head was not in the yard to see her off but Kerry thought she might have glimpsed him watching from a window, eyes unacademic. The soccer game had finished. She loved the solitariness of it, this second walk – could convince herself, con herself, that she was even nearer to Melissa, but the talk with her did not have to be whispered or concealed now. 'Was it me put you into peril, Melissa? Did I arrange your death?' The idea troubled her more than she would have expected. Kerry thought she had somehow managed to bury that fret, or at least shelve it. Some hope. Suddenly she grew very edgy. Paranoid? 'Why persecute me with your silence,' she howled, 'you evil little, dead little, ostentatious little victim? Could I do any more for you? And don't fucking well answer that.'

'Here's a lady who thinks she recognised you – recognised Melissa, that is,' Harry Bell said, when Kerry finished again at the same spot on the estate. 'Or recognised the school bag, at least. She's been away from the area for some days, or we might have heard from her before.'

'No disrespect, saying the school bag,' the woman replied, 'but, yes, it *is* what I noticed first.'

'Why I'm carrying it,' Kerry replied. 'I'm really glad it registered – makes being lumbered with the bag worthwhile. Damned heavy.' What was this snotty, interfering twerp saying – that *only* the school bag looked authentic, not the twenty-five-year-old thirteen-year-old? This woman obviously wanted to put a barrier between Melissa and Kerry. The woman was middle-aged, slight, small, bright-looking, more ugly than plain, her grey hair grubby, heaped high and much pinned. To Harry she would seem an angel, despite the bulging old shoes and recycled clothes. She was a witness, that terrifyingly threatened, precious species. She could see, remember, speak.

Harry's driver had brought the car down from the school yard and he and the woman and Kerry went and sat in it. Harry told the driver to leave for ten minutes.

'Of course like, a big age gap,' the woman said, able to look more closely at Kerry now.

'Of course,' Kerry replied. 'She was on her way through, was she?'

'Through?' the woman asked.

'Going down towards the town.'

'I thought so, at first. Children from the school do. They've got their own unpleasant, secret lives, haven't they? Not all of them. Some you might still allow into your home. But many, no. Some of them amusement arcades and so on down there. Don't tell me that's all about pinball. But then she turned around and went back.'

'Up to the school again?'

'Towards it.'

'Why?'

'Don't know. I didn't watch her for long. Why should I?'

'Absolutely,' Bell said.

'If my hubbie was still alive he would have most likely watched her from upstairs in the bedroom, the letching, sweating pipsqueak. One reason he took this house, if you ask me, so he could sniff at the jailbait when he was home off shift in the day. Only sniff. He didn't have the gumption to get out there, you know. Luckily, he died in quite a bit of pain around that lower area. I used to say to him when he groaned in hospital, ' "What price them schoolgirls now, then, Eric, dear?" These things always sort themselves out, don't they? I don't mind keeping in touch with his brother and sisters. Why I was away visiting.'

'Had Melissa seen someone behind her and gone back to meet him, her – whoever it was?' Kerry asked.

'Now and then I feel like getting out there myself and pleading with these girls not to let themselves in for anything,

94

relationships and all that – that's the charming long word they've come up with for it, I hear,' the woman replied. 'They could stay home with a good jigsaw. Do they want to end up like this?' She pointed at a couple of groups of women talking in the street. 'Or like the dead kid – made filthy play of before the finale?'

'Possibly someone called to Melissa from behind,' Kerry said. 'You didn't hear anything like that? Did she turn her head suddenly? Would you remember?'

'Or someone in front of her?' the woman replied. 'Someone she didn't want to meet. Some teacher, something like that? Was she supposed to be out of school at that time in the afternoon? Maybe she bolted back. They're wily, these kids, especially girls. But they're never going to be wily *enough*, not to beat this lousy life. That's the trouble with schools now, they make kids think things could be all right when they grow up, girls as well as boys. It's cruel. They don't give them enough of the Book of Ezekiel and the valley of bones. As I say, I didn't watch her. She was just a schoolgirl walking. They're around here every day. When I was away and I read about the killing in the *Mail* I did not even think of that child. But then when I saw this lady and the school bag today, I thought, Yes, although the very big age gap, and heftier arse and stouter legs, obviously.'

'I wonder if you ever asked yourself why your husband turned to peeping at young girls,' Kerry replied.

When the woman had gone, Bell said: 'Interesting, her suggestion that Melissa might have seen one of the staff and turned back because of that. Somebody been making a nuisance of himself with her?'

'We don't know it was a he, sir – supposing there was anyone at all.'

'But it might have been a he. These school romances do hit some teachers. The age of the pupil doesn't seem to bother them.'

'The woman wasn't talking sex, sir, was she? She only meant that Melissa might have turned around because she shouldn't have been out of school.'

'But *I* can talk sex. That headmaster, what I've seen of him –

some oddities there? I have to admit he's got no sex past that we know about.'

'You've checked to see if he's got form – a head teacher?'

'Of course.'

Of course. Kerry would have got round to it herself eventually, too.

Bell said: 'It's a school. If there's a sex crime run all the staff names through Criminal Records. True, long odds. He wouldn't get the job, would he, if he had that kind of past and he'd been caught? But he might be clever, and *not* caught. I'll tell George Ince to have a chat there. Get George's mind off informants.'

20

To: Avril Grant
From: Melissa Slater
Subject: Secrets Secrets and Secrets

Well old Avril how are things out there in cheerfull Portugal? I read in a Travel book they are always eating salted cod, well you can keep it. Have you found any true evol out there yet you lucky old thing? Tell me when you do.

Things are sort of great here and I have stayed right off sgurd – O very well done Melissa!!!! Give the girl a lollipop!!!! People such as hctiT and not even that creepy creep notsaG dont never even try to sell me something these days. Well I dont know what that creepy creep notsaG will do. He is still staring and staring, trying to scare me you know what he is like the creep.

hctiT is still all right. Now he does not say tell him what kids he can try but tell him what kids it would be WRONG to try because they are into church or the Baptists and have heard a lot against sgurd. Or these kids they got a mother or father who is always keeping an eye because they read it in the papers you know them articles – Is Your Child on sgurD the Tell-Tale

96

Signs and it would be trouble for hctiT if he tried kids like that, their father might report him or even come after him. Well my mother and father did not notice but some of them do. My mother and father was too busy to notice through getting stuff up their own hooters I should think in them days.

I think it is all right to tell hctiT what kids to leave alone. One kid I told him not to try was Liz and he said fine, but of course that creep notsaG pretended he did not know about that. That nice kid Florence is another one I said they better not try she is so nice and just a kid. I expect you rember her she was the one who was with us that night when we met them two syob at the Regis when it was Trainspotting. She is always asking me what it was like with them two after. She is nice but she is a nosy little cow. She says was it lovely and true romance like the name of that other moovy by Quentin Tarenteeno!!! I never tell her nothing and never about that window and what happened to that washbasin!!!! She would not understand She is just a kid. She said did I ever ask you about my d. I said to shut up you cow.

Also hctiT wants to know anything about Poison Breath, you know what I mean. He wants to know does Poison Breath ever try anything with any of the slrig or syob. It is so they could lean on him and it would be easier selling stuff near the school. He said why did I call him Poison Breath because he never heard no other kid call him that not slrig or syob. He said did Poison Breath come close at all that way some teachers do. Well I did not say nothing. I do not like talking about that and I know you hate talking about it as well. I think some things it is better not to talk about Av. I said I called him Poison Breath because I saw a butterfly drop dead when it flew past his mouth in the playground one day.

So hctiT gives me a bit of money for info and I expect Kerry will give me some if I tell her what she wants to know about sgurd and the school. Maybe I will save it all up and come and see you in Portugal one day. I still do not REALLY know if I want to be a ssarg because it is so creepy and horrible and dangerous. But what I think is that one day I might want to get a job in the police and be a detective. It might be fun in fast cars and they get payed a bucketfull. So if they know I helped them before they might think this is the right job for me. Somebody like Daisy who is Jessica might think police is not the sort of job to have because she will go to a college and then she can be a doctor or making TV shows. But being in the police they could give you a special car not all painted up like a traffic car but just plain and secret for watching people and then suddenly shouting out Police and showing a badge and telling them it can all be used in evident.

And I think somebody must stop people like notsaG getting stuff to kids who are still like babies such as Liz and Florence thats all. That is why I might talk to Kerry. So I have a meeting some days with her which I hope are REALLY secret. This is why I called this e-mail Secrets. It is a laugh really because one day I go to have a secret meeting with hctiT in his Saab and then the next day or maybe even the same day I go to have a secret meeting with Kerry in her old Cavalier. I hope I do not forget which is which one day!!!!! Kerry is the one who uses that perfume Red. It is a pity hctiT does not use a bit of perfume himself. He smells red but red and purspiry. But it was on the news the other day that a list of big sessarg really important sessarg was give out to crooks by somebody in a big office in London. This means they could get killed. This is scary.

That is all for now then Av. I do all my homework now and never bunk off school. I expect I will definately go to heaven!!! I hope you can see I been working on that grammar you wrote about last time in your clever clogs way.

Your best old pal,
Melissa.

21

Next day in her lunchtime Kerry returned urgently to the Page estate and the place where the witness said Melissa had stopped, turned then gone back towards Fortune School. The woman seemed to assume Melissa had actually re-entered

Fortune, perhaps frightened by seeing a teacher who might ask why she was away from classes mid-afternoon. But this was not the only possibility. The headmaster had said Melissa was missing from about 2.50 for the rest of the school day. He did not mention a return at what must have been 3 p.m. or later. Someone would have seen her, surely. And, of course, Kerry knew Melissa had been in time for the scheduled rendezvous with Titch in the town before 4 p.m. It was true that Bell thought the head might be implicated; and it was also true that Kerry herself had considered it a possibility not long ago. If this were so, nothing that he said should be taken as reliable. Recently, though, Kerry had pushed Rose much lower in her list of likelies.

There were other routes down into the centre. The main Murdine Road passed near Fortune's front gates and she might have decided to go that way, perhaps walking, perhaps by service bus. Or what if she had met someone else with a vehicle, before she met Titch with his? As Kerry had suggested to the woman witness, Melissa possibly turned because she heard something or somebody behind her, not because she saw a troublesome figure ahead. Perhaps there had been the sound of a car engine. Perhaps a car driver or passenger shouted to her. She might have joined someone else, spoken for a while and then been given a lift to the centre for the Titch meeting.

Who realised she could be intercepted on the estate? Wouldn't it have to be someone who knew not just her school, but also that she was going to skip a couple of lessons? Might Gaston Devereux have heard from Titch he was due to meet her? Although Harry Bell thought next to nothing of the information Kerry and Viki had brought from the Fortune interviews, the child Liz's story had been interesting, hadn't it – that protective intervention by Melissa when Gaston was trying to hook Liz with a free gift fix? Gaston might not be willing to forget such a humiliation. He could have come looking for Melissa. But, obviously, if he did come looking, not much had happened. She was still able to keep the appointment with Titch.

Kerry had on her ordinary clothes today, not Fortune uniform, and her hair was in her own style, not Melissa's. But she had a couple of pictures of the child and began knocking doors on the top end of the estate. Unless they walked down to look, people here would not have seen the re-enactment at the southern section. She asked those who opened to her whether they remembered Melissa alone on foot or had seen her talking to anyone, perhaps somebody also on foot or possibly in a car. Had any unknown vehicles been spotted waiting on the day? It was pretty hopeless. There were too many cars parked in the streets for an unusual one to be noticed. Nobody recalled seeing a child like Melissa walking alone. In any case, these folk all knew from the media about appeals for information, and anyone wanting to co-operate would have already reported a sighting.

Once off the estate and on to Murdine Road things would become even more difficult. This was a busy main drag lined by offices, hotels, filling stations and, for several blocks on one side, the Cardon hospital. Much of the road's population changed hourly. Kerry knew she would get no spotting of Melissa here, nor of a lurking car. She felt a bit frantic. The whole case had become more desperate for her during a talk with Mark in bed. He often liked to chat after lovemaking and did last night. Kerry sometimes preferred to drop into happy sleep. 'So, did you tell them, darling?' Mark had asked.

'I think I'm going to,' she said. Or not.

'For the best. Look, not to sound heavy, but if you'd persisted with the silence I was afraid . . . I mean, there was a chance it might change things between us. It could have meant I'd come to feel I didn't know you properly.'

That sounded as if he would have dropped her. Might drop her even now, since she did not mean to disclose what she knew. To be dropped – did that worry Kerry? After all, there would still be Vic. But, yes, Mark's words *had* worried her, and continued to as she knocked doors on the Page estate.

In the streets, children who had been home to lunch were making their way back to Fortune. When she knocked the door of a house near the edge of the estate it was opened at once by the boy who had given them their first school interview. He had on his blazer and was eating from a packet of crisps, obviously just about to leave and return to classes. He looked horrified, terrified, to see her and reached out with his free hand as if to slam the door. Kerry held it open. 'Lester,' she said, 'at least I don't have to show *you* pictures of Melissa.'

'What?'

'Is there anyone else in? Your mum?'

'What are you here for?' His face was agonised. He went into a whisper, so faint she could hardly pick up all the words. 'I told you everything. That was wrong. I know it was wrong now. You must not come here.'

'Wrong? You mean you told lies about Melissa and Titch Raybould?'

'No. Wrong.'

A woman called from a back room. 'Lester, who is it?'

'Nothing,' he called. Again he reached out to pull the door to. Kerry kept her hand in place. 'Go, will you?' he whispered. 'It's bad for me. You, you're bad for me.'

'How?'

'Bad for me.' He pushed an arm forward again, but this time the one with the hand holding his crisps. It was not an attempt to shut the door. With his other hand he pulled back the sleeve of his blazer and shirt. She saw thick, intercrossing weals on the underside of his arm between wrist and elbow. The boy left this evidence of a beating in front of her for thirty seconds, perhaps longer. There might be other evidence elsewhere on his body. Now, his face was a plea – for her to disappear. And she understood. It was the kind of thing you *did* understand if you managed child informants. She would have gone immediately then, but suddenly there was the sound of footsteps behind Lester and a woman appeared in the hall. Lester lowered his arm quickly and let his sleeve fall back into place.

'Police, aren't you?' the woman said. 'You're the one I saw yesterday doing your idiot stroll in your idiot gear through the streets. I made a special trip to watch, it was so funny. And I suppose you're also one of them who talked to Lester at the school, aren't you? You've no business coming to the house.' There was anger in her voice, but above all fear.

'It wasn't planned. I'm knocking doors at random.'

'So you just knocked this one *at random*?'

'Right.'

'We've seen nothing.'

'We?'

'Nobody in this house. I'm out several days a week, anyway. I work part-time in an accountant's. We don't want you here. People will see you talking to us.'

'I'm trying to find anyone who might have spotted Melissa up this way. We could have been wrong about her route.' Kerry produced the photographs. The woman had come to stand alongside Lester in the doorway but did not look at the pictures. She might have seen enough in the Press and on television, anyway. Kerry said: 'It's part of the same inquiry. After all, you gave permission for Lester to talk to us at the school.'

'I gave no permission. Would I? But he told Mr Rose I had said all right, the disgraceful little liar.'

It was wrong. The boy meant he should not have talked to the police at all, not that he had been spinning a tale to her and Viki. 'Don't you want us to find who killed the child?'

The woman looked about in the street and down into Murdine Road, obviously scared they would be noticed. 'Look, either go now, or come in. I'd prefer you went, but you're police and if you refuse I can't . . . Lester, get to school. It's late.'

Kerry stepped into the hall. Lester was about to leave. 'It was all shit what I told you at school, all make-up. Honestly.'

'Go, will you, please?' the woman said. She closed the door after him and led into a sunny room off the hallway. She was about forty, short, thin not slim, dressed in what Kerry thought of as office gear – a longish grey cotton skirt and pale blue shirt – her hair tight and formal and darkened, a little lipstick, a little blusher, low-heeled black shoes. Probably she could still make herself look pretty good when she wanted to, but maybe for not much longer. Kerry had the impression of some kind of immovable confusion in her, making her face startled at times, blank at times, enraged at times. And there was a sadness there, too, though she never allowed it to stay long. 'This is *my* house,' she said.

'It's very nice.' And it was. French windows gave on to a well-cared-for garden with a brick garage down near what seemed to be a lane entrance. The room had not much furniture in it, but enough and good. The floor was polished boards with a couple of tan rugs near the small round table which seemed to Kerry like rosewood, perhaps Regency or very early Victorian. A glass-fronted mahogany bookcase contained hard- and paperbacks which looked as if they had been read, were not décor.

'I mean *mine*. The house.' She spelled it out: 'M-i-n-e.'

Kerry tried to guess what the emphasis meant. 'Inherited? Or perhaps from – '

'A previous marriage. Right. Like Lester. Lester is still Lester Maitland. That's his father's name.'

'We didn't take surnames at the school. That was part of the understanding. To us he's just Lester.'

'In your notes.'

'Always notes when it's a police matter.' She tried a smile. 'So, are you still Mrs Maitland?'

'Sit, please,' the woman replied. 'Sometimes I call myself that. It can help occasionally.' There were a couple of handsome brown bucket armchairs, again in an old style, but re-covered. Kerry took one. Perhaps the furniture also came with the divorce share-out, or life policy if she was a widow.

'Understand about the house and you'll understand a lot,' Lester's mother said. 'I'm not much without it.'

'I don't know what you mean.'

'Perhaps.' It was said like, Don't bullshit me. 'When there are notes your bosses see a name and say, Let's go and talk to this one again. Once a person is in the notes you keep on coming back. How police operate. They tell you, His mother's got a nice house up there, so she won't want police standing on the doorstep drawing attention. Lowers values. Bound to ask you in, and you can really get a conversation going, squeeze stuff out.'

'No, not like that at all. A fluke.'

She sat down herself and stared for a while at Kerry, no friendliness in her face, but not much hardness, either, perhaps not enough hardness. She looked lost. 'Well, no, it's not Lester who lies. I have to lie, lie to my own kid, and of course he knows it. And not just lie. I'm in a tough situation here, you

103

know. A house is fine, but it's not everything, is it? Are you married, in a relationship? Children?'

Kerry resented it when the customers began asking *her* questions. That upended an interview. But she said: 'I live with someone. No children.'

'Not even police have to be married these days. God, what changes, though!'

'How do you mean, lie to the boy?' Kerry replied.

'Lie *to* the boy, lie *about* the boy. It's disgusting, I admit it. I did tell him he could talk to you at the school if he wanted to. Why not – or that was how I thought then. Stupid. Naïve – and I'm damned ancient to be naïve.' She gazed at the back of one of her hands as if the state of the skin proclaimed her age. 'I knew what he was going to say. It didn't seem much and, in any case, I wanted whoever did that to the girl caught.' She half stood, then lowered herself back into the chair. 'No, I'm not going to offer coffee. This mustn't last long.' She glanced from the window towards the garden, as if even in here they might be watched.

'That's fine,' Kerry said. 'I've just had lunch.'

'I doubt it. I wasn't brought up to be rude or mean, but I'm getting there. At any rate, I said yes to Lester, and then had to deny it. You see, I hadn't realised how much grasses were hated.'

Kerry said: 'Who are you married to now – living with now?'

'Right. He didn't like it. That's what I meant about the house.'

'The house?'

'He's younger than me. Quite a bit. Ever been hooked on a younger man?' Her face grew joyful, acquisitive for a second, and then seemed to slump into weakness and daft need. 'No, I don't suppose so. After all, you can still play a teenager.'

'*Sort* of play a teenager.'

'Some might say he's only with me for the house, a roof more than a bed. They *do* say it, envious bitches. Somewhere to lay his head, according to them – and only incidentally to lay me. What kind of relationship would that be?' She leaned forward and hissed the words at Kerry. They seemed rich with contempt for herself, as though the slur about the house might be accurate but to be swallowed. 'I'd be sort of buying him, wouldn't I? He's shagging the landlady who forgets the rent – an old, old yarn, and one that only goes on until he finds different digs, a different landlady. I've got to make him want me properly, haven't I, not just the property? I've got to learn how he sees things, and go along with it if I can. And I can, will. That's how relationships are, isn't it? People adjust then grow more together.' She hissed the questions, too, as though determined to sneak them into Kerry's mind, though without wanting answers, because the answers might not be the ones she required: one hundred per cent yesses. In fact, Kerry was uncertain what answers she might have given. There was a case for trying to humour the man you lived with. Perhaps she feared the end of a relationship as much as Lester's mother did.

Mrs Maitland said: 'It's a strain for him, taking on someone else's kid. I've got a situation to manage.' She tried to give a worldly, such-is-life shrug. It didn't work and looked more like the start of a small fit. 'So, the beating for Lester,' she went on. 'Look, I'm being frank. This is off the record.'

'He did that?'

She swished her arm through the air. '*I* did that. He only watched. He's got quite a tender side. Would I be with him if not? And he has always said he would not come between me and Lester. He read a book on stepfathering.'

'So, he makes you do it instead while he spectates. Kinky. You beat the boy for doing what you said he *could* do. That's adjusting?'

She took a couple of vast breaths and worked a great slab of blankness into her face. It was there to oust pain and frailty. She set her voice somewhere between offhand and businesslike: 'I think Lester understands. I'm going to make it up to him. He's marked here and there. Did he show you? He's quick. But the marks will fade soon. There's no point in apologising to him and offering recompense while the weals persist to remind him. That would be callous and farcical. But, yes, he's quick and understands it's best for all of us if – best for all of us if there's a full family, not just me and Lester. How it was before. Single parenting. No good at all. And Lester knows that on its own the house can't hold everything together, not as a permanency. We both long for a permanency, even if it means

105

sacrifices. Of course it means sacrifices. I've explained that already to Lester, but he could see it for himself. When he was getting the beating for talking to you, and the three of us were in the room, it was a kind of family thing. Kids get beaten in even the most secure households. I'll say sorry and give him some treat but ask him to keep that secret. In a way this could bind us even more.'

'Really?'

'It was not a terrible beating. Just something to show I've moved a little way in my outlook. Symbolic. Look, now, we don't want aggro from the Social Services. It was to make everything here stronger, better. I expect you can see why you should not come to my house, why you should never try to speak to Lester again.'

'I didn't want to speak to him.'

'Or so you tell me.' Her voice had grown dry and tough. The accent and vocabulary said a middle-class education and income at some stage, even upper middle-class. The selfishness and fraudulent pace of her foul arguments might even indicate a public school and Cambridge. Now and then Kerry did run into households like this: a woman on a bit of a social slide after the end of a marriage, who tied herself to a glamorous, dubious, possibly crooked man. The woman's child, children, might be placed in a grim and conceivably dangerous spot. She should name this house Cockatallcosts. Kerry sympathised.

Lester's mother said: 'I hear your job is kid informants,' she said.

'Hear it from your young, tender partner, the family man, yes? Would I know him?' Kerry asked. 'He seems to be into crook culture. Thinks he's into police culture.'

'Oh, there's a real goodness to him and even a kind of honesty. And such a smile – so wholehearted and true. But, OK, he'll be in your records.'

'He's got form?'

'He says that kid, Melissa, was a grass, and look what happened to her. He hears a lot, even now. I believe it, half believe it, anyway. So, how could I acknowledge I'd given Lester permission to talk to you? That's admitting I'd endanger my own child. *Was* she a grass?' She spoke the word gingerly, as if it came from a foreign language, and as if she had only just let it into her store – like a schoolkid swearing for the first time to get accepted in the playground.

'No,' Kerry replied.

'How do you know? Because you're in charge of child grasses?'

'We would have been briefed for this murder inquiry.'

'I thought grassing was kept very secret, even from other officers.'

'There are certainly rules about informants, when the inform-ant is operating and at risk. This is a dead child,' Kerry said.

'I'd noticed. I'm told the police know who did it – that is, the high-rank people know, but they'd never wanted him grassed on in the first place because there was an "arrangement" with him – with the one who did it – someone really big-time. Reciprocity – police/villain. You'll deny this, obviously, but I'm learning. They don't even *care* about the death or abuse, those top police. In fact they might have given the nod because you and your child tipster were getting to be a nuisance and they couldn't actually stop you without giving themselves away. It sounds disgusting, but I've read of worse. We don't say you're bent, you personally, you see, only those ahead of you on the ladder.'

'Kindly. What sort of form? How old?'

'Thirty-one, that's all.' She sounded excited by it, proud of pulling such almost-youth, and fearful. Even someone with a wholehearted and true smile might have an unpleasant side, *plus* that moving-on side she dreaded. 'You see how it is for me?' she asked. '*Your* love life – I expect it's all tidy and packaged, even though you're not married.'

Kerry loved the words, 'tidy' and 'packaged'. Christ, how nice if they were true. Didn't she have heavy relationships going with two men? Guilt. She had read somewhere, or heard it in a biopic on TV, that Marilyn Monroe liked sex the way men liked sex. Kerry thought this might mean Monroe could enjoy more than one liaison at once, without blaming herself. Without blame. That was a damn tough one. She still slept with Mark, foreplayed and fucked Mark over wonderfully pro-longed spells of the night, and she had been to bed with Vic

107

and foreplayed and fucked him over a wonderfully prolonged spell of evening. Of course, for Kerry it amounted to more than just going to bed, but that was certainly included. She wanted to give herself to both. She wanted both, Kerry did not expect this to continue for ever. What did continue for ever in relationships? Mark was lovely and passionate and considerate with her because he was that sort of man, and no amount of new, boardroom bullshit would ever sink those qualities. Vic was lovely and passionate and considerate with her because he was that sort of man, and perhaps because he had had longer to learn how to be considerate. And he needed to offset the tobacco reek. Possibly she would have to decide between them one day. More likely the choice would not be hers. Vic might tire of her or of the arrangement and/or of her frowns when he lit up again. Mark might find out about Vic and leave. Oh, he definitely would leave then. Or he might leave because she still kept silent about Melissa. She could get anxious about losing Mark no question. After all, was this new bond with Vic only a run-of-the-mill extension of an occasional work partnership, a clichéd office romance? Was Kerry stupid to risk what she and Mark had built together for something so commonplace? She did let this thought trouble her now and then, despite Marilyn Monroe, but so far could shelve it, thank heaven. Definitely not something to tell Lester's mother.

'What kind of form has your partner got?' Kerry asked.

'A bit of car theft. A bit of burglary. Very minor pushing. Nothing grave, believe me, and he's righting himself now. I have his promise.'

Kerry's mind quickly went through the likelies, especially the going straight bit. 'Jason Gill?' She tried to keep incredulity and pity out of her tone. This was a question, that's all, no judging.

'You could have found out anyway, even without the hints.'

'I've never actually come into contact with him.'

'But the name – it's known.'

Oh, Jesus, it was known all right. 'I haven't heard it lately.'

A lovely grin rippled slowly across her face. Suddenly, she was alight again, five or six years younger, confident. Even her hair seemed to get a better shine. 'He's trying. He's working with his brother, totally straight. No drugs – using or pushing, and a total break from the big dealers.' She abruptly lost the confidence and the smile and became jumpy for a second. 'He *is* straight, isn't he? Bernard Gill and Co.'

'I know nothing against.'

'Jason's is an ordinary muck and shovel job and he's sticking it.' She looked down towards the garage at the bottom of the garden. 'Please go now. He gets off early if the work's finished.'

'Not the kind of breadwinner you're used to? But great, just the same.'

'His brother has told him there's a future – something higher – if he . . . if he stays . . .'

'Clean. Muddy but clean,' Kerry replied. 'Neither of you saw Melissa up this way? A glance from the window.'

'I've told you, we're both out working most of the time.'

'But now and then he's home early. If he was around the house he might look out and see her,' Kerry replied.

She did another series of gulping breaths. 'Now, wait a minute.'

'Just a sighting, that's all.'

'You're sure that's what you mean? We don't even know it *was* one of his days off.'

'No, we don't,' Kerry replied. 'But suppose. He'd probably recognise Melissa from the publicity.'

'He hasn't mentioned her.'

'Possibly no go then,' Kerry said. 'Do you run a car?'

'What?'

'A car.'

'A Fiesta.'

'What colour?'

'Why?'

'I'm trying to build a picture,' Kerry replied.

'Of what? Who's foregrounded? Listen, when I said he . . . if I gave the idea he hates all grasses . . . this is just something he was born with or has picked up from – '

'The culture,' Kerry said. 'I do understand.'

'What's that mean – "I do understand"? *What* do you understand? Think you understand?'

'He's got a really loyal one in you. But all I'm asking about is a sighting, you know, a possible sighting.'

'Jason would never – Did you come here to ask about him, not to see Lester?'

'I'm here by accident.'

'You knew Jason lived here?' Suddenly, she went into a bitter, sing-song tone: 'Police say, He's got form, a girl has been killed and might have walked past the house, so Jason must be in the frame. How you operate.'

' "In the frame". You're picking up the vocab.' Not long ago Mrs Maitland had perhaps believed in the police, like some middle-class folk did even now. Jason had given her intensive tuition, though, and, for the sake of keeping him, she 'adjusted', kow-towed, brainwashed herself, hammered her child. Mrs Maitland shook her head, her face miserable. 'You think I'm mad to let him near me, don't you? *You* wouldn't do it.'

'Nobody can legislate for these things,' Kerry replied.

'*You've* got some problems?'

'Not at all,' Kerry replied.

For a second Mrs Maitland's face had relaxed again, became almost friendly. Then it closed. 'No, of course, you wouldn't.' That businesslike curtness of the well-heeled once more.

This was another time Kerry would have loved what Mrs Maitland said to be true: the no problems bit. There were problems – self-induced, maybe, but problems just the same. Last night, Mark had stayed sitting up in bed for an age, elaborating his impeccable, public-spirited case against her. He would not have called it that. She would and did. 'Had you gone on with your silence I feel it would have shown an appalling ruthlessness, you see, Kerry. A willingness to put your personal advantage ahead of the interests of a dead child and her family.'

'No,' she had said, shouted. 'Not like that.' But *had* it been like that? Was it still? She would continue with her silence. Of course she would.

'How it could appear, love, the career obsession,' Mark said.

So bloody clear-sighted and able to express what he saw. And right? Half right? Mark was bound to get on. Business needed such communicators. This was not sarcasm, was it?

'I tried to imagine my feelings if by some accident it came

out that you had been suppressing evidence and Bell decided to get harsh with you,' he said. 'That is *really* harsh.'

'The courts?'

'In that kind of situation, I *hope* I'd have had the strength to back you, regardless. I'm sure I would have. Yes.' He had become loud and fervent. She longed to believe him. But in her job believing people did not come easily.

'I've got to say this, Kerry – it did . . . well, it did revolt me to think of you doing that mock-up walk when you knew it couldn't produce anything worthwhile. Garbed like that. A lampoon of the child's memory.'

Fuck you, fuck you, fuck you, Mark – but not in any sweet sense of fuck . . .

Mark said: 'Heartless. This is not at all the Kerry I know. Knew.' He had bent and kissed her on the forehead. Oh, great.

'The mock walk *did* produce something useful, actually,' she had replied. 'We've all had to rethink.'

He did not answer, seemed to have decided what he thought of her and would stick with that. She saw then that to hold Mark, if she wanted to hold him, it became even more urgent that she should nail Melissa's killer by her own methods and special knowledge. Vic's aid might become increasingly crucial. Oh, God, the grim tangle: she's ask him to go on helping her so she could feel secure with Mark and possibly ditch Vic. Sleep, for Christ's sake, sleep. And eventually last night she did.

Now, Mrs Maitland said: 'Look, I've talked square and full, maybe much, much too full, talked because I want you to see you mustn't be in touch with Lester again, ever. I can't lose him, can't.'

'Who?'

'I meant Lester. But also Jason.'

'He's filled you with poisonous rot,' Kerry replied.

'He gives me his confidence. I'm grateful for that.'

'He manipulates you,' Kerry said. ' A long time since I've seen anyone so fucking pathetic, woman or man.'

'*Do* you run child grasses?'

'Not at all,' Kerry said.

'Did you know the dead girl?'

111

'Not at all,' Kerry replied.

'Lies.' Mrs Maitland stood up properly now. 'Don't come back. This concerns my son. When you've got one you'll understand.'

22

'Ah, don't tell me, don't tell me – you've *got* to be police,' Jason Gill chortled.

Kerry had been too slow leaving.

'How do I *know* you're police?' Gill asked, still driven by merriment. 'Is it the way you stand there, staring about, like you own the place and want to kick everyone else out? It's not the clothes. I've seen all sorts in gear like yours, and making quite a decent show of it – cockle gatherers, charwomen. And not the eyes. Anyone can have eyes that believe nothing, but look like they want to believe the worst.' He did a big theatrical lean forward and pointed at Kerry, his hand grubby. 'Hang on, you're the officer who did the little girl's walk yesterday.'

'Should you be talking about clothes?' Kerry replied.

He laughed a huge, wholesome, serves-me-right laugh, the jaunty, handsome, recidivist, pushing, thieving slob. At headquarters he was idolised for his speciality, collapse under questioning. 'I don't wear my tuxedo to work,' Gill said. He had on old jeans and a filthy grey-beige anorak over a roll-top grey sweater, the roll greasy with age. God, this would be brilliant, thorough cover if he was still doing something crooked. Kerry recognised that in days when she used to need a bit of rough once in a while this bit of rough might have been welcome: meaty lips, shortest of short-term eyes, square chin suggesting the strength he did not have – maybe the best circumstances to have a square chin. But Mrs Maitland needed more than a fly-by-night, she yearned to make a lovely life with him. It meant suffering. She seemed to know it, really. Kerry loved the glare of his cropped thick yellow hair, probably peroxide, a smart creation. He could have done with a short pony-tail. She

112

thought most fair-haired pony-tails gave dash, except on men over sixty when dash had died. Gill was wearing black welling-ton boots as he came up the garden but must have kicked these off at the rear door of the house and stood now in navy socks.

Through the French windows, Kerry had seen the old blue Fiesta drive into the garage at the other end of the lawn while she and Mrs Maitland were still discussing Lester. 'Shit, I told you you should go,' Mrs Maitland had said. 'But wait now. He might have glimpsed you. There'd be an inquest if you slink out through the front door while he's docking. He sees conspir-acies.' She half turned away towards the garden. Kerry could still see part of her face. It was a huge smile of welcome. Her voice took on again the managerial rasp that made the *haute bourgeoisie* haute. 'I'll say I saw you in the street knocking doors and asked you in,' she told Kerry over her shoulder. 'He'll like that. He'll think I was trying to find out what you were up to, not assume you'd come looking for us.'

'I hadn't.'

'Stuff it, will you? And Lester wasn't here, remember that. He'd gone back and you didn't see him. I'll square it with Lester.'

'Sorry to have caused this,' Kerry replied.

'You hung on deliberately, you eternal fucking snoop.'

Yes, of course she had hung on deliberately. Snooping *was* an eternal sort of game. So was crookedness. Did Jason really go non-swerve straight these days?

Now, as he stood leaning against the bookcase, Mrs Maitland said: 'Sergeant Lake was doing random door-knocking up here.'

'Thoroughness is her thing.'

'The dead child,' Kerry said.

'Searching solo?' he asked.

'An idea I had,' Kerry replied.

'And ideas. Thoroughness and ideas, she's famous for them,' Gill said. 'She's got an accelerated promotion mind.'

'I told her we long to help,' Mrs Maitland replied.

'Absolutely.'

'Did you see Melissa?' Kerry asked

'Would I have known her?'

113

'Would you? Her picture's been in the media.'

'But that was afterwards, wasn't it? She came up to this part of the estate? I thought it was where you flashed your thighs yesterday, otherwise why do it?'

'If you were home early from work and possibly looked from the window,' Kerry replied. She held up a couple of the photographs to him. 'A pretty kid – memorable.'

'I prefer the older woman, don't I?' he said. 'Depth.'

Kerry put the pictures away. 'Wonderful to hear you've gone legit, Jason.'

'Responsibilities,' Gill replied, ' – with the older woman. But I never think of her as that. Older than a kid, obviously, but that's all.'

Mrs Maitland said: 'Jason, don't flannel me.' But she was pleased.

'Responsibilities can take over a man,' Gill said. 'And you, sergeant – still shacked up with the catering tycoon? Have the jungle drums got that right? You're not going to give the rest of us a chance? Honestly, I could smarten up – duty-free Dior Eau Sauvage in the armpits, nicer socks.'

Kerry saw Mrs Maitland's body tense for a second.

'But he brings home free sausage rolls from work, I expect,' Gill said. 'Who can compete?' Mud streaks on his cheeks made Gill's grin impish, and he would know it. At thirty-one impishness was still just about on. His pose against the bookcase had been carefully picked. It said, Look – dull, dead books, and, in contrast, me, full of sweaty, grimy, ready-for-it vigour. He said: 'One thing I've never had and would really love to have is a policewoman sit on my face.'

'Why? Your nose bigger than your dick?' Kerry replied.

'I'd join you for a real chin-wag – but mustn't get mud on the furniture,' he said. 'And Lester talked to you at the school, too. The whole family involved. I'm proud. We both are, aren't we, Ann?'

He was middle height, slim, nimble-looking, a burglar's frame. It would be wasted on a shovel. Handy for pushing, too. There were times when a dealer needed to be quick and unobtrusive. Gill spoke a lot to Kerry but watched Mrs Maitland for most of the time, probably trying to read the realities of what had happened here before he arrived. She would still get an inquest from him once Kerry had gone. So might Lester.

'Are your people going to like it, you digging around on your own, however gifted?' he asked.

'Which people?'

'But you might be heavily committed to this, because the child was special to you somehow?' Jason Gill asked.

'Ann's already tried that,' Kerry said. 'It's murder. I'm committed to it.'

'The kids at school gave Lester a tough time for talking to you. They see it as grassing, I gather.'

'I'd hate to hear there'd been more violence to him because of it, or because of anything else,' Kerry replied.

'Exactly,' Gill said. 'Barbaric.'

23

Quinta-feira

Dear far away Melissa,

What do you think of that, then, meaning Thursday in the Portugalingo? Except for Saturday it is the only day I know so far so I had to wait till Thursday came before I wrote to you. But I am going to do a big swot afternoon to learn the others.

I thought I must not do e-mail this time but a proper letter. It is easier like this. And I get a bit fed up doing the code. I expect you do, also. It seemed fun at first, but then all the fiddling, and it is so easy. Maybe we ought to change it. We could maybe move the alphabet 6 letters forward. So then boys would not be syob but wjtn. Anyway in a letter no need for code, is there? I will put PRIVATE on the envelope. The thing is, Mel, I have not seen any really nice ones – I mean boys, syob or wjtn. One of the teachers is VERY nice, though. He is English. He comes from Exeter or Derby, one of those funny little places and he talks in that funny way they have in those places. He has got plenty of lovely shirts, blue, gold, green, black and when he wears sandals he never wears socks. His toes look VERY personal.

Of course he is older. He does not seem to notice a girl like me in the class, except just as a schoolkid. He is not like Poison Breath. You cannot wear padding in a school like this, they would go mad. So I had a good idea to show him that I knew about older men. When he told us to do an essay called A Personal Adventure I thought I would write about that time we went to see *Trainspotting* and the true adventure of getting away from those two boys who were men really that we went with. I know you remember. BE CAREFUL IN CASE YOU SEE THEM, MEL.

I thought this essay would show this Oporto schoolteacher that I know quite a bit about older men but not in a cheap slaggy way which I know he would hate. They all do. Not all of them want to be first, not TOTALLY first. They know things have changed since Queen Victoria. But they want to be early. He has got lovely dark eyes and long fingers that I have really noticed when he is holding the whiteboard felt pen. His first name is Theobald which could be the kind of first name they have in Exeter or Derby. So the other pieces of paper in this letter are what I wrote for Theobald with his marks on it by the side and at the bottom such as Do not write words all in capital letters, and Explain more clearly how you climbed up to the window, and Good use of commas, and Badly not bad, and Quite a Good Effort B+.

I thought it would be easier than to write you a big long letter!!!! I did not tell it all of course!!! I do not think Theobald knows much about life although older. Also this is school work. It is not just a sort of message to Theobald and it is important to be careful in what is known as a Catholic country.

A Personal Adventure Avril Grant

One evening, accompanied by two friends, Melissa and Florence, I went to the Regis cinema complex to see a film called *Trainspotting* which is quite famous worldwide and rude but also important. Whilst standing in the foyer we met two boys who were not really boys at all but grown men and more than twenty. We did not speak to them not at first but they spoke to us. One boy was called Colm with dark curly hair. Also he had nice long fingers and nice long fingers are something I always notice, they make me think a man is not piggish. The other boy was called Jake but his real name was Maurice and one day he might be a great poet even with very short hair.

Then Florence said she did not really want to see *Trainspotting*, she would rather go home so Melissa and I went into the cinema with the two grown men. They said they had seen the picture before but they wanted to see it again but when we were sitting down they did not seem to want to see it at all especially the one with me. He started stupid behaviour which I did not like and people sitting near were complaining and quite right.

Although I said at first that I would spend a little time with the grown man who was with me after the film I did not want to any longer because of his BEHAVIOUR. I was afraid. Not all men with nice hands are not piggish but I am sure some are not. I said to Melissa we should go to the toilet. These grown men did not like this. They wanted to keep hold of us. I know the one who was with me wanted to keep hold of us. But I said we had to go to the toilet to do our faces and so on. I knew they would wait right outside in case we tried what is known by some as a runner.

There is a window a bit high up in the Ladies' toilet in the Regis. This is well known. Even though it is a new cinema and has security guards children sometimes climb into the cinema through the window, mostly boys. They do not even care about going through the Ladies. But this night we had to climb OUT of the Regis not IN. So we did it like on the wall bars in P.E. I bent down and Melissa stood on my back and got up to the window and opened it. Then she could sit on the window sill and lean down with her hand and help me with a tug up. It was hard but there was a washbasin to put my foot on for a lift. There was not really enough room on the sill when we were both sitting there for a second. I hurt my leg but not very bad.

Then we dropped down into the dark lane outside and we

really ran in case those grown men guessed what we were doing and came looking in that dark lane. They would be very ratty, I knew it. I was a bit glad I would be leaving soon to live in Portugal because I would not have to meet these grown men by accident one day. I am sure that many grown men do not have such behaviour here in Portugal or in other countries, but those two did.

This was the personal adventure of Avril Grant.

24

Friday

My dear old Avril

I think the teacher should give you A+ not B+ for that adventure, it was great. It was clever to say some men with nice fingers could be nice because you said the teacher got nice fingers. This was like a love letter but it was not one because it would not be right to send a love letter to the teacher too soon. I do not believe what some kids say here that your dad wanted to start that factory in Portugal so he could get you away from my dad. I think you would of told me anything like that being an old friend. My dad is not ugly but he is bound to be old having a daughter as old as me. I expect you can get the pill out there all right. Can you? If it is a Catholic country can you get it all right being so young? I heard they are fussy because they REALLY believe in birth them Catholics.

I do not want to change the code it is too much bother. I think it is good like it is. I do not think everyone is as clever as us and they will not be able to see through it. I will do it e-mail next time but all right I will do this letter this time. My mother and father did not open the one you sent and I hope your mother and father will not open this one because of private matters such as the pill. Parents are so nosy some of them. It is called caring.

I think you was clever not to say in your adventure that you broke the washbasin off of the wall in the Regis when you stood on it. That was a laugh when I think about it now in a new cinema but not then because of the noise. I thought the cinema manger might come in to see what the noise was or them two. I bet the manger came in there looking when he heard about the damage. It would of spoiled the adventure if you said about the washbasin. It would not of been like an adventure more like Laurel and Hardy and he might not like you so much if he knows you break cinemas, even if it was so you could get away from them two. Teachers hate it if things get broke. I did see them once I told you. I have not seen them again. I am glad really because I was afraid they might get nasty because we done that runner.

Well Avril I been talking some more to the officer called Kerry and I think she might let me help her soon for money. She said she wants to know everything about Titch and so on and where he gets his substances. I rember them well!!!! This would be a very very big dealer and it would be a REALLY big job to catch him needing the aid of none other than Melissa Slater!!! Give the girl a lollipop!!!

I think maybe that big skinny girl in the sixth called Jessica or Daisy has seen me with Kerry even though we try to be secret. Now Jessica wants to be called Jessica again because she found out some very classy familys call their kids Daisy because of all the daisies in the big gardens around their manshions I expect. She said did I know any police and I said what do you mean? This was private in the geog room when the other kids had gone. She came in and told me to wait until they had gone. I thought is she gay? I did not fancy it. It was not like that though. She is against police thats all. She said anyone who grassed was outside of their comunity like a leper and even the police thought they was crawly. She said the police did not help the comunity they only helped theirselves and so the comunity had to look after all the people in the comunity theirselves. She said Fortune School was a comunity and she would hate it if there was grasses in it such as me. She was bending over to talk to me really sticking that hooter nearly in my ear as close as Poison Breath but no touching. I said I did not know what she was talking about and she said,

are you sure? That means she thinks a lie. She is clever. I said
well thank you very much Jessica and now I have got to go to
Technology. She just said be very carefull. I said did she mean
when I was crossing the road. It was a joke. She said be carefull
all the time.

The other part you left out in the adventure was when the
manger came because of all the aggro from all the other people
because of the behaviour when we was watching Trainspotting.
I think that was right you did not put that in the adventure
because it does not make it sound like an adventure but mucky.
If he came in the Ladies and found you because you broke the
washbasin he would of really been so mad. I expect he found
out about it later. I decided I will not go to the Regis for a long
time. He might rember me.

Well Avril I must go and watch East Enders now.

Love from your old pal,
Melissa.

PS I hope there are not mistakes in this because I am not trying
for mistakes. Why would I do that you stupid bitch-cow?

25

'I think you ought to get here,' Vic Othen said.

'Where?' Kerry said.

'Titch is here. My flat.'

'Well, I don't know.'

'I think you ought to.'

'Difficult.'

'I can't handle this on my own, Kerry. I think you ought to
get here.'

She was talking on a mobile, crouched in her chair and
apologetic as people on mobiles often were, one part of them
with the distant caller, the other still tied into the folk around.
Yes, difficult. It was a restaurant night out. Mark's chief,

Stephen Comble, treated board members and their partners to these celebratory meals now and then from company profits. In the three and a half years Kerry had been with Mark and known the firm there had never not been profits. The board could feel good. 'It's when the caterers are catered for,' Stephen had told her once. He was a nice old man who still made an effort and still made money. Even in a possible slump people ate and some ate good.

She enjoyed these occasions, enjoyed the great menu and wines, enjoyed even the smugness a little, enjoyed the serenity and harmless, civilised, bright talk. This talk continued comfortably around the table now while she spoke into the telephone. Stephen and the others accepted the tiresome demands of her job, or at least never showed that they did not accept them. They knew the world was not run by caterers only. Stephen's manners were famed, natural to him, probably, but also polished up during the decades he had fed worthwhile stuff to worthwhile families and firms.

Vic knew where she was tonight and what it was. She found his voice a pestilential intrusion, the rapid low tone, the battering interrogation-style repetitiveness. Jealousy? Envy? Was Vic that excluded urchin, nose against the window to watch the lucky ones feasting inside? Now and then, Kerry could fancy a steady, well-to-do, nicely organised life, no furtive hectoring phone chats during the melon and Parma ham. She liked showing off her clothes. She liked nabbing a share of the deference old Stephen was given in a place like this. It might even be her proper habitat. So, fuck Titch. There would be no deference from him. Perhaps he had collected – created – his alibis. Would that require such urgency from Vic, though? Or had he deliberately invited Titch again, to give an excuse to ring her and scrag the party? It was the sort of thing she would have done herself if a man she wanted had gone off with a different crew. So, she would be evil with Vic if *he* had pulled that trick.

'I wonder whether this might wait,' Kerry replied. 'I'm tied up at present.' She said this with good volume so Stephen and the others would know she was resisting. What point telling Vic she was tied up, though? The sod knew this. Why he was ringing, probably. But she had loved it when he said he could not manage alone. This was the great historic Vic who ought to know how to manage everything. Vic needed her fast-track brain and confidence. It was natural. It was a fucking nuisance.

'He'll hang on for an hour, and I had to fight for that,' Othen said.

'What does – ?'

'He knows,' Vic replied.

'Knows?'

'Knows.'

Mark gave her an occasional stare across the food, part loving and considerate, part impatient, part possessive, part helpless. He was only a junior board member and his politeness did not match Stephen's yet. Another of the reasons Kerry liked this socialising was that in company Mark could not do any of his awkward analyses and quizzing – not ask again whether she had told Harry Bell yet. It was a fair question and one she did not want to hear.

She tried to work out what it meant, 'He knows.' Of course, Titch knew Melissa had been seen in his car on the day. Kerry and Vic had told him. What else could he *know*? People did not give too much sensitive detail on mobile phones. Someone as weathered and careful as Vic would not risk many specifics, no names, not even for the holy cause of wrecking her evening out and tearing her away from Mark. God, if you went to bed with a cop you'd better get set for some malevolent follow-ups, especially an older cop.

'This is really awful,' she said to Stephen, 'but I have to leave.'

'Oh, dear, Kerry,' Stephen's son Peter replied.

'And such a lovely do,' Kerry said.

'*Really* so urgent?' Mark said. He might think she had asked someone to phone and free her from this dull business feast.

'We must be grateful we have people like Kerry – people sent for to ensure our protection and the furtherance of law and order non-stop,' Stephen said.

Alex, Peter's wife, said: 'Is this to do with the – '

'I don't really think we should ask,' Stephen said. 'Perhaps Mark could bring something home for you in a doggie bag.'

'What a lovely thought, Stephen!' Kerry cried. 'That would be a consolation, some consolatation, though I shall miss the companionship.'

'Perhaps you could get back after . . . whatever it is,' Mark said.

'Possibly,' Kerry replied.

'We'll linger even more than usual over the coffee and *digestifs*,' Stephen said. 'We shall miss you.'

Kerry left the restaurant. Passing between the tables she felt a mixture of high importance at being on call and almost crippling rage that a shit-heap like Raybould could twitch a string and make her run. Probably self-importance came out stronger. She knew that with her it generally did. She could understand Mark's anger. Didn't he represent a saner, sprucer life? Was it loving, decent, to leave him unpaired at the Comble PLC beano, swamped by the benign family?

When she reached Vic's street she looked around for the Saab but could not see it. A big grey Mercedes estate car was parked near Vic's Peugeot, though. Perhaps Titch had come to regard the Saab as marked and brought something else out of the pool. A chauffeur-heavy sat behind the wheel and turned his head with minder swiftness to note her arrival but did not stir. He must have been forewarned. Titch ran a beautifully organised company. He might have won *Business News* trophies if he could only say what his trade was. She went in.

'You're looking really festive, Kerry,' Raybould said. 'You must have known we were into a bit of a celebration. I think things have been building towards this for a long while.'

She had on a long, silk, old gold Susan Wolf dress, buttoned down the front and with cap sleeves, bought from the Nearly New shop. Mark said she must look at least ten times as good in it as the woman who wore it first. Mark knew how to praise. Why couldn't she be satisfied with him?

Titch was accompanied by what she took at first to be another minder, a square-faced, square-bodied man in his forties who reminded her of Michael Corleone's bodyguard and general hitman, Al, in *Godfather 2*. But this minder had a lot of lines to speak and seemed here to advise Titch, not only to shield him. He was dressed like a soccer manager in a TV interview, sleek grey suit, possibly custom-made striped shirt, discreet cufflinks, unadventurous tie. He did not have class but he had a class outfit. Titch was in another of his brown suits, the jacket with a strange, loose-fitting pleated back, a back with rank to it, possibly the kind of thing squires or bailiffs wore at one time. She detected not a feeling of celebration here, as he had called it, but of expectation, as though mighty business deals were to be finalised. She felt some fear. Raybould introduced the aide as Wally Yapp. Kerry did not know the name or the face. The face could smile wider than Al's in *Godfather 2*, but he still looked like someone who'd kill your brother for you.

'Titch thinks the situation has moved on, Kerry,' Vic said.

'We see you as needing, help, Sergeant Lake,' Yapp said. His voice was sharp, definite, medicinal.

'I hadn't realised how matters were when we met last time,' Raybould said.

'Which matters?' Kerry asked. 'You were going to look for an alibi.'

Yapp laughed: 'Can't be done.'

'Ah,' Kerry replied.

'You personally saw Melissa enter the Saab, didn't you, Sergeant Lake?' Yapp said. 'This is new information for us.'

'Why are you, as it were, sitting on it, Kerry?' Titch asked.

'You're in a terrifying spot, Sergeant Lake. I know you appreciate that. Your seeming calm is a remarkable achievement. This is nothing less than poise.'

'No wonder old Vic here has fallen for you,' Titch said. 'Why we had to see you together. Wally said as soon as matters grew clear, "It is a matter that must embrace them both. And they will *wish* it to embrace them both, if what you tell me of their relationship is right, Adrian." I accepted this.'

'Now, I'm sure it *is* right,' Yapp said, 'not simply because Adrian's judgement in such things is always brilliant, but because I have observed you here together this evening, Detective Sergeant Lake, Detective Constable Othen. This is lovely and inspiring to watch and obviously not merely a police work partnership. Substance.'

'Kerry has another commitment at present,' Raybould said.

'Nonetheless,' Yapp replied.

Kerry felt the nice, charmingly spoken words begin to enmesh and strangle her, and knew it was what Yapp wanted her to feel. This was how things could be when you thought you had nailed someone as enduring and big – money big, reputation big, trade big, power big – as Titch Raybould. You might suddenly find you were nailed yourself. It had never happened to Kerry before but she knew of detectives who felt the ground give way at just the moment they moved to make a major collar. Some of these colleagues were out of the service now, thrown out. One or two were in jail. *Christ, save us, Vic. Save me, Vic. You've bobsleighed through shit like this before and finished still a dandy, stinking only of Marlboros.*

'I don't know if you understand how these revelations have come about,' Titch said.

'Adrian's always very keen everything should be in the open,' Yapp said.

A kind of inertia crushed Kerry. She felt all she could do was listen. Titch and Wally had taken charge. It was Vic's territory – her territory, too, since she had climbed into his bed here – *their* happy territory, but it had been colonised, in the way evil did colonise and win if there was a moment's slip of resistance. All Vic could do, even Vic, was move around pouring everyone tea in mugs, like a serving boy.

Titch had a place on the settee again. 'First, an apology, Kerry. When I was here last I accused you of having been bought by Ivo Kyle or Bright Raymond, to help do me right down. That was a disgraceful suggestion, and I withdraw it absolutely. I do not believe you would link yourself with degenerates like that, and nor would Vic.'

Yapp paced a bit with his mug. 'I'd confirm Adrian really reproached himself for making that suggestion – assured me it was only said in the heat of dispute, a mere point-scoring effort.'

'I want to say, Kerry, that nobody could better understand the true nature of your predicament than myself and Wally, in the light of new knowledge,' Titch said.

'We talked to a child called Lois Fauld,' Yapp said.

Titch held up both little hands at once and spoke very hurriedly, very gently. 'Now, don't agitate yourself, Kerry.

When Wally says "talked to", that's all it means, *talked to*. Lois is quite all right.'

'Oh, certainly,' Yapp said.

'Lois is one of your kid grasses, isn't she?' Titch asked. 'I gather she called on you lately in that way they have.'

'And, of course, Melissa was another,' Yapp said.

'Lois?' Kerry said.

'I knew all along you could speak,' Titch replied.

Yapp said: 'She's been asking questions around. We heard. I mean, her name was familiar as a likely grass before this, but lately she's really been giving herself exposure, touting these questions. The interesting thing about Lois is she gathered a couple of rumours that Titch and Melissa Slater were seen in his Saab together, and, as we now have to concede, this is correct. We came to the conclusion it must have been Lois who told you about the car trip, Kerry. Well, we know it was. We asked her and she admitted it. The home visit.'

'What do you mean she's quite all right?' Kerry replied.

'*Quite* all right,' Yapp said. 'Does Adrian hurt young girls? I should hope not. Would I, personally, be party to anything like that? Lois is quite all right and a bit richer, though she's not going to be much use as a grass to you from now on, is she? Actually, you're better without her. Not unintelligent, but clumsy. Obvious. Single-parent child. Adrian insisted she give some of the money to her mother. We had to assure Lois that we would not tell you she'd coughed, Kerry. She thinks *so* much of you, regardless. Will you act dumb when you see her next, please? Thank you. You're used to fooling her, aren't you? Or trying. She's a sharp one, that. Astonishing for such a youngster – clumsy, yes, but perceptive. She got the idea that when she told you about Adrian and Melissa in the Saab you already knew. You'd been hiding the knowledge. Still *are* hiding it. Lois says you jumped in with so many questions about how she could be sure – talk of make-believe and chain letters, we gather – so much of this, and no move to do anything about what she said, she decided, yes, that she was not telling you even a fragment you were not aware of. And Adrian and I are inclined to believe her, Kerry. You knew about the rendezvous, didn't you, because Melissa was on your informant list? It seems so simple now, yet it did not strike Adrian until very recently. We think you must have been upstairs above a shop in that little street where they met, Meteor Place, chosen by Adrian as being too small for security cameras. Probably in the delicatessen. And no doubt now, Kerry, you'll be feeling bad still about letting the child go into possible hazard.'

'*Actual* fucking hazard,' Raybould replied. 'Not from me, though.'

'Goes without saying, Adrian,' Yapp said. 'I'm sure Detective Sergeant Lake and her colleague would recognise that. Naturally, Adrian did not ask in the delicatessen or other nearby shops whether they'd had a woman detective voyeuring upstairs recently, or they might have been on the phone to you and you'd know too much before we were ready with our offer.'

'The timing has been very much Wally's thing,' Raybould said. 'What I pay him for, and for the sort of lawyer's outlook he can give, having quite definitely been one, with full qualifications.'

'We see your present, appallingly hazardous position as arising out of a strength in you, not anything shady or weak, Kerry – that strength being a real tenderness towards Melissa Slater, to such a degree that you could not bear colleagues to think you had deliberately put her in a position to be slaughtered. As they would see it, in their grossly simple style. *So* understandable in you. Yet it has, of course, obscured the investigation, and they would be annoyed about that. They plug on, but with any real hope? That re-enactment, for instance. Then the buzz about Harry Bell sending Ince to work on the headmaster. Are they getting anything out of that? Hm? But we do not believe your actions spring entirely from good feelings towards Melissa, worthy as these are. We like to think, Adrian and I, that you did not want to expose him to a possible accusation and framing. Some of your colleagues would be happy to see Adrian imprisoned for any charge they could come up with. And we admit that he might have been in difficulty had you revealed what you know. A "last seen with" report would hit a jury damn hard.'

'Grateful, Kerry, Vic,' Raybould replied. 'In a way I should feel fucking harsh towards you, I know that – putting that kid in to get close to me and report back. You must have coached her brilliantly.'

'Melissa Slater an informant? Never,' Kerry said.

'Never,' Vic said.

'Well, OK, as you say. And if you *both* say, it's bound to be so, isn't it,' Raybould replied. 'When two officers say the same thing this is second only to the Gospels as truth. Anyway, I consider you did splendidly, Kerry, and although I had a little wonder now and then about that kid I admit I never really considered she was one of yours.'

'She wasn't,' Kerry replied.

'Not at all,' Vic said.

In Kerry's head a longing, a compulsion, to escape from here, a need to throw off the ghastly helplessness she felt and saw in Vic, too. She was a gifted leader, all her personal assessments said so, but these two, Titch and Wally, had the leadership now. She must listen passively to their view of things and try to guess at their plans for her. Or half listen. Less. She sent her mind on a little journey in search of recent moments when she still seemed to have charge of a situation, was not submerged by it, like now. On another quick visit to the school, just before she met Lester and Mrs Maitland, Kerry had asked the head and others whether anyone had seen Melissa come back to Fortune. This would be after she turned around suddenly on the Page estate, according to their woman witness. Nobody had. But, while Kerry was on her way down a school corridor crammed with kids changing classrooms, Florence Cass had reached out a hand and stopped her. 'I want to talk to you, by ourselves,' she muttered. 'About Mel, Avril and me and the cinema again. But this time no teacher.'

'Shall I come to your house?'

'No, no, no.' She almost screamed the refusal.

'Come to mine?' Kerry spoke the address. 'Evenings. If I'm not there my boyfriend will know where I am.'

'Is he safe?'

'Safe?'

'You know, safe. In the place with him by myself.'

Kerry could have smiled, but did not – this undeveloped mite. 'Oh, safe. Yes. He likes them mature.'

'Yes, you are. Bus fare?'

Kerry had given her a £2 coin, then bent and wrote her address on Florence's wrist in biro. The child moved on with her friends to a lesson. This was forty-eight hours ago and so far she had not appeared at the flat. Perhaps the address had been wiped off. Perhaps she had changed her mind. Perhaps something, somebody, had prevented her. But, at the time, she was desperate for Kerry's help. That pleased her, heartened her now. She had been a focus then, not a victim, colleagued by another.

Yapp was saying now, 'The reason Adrian felt so distressed at having accused you of being paid by Ivo or Bright Raymond is that he's convinced neither of you would take from anyone.' He sat down in one of the easy chairs and gazed at Kerry over the rim of his tea mug. 'Not in character.'

'In the least,' Raybould said.

'Right,' Kerry replied.

'Never,' Othen said.

'And yet I know Adrian also feels a genuine gratitude for what you have done, or rather *not* done, Sergeant Lake, and remains aware that, given your . . . your, well, possibly serious domestic changes, you might be in temporary financial trouble soon.'

'I don't say anything against this flat,' Raybould told them, staring around it, his small face vivid with half-cock approval. 'How could I when I seem to spend so much time here!' He had a heavy giggle about that for a while, his fragmentary shoulders heaving like moth wings. 'Ideal for someone like Vic, alone. But two people, that's not the same thing at all, and especially if one of those people is used to what I imagine are quite comfortable quarters with a high-earning laddie like Mark Taber. This is no reflection on Victor, none at all. He has chosen to go his way and a distinguished way it is, in its own fashion, if you like that sort of thing, or why would a girl like you, Kerry, want him so much?'

'We are referring to *temporary* financial problems, Sergeant Lake, I must stress that, and so would Adrian,' Yapp said. 'Until things settle down and all the changes are efficiently made. In other words, we are thinking about a *loan* to you. And only a loan. Definitely a *repayable* loan, in due course. Adrian is not going to hound you for settlement, but unquestionably a loan, not a gift. He has in mind, I think, something around twenty grand, in the first instance.'

'Which if you were looking for a new place might help with any bond money needed or refurnishing and so on,' Raybould said. 'I feel a kind of duty, Walter – Kerry being a kind of benefactor to me, Victor an ancient pain in the arse, but likeable with it.'

'What Adrian wishes to avoid above all is any appearance of your being on the take, sergeant,' Yapp said. 'The money would be in cash, of course, and untraceable but that should not be read to mean there's something underhand about it. Simply, Adrian would want to guard against misinterpretations by your colleagues should one of his cheques appear in your bank account. As we've said, some of your workmates are inclined to judge hastily, and they have their ways of penetrating supposed bank confidentiality.'

'It's possible twenty would not turn out enough and there would need to be top-ups,' Raybould said. 'That is certainly reasonable. In a move like the one you're contemplating, Kerry, expenses can arrive from all sorts of unforeseen directions.'

'We're convinced neither Ivo Kyle nor Bright Raymond could come up with this sort of money in cash,' Yapp said. 'As we see it, Sergeant Lake, this is a totally self-sealing situation. That's what Adrian had in mind when he spoke of a celebration. Secrecy is assured. You, obviously, cannot make any move against Adrian for offering a money facility to you and Detective Constable Othen because to do so would entail disclosing the circumstances under which the offer is made – that is, your failure to speak about Melissa Slater in the Saab. I certainly don't regard pointing this out as in any way akin to blackmail, yet it does give us a degree of leverage. At the same time, though, *we* cannot get oppressive with *you*, should you fail us in some aspects despite the twenty grand for a drink, which I'm convinced you never would. We could not threaten to expose that you've taken money loans and drop you in it, because if we do it is almost sure to come out that Adrian is in an almost indefensible position, having been seen in the car with Melissa at a difficult time like that.'

Raybould said: 'It was Wally who pointed out the unique fucking beauty of this . . .'

'Interdependence,' Yapp replied.

'He's worth everything I pay him,' Raybould said. 'He's got the strategy, he's got the words.'

'In politics such a set-up is known as checks-and-balances,' Yapp said. 'It's the way the US Congress operates. But listen to me giving a lesson to someone like Sergeant Lake who, I understand, was at Oxford before joining the police.'

'The money's in the car now,' Raybould said. 'I could get on the phone and ask Tarquin to bring it.'   .

'He looked a Tarquin,' Kerry said. 'No.'

Yapp stood and put his empty tea mug on a side table. 'That's all right, Sergeant Lake,' he said with kindness. 'We realise you need to think and consult. We didn't really expect an instant response – why Adrian considered it would be presumptuous to bring the money actually into the flat with him, as though the deal were cut and dried. He wants to make it clear that we would expect nothing of you, either of you, because of the payment, nothing beyond the continuance of things as they are. Silence. Certainly no favouritism or special blind-eyeing. Not at this stage.'

Raybould also stood now. 'I know you'll think about it, Kerry, and, really, that's the best we could hope for.'

'Where did you put her down? When?' Kerry replied. *Get some fucking initiative here.*

'These are questions which might certainly need attention later,' Yapp replied.

'Why the hell do you have to be coy about this, Titch?' Kerry asked. 'Because you could land Gaston in it if you say what happened after Melissa left the car?' She paused and then gave some volume. 'Or Wally?'

Yapp was walking towards the door. He did not turn.

Raybould had begun to follow. Ferociously he spun his

miniature body now. In the pleated suit he became a tiny, fierce brownish blur, one dead rose bush leaf toyed with by Expelair. He faced her: 'We will regard that kind of question as on a par with my suggestion that you were taking from Ivo or Raymond – an outrageous, under-pressure impulse which I'm sure you will regret almost immediately.'

'No,' Kerry replied. Then she said: 'Christ, Titch, *did* you put her down somewhere? I haven't got it wrong about you, have I? You *are* the wholesome crooked baron we all think of you as? Is that what Wally meant about keeping things as they are – my silence is not just about you and her in the car, it's about you slaughtering her, is it? Fucking *is* it?'

From the door, Yapp said: 'She grows abusive, Adrian. In the long run their job turns them all grubby and savage. Yet I fear these are the folk we have to make agreements with, live peaceably alongside.'

'A grief,' Raybould remarked, 'a terrible, enduring grief.'

When they had gone, Vic said: 'You look bad, Kerry.'

'I feel like I've taken a hammering and couldn't even yell about it. No, I feel like a gap, an emptiness, a negative.'

'There was nothing to say. They've got us tucked up, haven't they?' He chain-lit another cigarette.

'I've led you into something.' That could please her a little. At least it *was* leadership, though disastrous leadership, in the great British Charge of the Light Brigade tradition.

'We'll get out of it. We find who did it.'

'He'll come flashing his wad again,' Kerry replied, 'to buy more quietness.'

'Of course. So what?'

'Because it's him?'

'I don't think of Titch like that,' Othen replied.

'Why? My God, I have to go and see the other kid really is all right – Lois.'

'Titch wouldn't lie, not on that.'

'Why do we talk about him as if we're sure we know him and can be certain what he's capable of?'

'How police work works,' Othen said. 'Villains act to form. Drug dealers deal drugs, and do all that's necessary to keep dealing, such as killing competitors, not little girls. Kid killers kill kids and sometimes rape and bugger them. We have to believe in patterns, Kerry, or we're nowhere.'

'We're nowhere. People change. They're in a state of becoming. Kierkegaard said so.'

'Don't pull education on me.'

'He could have been thinking of Titch. I must see Lois. Must.'

'Too late tonight,' Othen said. 'I expect you ought to get back to the restaurant.'

So they had returned to his damn considerateness and nauseating self-effacement.

'Yes, I ought to, half promised to,' she said. 'But you're low and needy, Vic.' Mark might be needy, also, but she thought Vic was worse. He'd got it right – they had both played nothing roles. They had to restore each other. 'I can stay a while.'

26

To: Avril Grant
From: Melissa Slater
Subject: All the usual

Saturday

This big old baggage from the sixth form Jessica who used to like to be called Daisy really scares me sometimes Av. She is still on at me saying it is wrong to be a ssarg. I wonder who she tells about it. I wonder who she knows.

I do not know if she uses. A lot of them clever ones talk about it and shout it should be legal but they do not use any. They are just loudness. Maybe she knows some pushers and talks to them about me. People like that really hate a ssarg. She might of told that turd notsaG. He would really be evil. He is already evil and still following me around. But if she told him she knew I did talks with Kerry he would be REALLY evil. Maybe Jessica fancies that turd notsaG. If she got a face like that and the hooter she might want to be real nice to him so he will notice her the scragbag, and this might mean she would tell him about me. My m. and d. seem better with each other now but she looked REALLY ratty on Tuesday when he said to me did I ever hear about you these days and so I pretended I did not hear him and he did not ask it again. I did not WANT to hear him Av.

Sometimes that one we met in the cinema comes up to near the school by himself. He is the one with dark curly hair called mloC that Irish name. He comes on a m-bike. I dont know where he got it. He wanted me to go for a ride on the back but I said no thank you because I did not know what he was like. He might try BEHAVIOUR. He said come on but I would not. He was laughing. He was not being nasty when he said come on and he was not all teeth. I do not think it is a BMW but it is great and full of roar. I would not mind a ride one day. He seemed all right but a bit ratty because of getting out of the Ladies. They really thought they were all right for something. I can tell. It seemed funny he was with YOU in the pictures but now he comes to see ME. Of course he CANT see you because you have gone so I esspect that is why he comes to see me. This is two nem up the school to see me. There is mloC and that turd notsaG. Maybe they will have a fight about me like old time sirs about a maiden. I do not know where the other one is the one called ekaJ. He does not come up the school no more. Old Poison Breath might get jealous if there was THREE. It would be like that Othello getting REALLY angry and rolling his eyes about on video in Lit!!!! You are lucky to be away from PB. DID something happen with my d. when he was doing a lot of snort Av? What is the teacher's breath like who you wrote the great adventure for? People in places such as Portugal eat garlic to make the rubbish they eat seem tasty so their breath could be slimy. But you said he is from Britain so I esspect he asks them not to put too much garlic in his food where he is staying such as salt cod.

Well that is your lot today Av,
From your dear mate Melissa

27

'How much did it cost you to get here?' Kerry asked.

'Forty pence,' Florence said.

'I'll drive you back. So you'll be making a good profit.'

'Not right to my house, please.'

'No, of course not.'

'Three streets away. I'll walk then. I know a way where it's pretty safe if you don't hang about. Even a girl. You won't believe it, but some of the street lights are still there.'

For a child, and a child who looked so childlike, that was quite a sentence, Kerry thought: *You won't believe it, but some of the street lights are still there.* Irony and rhythm at thirteen plus? Florence might be more than she seemed. Her eyes seemed a sharper blue than Kerry remembered. Florence had come into new territory and she was alert and artificially polite. She had a strategy. Her movements and gestures were confident. They said, Watch this, you'll be flabbergasted. Perhaps that school gave them spirit

'I'm glad you came,' Kerry said. Mark moved about somewhere in the flat and Florence looked towards the sound and stayed quiet. 'It's all right,' Kerry told her.

'I want it private.'

'He won't come in here as long as the doors are closed.'

'It's his place, too, though, isn't it?'

'But he knows I'm talking to someone. Listening to someone.'

'Is it fair – to keep him out of his own room?'

'It's not very often.'

'Other people come?' she asked. 'Grasses, to be secret?'

'He understands about my work.'

'Is he the police, too?'

'No.'

'Is this what I say here tonight grassing? Well, I don't suppose you will answer that. You *can't* answer it yet, because you don't know what I will say.' She glanced around, noting the furniture and big TV plus Mark's hi-fi stuff. Kerry saw again that these were very undim eyes. 'No, not police,' Florence said, as though she could read that from the gear. 'Is he rich?'

'Not that either.'

'I don't see why a woman cop can't have a rich boyfriend.'

'No.'

'It doesn't mean you've been bought. You know that old, old song, *Only a bird in a gilded cage*? Is he old – I mean, you know, old enough to be rich – older than you?'

'Not much.'

'It would still be all right,' Florence said. 'Is he Brit – I mean, Brit Brit?'

'Yes.'

'It would still be all right, even if he wasn't.'

'Of course,' Kerry replied. She had given her a can of Tango and had one herself. They both took a drink. It was early evening, November.

Florence said: 'Some words I don't like to say when the teacher is there.'

'No, I understand.'

'Such as cunt,' Florence replied. She spoke it like a small explosion, a real rasp on the first and last consonants. It did not sound like a word for something pretty.

'Right. Somebody said that to you?'

'Shag.' That came out strong, too. 'Prick. Prick is nearly all right. I don't know why – not when cunt doesn't seem a bit all right.'

'I expect teachers know these words,' Kerry said. 'In their way they are about beautiful things. But it could be . . . awkward, speaking them to your school staff, yes. When did you hear them?'

'Oh, I would never say cunt if Mrs Ferguson was there.'

'No.'

'And I would not like to say shag to the headmaster.'

'No.'

'I expect Mr Rose does know the word shag but he would not like to hear a girl say it. Not a girl like me, I mean. He calls us "School". I expect you heard him. That means he wants us to be proud of it, not talk dirt.'

'Yes, some people might think "shag" is crude.'

'Girls do say it,' Florence replied. 'Not the girls who do it. They say have it off or fuck. Well, they don't talk about it much at all. The boys do. But other girls – they want to sound big.'

'What do you mean, not a girl like you?'

She shrugged and looked irritated. 'Some girls he thinks are moving towards lovely womanhood. Mr Rose tells them that. He says they should behave like that. Well, I mean . . .'

'You will, soon,' Kerry said. 'But not too soon. Enjoy being a girl.'

'Mr Rose probably wouldn't mind it if one of the girls moving towards lovely womanhood said shag when he was there, because they are like grown up. He might lick his lips and his eyes get a bit bigger, I should think. He can't help it. You've got to try to understand men like that.' Her face tightened into a show of bad temper. 'But those girls moving towards lovely womanhood don't know everything.'

'Of course not,' Kerry said. 'They're only your age. It's just that some grow quicker than others. In a year or two it will all have sorted itself out.'

'Will it? Honestly?' She whispered this, as if to speak louder might fracture the rightness of the forecast, like a tenor's high note cracking wine glasses.

'Definitely.'

Florence smiled and nodded. 'It's not really important I could not see *Trainspotting*.'

'It will come back when you're a bit older, I'm sure.'

'And I did not really care about those boys wanting me to go home because I was spare. Well, not boys, really. Well, I *did* care, but I did not care as much as you thought I cared because I was almost crying when I told you about it at Fortune. I cared but not very, very badly. They were cruel. Not Mel and Avril. The boys, men.'

'Maybe Mrs Ferguson was right and you did the best thing, not going into the cinema with them.'

'That's why I would never say cunt to Mrs Ferguson. She

137

wants everything to be clean and nice. She *is* nice. She doesn't want to hear words like that, not when somebody is called it. She does not know about going to the pictures these days and that sort of thing. It was different when she was a girl. She told us once about an old film called *The Bible*, it still comes on the Movie Channel.'

'What happened?' Kerry replied.

'Adam and Eve and then right up until Jesus.'

'No, I meant what happened at *Trainspotting*?' Kerry replied. 'It was different from what you said at school?'

'That's because you're a detective.'

'What is?' Kerry asked.

'You could tell it was different from what I said.'

'Because you could not say cunt and shag and prick then?' Kerry asked.

Florence took another nip of Tango. 'I did not go home after they met those boys, those men,' she said. 'When I said I was going to go home I went away from the cinema but if I went home my mother would ask me what went wrong and why I was home so early. I would feel ashamed if I had to tell her. It would make her think I was just a kid, but Melissa and Avril were moving towards lovely womanhood and men fancied them.'

'Yes, I see why you might feel like that, but I don't think it was necessary.'

'I went to see a Walt Disney called *Hercules* in the Olympia instead.' Her face tightened up again. 'I can get into Disney stuff by my fucking self, you know. But I did not stay to the end because I wanted to see them when they came out of *Trainspotting*. Sort of watch. Do you know what I mean? I want to grow up. Brainwise I was all right, as good as Mel and nearly as good as Avril. But brain is not everything. I wanted to see what it was like when boys who were nearly men thought you were grown up. I don't mean peep-spy, nothing dirty. I wanted to know what it was like to be only as old as me, well, younger, but grown up at the same time, like Mel and Avril.'

'That's quite a natural thing to do, Florence. And when they came out, did you follow them?'

138

'You think I'm dirty, don't you, a peep-spy?'

'I think you're too eager to leave childhood behind, that's all.'

Florence considered this for a while. They were each in one of the tube-framed easy chairs that had come from Mark's previous place. Florence sank down a bit further, her hand holding the Tango can hanging over the side, like a warning picture of a drunk. She had on jeans and an orange sweater under a navy and white waterproof jacket. Even now she looked less than thirteen. 'Well, Mel left childhood behind,' she said.

'I know you miss her and want to help,' Kerry replied.

'Is this grassing?'

'We don't call giving important information grassing,' Kerry replied.

'You wouldn't. But it is, isn't it?'

'Did you follow them?' Kerry replied.

'No, because I couldn't, because they did not come out.'

'You were too late?'

'They did not come out, not through the front doors, Mel and Avril.'

'Is there another door? An emergency door?'

'There might be,' Florence said.

'And the two men?'

'They came out from the front doors. They were *so* ratty. I could see it.'

'Where were the girls?'

'I don't know.'

'But you saw them the next day at school and talked about it.'

'I didn't ask them. I did not want them to know I came back.'

'In case they thought you wanted to spy?' Kerry said.

'It would be like some nosy little kid. Always, when I talked to them about it or to Melissa on her own I used to ask was it lovely and romantic? What's known as playing them along. They wanted to act like they were moving into lovely womanhood, all that. And they would not say very much, only smile and nod, so I would think they all left together and that they had a great romantic time, rings in a couple of years.'

'I don't understand,' Kerry said. It was true. She knew it was important to understand.

'I think maybe they got scared, Mel and Avril. Maybe something not very good happened when they were watching *Trainspotting*. These were like men, the two boys. Do you know what I mean? I've read about it, they get these *needs*.'

'You spoke to them?' Kerry asked. 'They saw you?'

'How did you know? Is this also because of being a detective?'

'This was when you heard the words, was it – the ones you couldn't say in front of a teacher?'

'I didn't *want* them to see me. You don't think I *wanted* them to see me, do you? I didn't want to get picked up by them instead of Mel and Avril. They would not want to pick up somebody like me, even if they lost Mel and Avril.'

'You mustn't say these things about yourself. You – '

'I was standing behind a bus shelter to watch, but one of them saw me and then they both came over. I was scared. This was truly scared. It was quite late. These are two evil ones, I mean it. One of them said where are they? He just said it ordinary at first, not nasty. When I said I didn't know he started to get really nasty and he said where are they you lying little cunt? There weren't any people around then because the bus had just gone. He said where are those couple of prick teasers you lying little cunt? What you here for, anyway? I thought you went home. Are you here to meet them? He showed me a knife. It was to scare me, like he would cut me if I didn't tell him where they were. He had the knife in a sheath in his jacket pocket. He pulled the sheath out and then he pulled the knife a bit of the way out of the sheath. The other boy was watching, not laughing or saying anything, a bit dozy, really. I said I did not know all about those grown-up things I was just a schoolgirl. Honestly I am, I said. The dozy one said what school and I said Fortune. He said are those other two schoolkids as well? I said I did not know because I was afraid those men would come looking for Mel and Avril at the school. Of course you know, the dozy one said. No, I said, I only just met them in the cinema and I did not know them. You're lying you little cunt, the one with the knife said. You are all from

140

that school. He said it did not matter. He said if we find those two tonight or whenever we'll shag the arses off that couple of prick teasers. We will swap them about. Even before he said that I thought he wanted Melissa more than Avril, you could tell it straight away, the way he looked at her in the foyer, but he was with Avril because Avril was quicker, that's all. She wanted him, not the other one. I said I didn't know where Mel and Avril were. I don't think these boys were from here, I think they came from away. I don't think they knew about the Regis. He said Mel and Av went to the toilet but they did not come out. I did not tell them there was a window in the Ladies where kids came in sometimes so they did not have to pay. Maybe Mel and Avril went out into the back lane that way. I didn't know if they were still there hiding and scared so I didn't say anything about that window.'

'That was good, Florence.'

'In the end I think they believed me. He put the knife and the sheath away and they went away. I think they were still looking for Mel and Avril, but they did not go down into the lane.'

Kerry said: 'You must tell me about these men. Did you hear names?'

'Is this grassing?'

'It's information, Florence. Your friend is dead. That's why you're here, isn't it?'

'I was not with them, only at the very beginning. I didn't hear names. This was what is known as a foursome.'

'Oh,' Kerry said.

'Did they have foursomes when you were young? Younger?'

'Sometimes.'

'They were getting close. They did not want me.'

'You can tell me again what they looked like, can you? About twenty, twenty-one?'

'One fatter than the other. The fat one, brown hair, nearly skinhead. This is the dozy one. The other dark hair, a lot, not dozy. Well, nice really. Nice-*looking*. *Really* nice-looking. Like Mel Gibson. But not nice. Some boys are like that.'

'Tall, short?'

'Ordinary.'

'You said they were from away. Why? Accent?'

'What?'

'Did they talk like us?'

'You don't talk like me.'

'Did they talk like you?'

'Different. Faster. Louder.'

'Cockney?'

'It could be something like that. Like a town, like a big town, not like farms.'

Mark was running a bath.

Florence said: 'Is he getting ready? You're going out, are you? I heard some people always have a bath before they go out, to be fresh. Bath salts, everything.'

'Yes, we might go out. I'll drive you home first, though.'

'Not with him in the car.'

'No.'

'I don't want people to know I came. Was it grassing? I didn't get any money for it, did I? Only the £1.60 from the bus fare.'

'Do you want money? Do you want to be *A bird in a gilded cage*?'

'No money. It's grassing if there's money.'

28

Kerry slowed the car near Lois Fauld's house but did not stop. The place was entirely dark. 'What's happening?' Florence asked. 'Why are we going this way?'

'I just wanted to look at something.'

'What?' Florence asked, staring from the passenger window. At least her bafflement showed that less than the whole world knew Lois was a voice. Used to be a voice.

'It's all right,' Kerry said.

They were on a detour. Driving Florence home, Kerry had taken a slightly roundabout route so they would pass the house. It was a twitch, nothing more, a self-comforting gesture, on a par with that delayed and useless tailing of the Saab. Kerry could not call at the house and ask whether Lois was all right after her talk, talks, with Titch and Wally Yapp. Kerry's arrangement with Lois was private from her mother, and must stay like that. Perhaps Kerry would see Lois in the street, entering or leaving the house. This would do, this would be ample. Kerry wanted only to check she really was undamaged. Although Titch would probably not lie about such a thing to her, Kerry would still prefer to have a look at the girl, see for herself. But it was unlikely Lois would want to see *her*. Lois had spilled what she was not supposed to spill, and might feel guilty. As Titch or Wally had said, Lois's days of informing were finished. That would be regrettable but bearable, as long as Lois herself was not finished. They must have done something to make her give them so much. Threats? Even if she did see Lois, Kerry could only reassure herself about the girl's physical state. No knowing what they had done to her mind. Or perhaps it was just money that worked the trick, as Wally had suggested. Lois did like money. Kerry hoped that might be the answer.

She let the car pick up speed again and in a few minutes drew in to put Florence down. The child did not get out immediately but steepled her hands in front of her and turned to speak direct at Kerry, like a priest about to homilise. 'Will you search for those boys, men? Do you think one of them came back still angry and evil and found Melissa? Like punished her?'

'Came back from where?'

'From wherever. If they're not from around here. They might have a car or a motorbike.'

'We'll try to locate them, yes.'

'And, if you do, there would not be any need to say I told you?'

'No.'

'But they'd know, I expect.'

'Not necessarily.'

'People like that have relatives and mates.'

'We'd look after you.'

Perhaps Florence was thinking in that sly, wise style of hers,

The way you looked after Melissa? 'You could go to Portugal and ask Avril or ring her up. Perhaps she knows names. She's safe out there.'

'You're safe, too.'

'I'll get out here.'

'I'll watch until I can't see you,' Kerry said. Florence left the car and began a huddled, quick, little girl walk. She was almost correct about there being street lights. There was one. Just before entering the full darkness, she turned and seemed to hesitate but did not make any signal. She looked very small, very capable. She disappeared. Kerry started the Cavalier and followed the same roundabout route back to the flat. The Fauld house was still black and the street deserted.

Harry Bell had told her to take a night off and she and Mark were going to see a touring company production of Orton's *Loot*. It was about a comic, corrupt policeman. Kerry had chosen it. Plays or books undermining the police made Mark uneasy. On their way to the theatre in his Audi Kerry said: 'There'll be no need to disclose about Melissa and the Saab. In fact, it would send the inquiry in the wrong direction. I've been given some other information tonight.'

'Oh?'

Her behaviour worried her, disappointed her. Earlier today she had decided that if Mark went on making a big matter of her silence over Melissa she would swoop on the chance and push it as a big matter herself, perhaps a final matter between them. It represented something more than itself, didn't it? Did it? What? She was not sure but had felt relieved once she settled in her head that she would defy him, regardless.

But, suddenly, Florence turns up with a way of escaping any set-to with Mark, any finality, and Kerry clutches at it. All finalities terrified her. And so, a cosy theatre trip, dolled up and bathed, their only disagreement about whether it should be *Loot*. 'Yes, some real leads,' she said. 'As I've always thought, Titch and the Saab are irrelevant. Someone came along after that.'

'You know who?'

'Working on it.'

'Grand, grand,' Mark said.

144

'And when we come home I want you to shag the arse off me,' Kerry replied.

'Grand, grand.'

29

To: Melissa Slater
From: Avril Grant
Subject: Life

Sábado

He said I can call him Theo which is not so bad as Theobald. I said please do not ever grow a moustache. Many Portuguese men have moustaches. It is no good for somebody small because a moustache looks too much and it might make them fall head first. Theo is not small but he does not have the right kind of face for a moustache. His face is enough already, and a moustache would look like a turd in a lake.

There is a little coffee place and a stall where you can buy cakes in the school and then sit at nice little tables outside. Theo came to sit with me there because he said he wanted a talk about my personal adventure. He said it was really good and he never gives anybody better than B+ in case they get proud. He said my adventure was exciting and a real view of how dangerous life is in the present GB, such as a visit to the cinema. He gave me a touch on the wrist with three of his fingers, they are lovely and perspiration-less. It did not last long but it was a touch and he meant it I know, not making a mistake to touch his papers and me just by mistake.

I told him my friend said it should have been A+ and he said which friend and I said in GB. He said do you show her things like that personal adventure and climbing up a toilet wall and I said it was all right because you were the girl who was with me. He had a good chuckle. The Portuguese do not chuckle, it is British. He said he thought us two must be really true friends to look after each other like that. I said true true friends. I did not say we were true and for ever friends EVEN THOUGH the two ds have got a hate on. He would not understand that and I did not want to tell him about what my d. said about your d. and me and coming to Portugal. It is best to forget all that now. My d. always looks on the bad side. He could be sick. He should see a Brit. head doctor when he is over there. Theo had some papers with him with his notes on because it would not look right if he was just talking to me at the table, he had to make it look like school stuff. They are fussy about teachers with girls. It might be the Pope or because they had a revolution and women and girls are like equal with men. They would stop Poison Breath being a headmaster in Portugal although his breath would not be noticed here, it would be normal.

I do not think Theo has a girlfriend. He seemed a bit lonely. There were sighs. He was not like a teacher then. I did not say 'Shall we go to the cinema one night?' not yet, I think he would be scared. He was fiddling with the bits of papers through nerves. But I do not think it was nerves when he touched me. I hate any name with bald in it. It makes me think of that Bible story in Religious Education with that nice old lump Mrs Ferguson when the children said to Elisha, Go up thou bald head, so he made two she bears bite forty-two of them for such cheek.

He said was I worried when I was in GB in case those men from the cinema came back and I said I did not HAVE to worry because soon after this my d. started saying he was taking us all to Portugal owing to certain important business changes. He said was my friend worried in case those two came back and I said you might be a BIT worried but that old Mel knew the score and was careful.

I think you were so right not go on the back of that m-bike for a ride. This would be ASKING FOR IT. I do not mean dangerous because m-bikes are dangerous because of speed and only two wheels, but I think he might have a efink which he keeps in a htaehs in his pocket. I could feel something like that press against me when there was that behaviour in the pictures with closeness. I do not think that because he was smiling and being nice when he asked you to go for a ride that

146

he really is nice, it is a show. There would have been BEHAV-
IOUR when he took you somewhere on the m-bike such as
woods. It would be no good screaming. I am not jealous of him
coming to see you because I think Theo is better and here. If
you were on the back of the m-bike holding on to him you
might be able to feel if he's got a efink in his pocket unless he
has got leathers on. Anyway it might be too late if you were
already on the back of the m-bike.

I do not think it would be a good idea for you to come here
if you save up money when you are a ssarg because my d. is a
bit funny about your d. and about you. My d. might blame you
for it even though you did not know a thing, Mel, and he is
sometimes very very tricky. Your d. is not REALLY so bad, I
think I will always think that and he would never touch you in
a personal way being his daughter. Here the only game for
girls is volleyball, I am quite good being tall and able to bang
the ball down hard over the net. It scares them paralitic.

Theo comes down to the gym sometimes to watch us playing,
you can tell he likes it, a lot of stretching and the gym skirts.
Some girls don't like it when he comes there but most of them
do with plenty of swirling. I would never mention Poison
Breath to him because he would think I was saying he was the
same and he would be so hurt. His hands are much nicer than
Poison Breath's.

I think you are right and everyone will hate you if you
become a ssarg but only if they find out. Use the money for
something else such as clothes or CDs. Buy some CDs of the
Two Way Mirrors, they are terrific and rude.

So, all the best amiga

Av

30

Kerry had a call to Harry Bell's room. Something on the
headmaster? But in the lift another thought hit her, Christ,
those fucking delicatessen people have been questioned by

Hilary or Greg or one of the others in the street sweeps and chattily mentioned that they had a woman detective loitering upstairs one day on surveillance. Now, who would that be? Bell could be genial and devious and kindly and relentless. *So, who were you watching, Kerry? What did you see? Is it something you should have told us about?*

But when she was in a chair facing him in his room he said: 'Kerry, I've had a phone call from a Mrs Ferguson at the school. Religious Education. It's to do with the kid Lester Maitland that you and Viki interviewed.'

'She's the teacher who sat in.'

'This is something since. She thinks he's been beaten. Weals on his arms, although he tried to keep them hidden. She wondered if it was to do with what he told you. She wondered if it was because he had spoken to you at all. Bit of a leap? I don't know. There was parental permission for the interview, I take it. Why a beating, then? Could be for anything. Perhaps he pinched from the fridge. And what he told you was not very much, was it – just that Melissa seemed to get a bit of eye contact with Titch Raybould one day? Build a case on that? But this is a woman who seems to know the kids. She might have something.'

'I'll talk to her, shall I?' There was no real reason why Kerry should hide that she knew of the beating and had spoken to Lester's mother and her boyfriend. But the habit of secrecy had begun to claim her, soothe her, disable her, establish her. Other people's ignorance made her feel strong and hearty, especially the ignorance of superiors. Perhaps she was turning into a real detective. She would work on being a poor communicator.

'The teacher saw only the very edge of the wealed area,' Bell said. 'It was like a revelation. She might be mistaken.'

'I'll go carefully.'

'Gently. The class were acting that miracle where Christ tells the disciples to let down their net on the right side of the boat if they want a catch, after they've had no luck themselves,' Bell replied.

'Oh?'

'Lester was Christ and had to point out the good side of Mrs Ferguson's desk – their boat – to Simon Peter. His shirt-sleeve was pulled back a bit in the gesture. He covered up as soon as he realised. One man's miracle is another's give-away. She tells me Lester lives with his mother and the mother's boyfriend, Jason Gill. We know him, don't we?' He pointed with his thumb to a dossier on the desk.

'Small-time burglar,' Kerry replied. 'Small-time pusher. He's going straight, allegedly.'

Bell opened the dossier. 'No violence in his form?'

'Not that I can recall,' Kerry said. She wanted to turn Bell from all that. It couldn't lead anywhere, could it? 'I wondered, sir, if we should be looking in a different direction altogether. There was an incident at the Regis cinema involving Melissa and another girl. It's – '

'People change, develop,' Bell said. 'Gill might have decided it's time to think bigger and rougher. Perhaps we should have a word with him as well as Mrs Ferguson and the boy. He talks a lot, doesn't he, if he's given any pressure? Gill the Spill they call him, according to these notes.'

'I don't see Jason as a child killer and abuser, sir.'

'I see him as a career nobody, so far. Thirty-one years old. That's getting on, for a villain. He could be thinking about maturing while there's time. I wonder if he's doing some serious, quiet duties for Titch – to plump up earnings, being a family man now.'

'Duties, sir?'

'Oh, you know, suppose Titch got a hint Melissa was grassing. They're targeting schools, aren't they? A kid who talks could knock the business into recession. She might know something about his operation. She's been a user.'

'She wasn't talking, sir.'

'But was lined up for it, yes?' Bell asked.

They were suddenly into that terrain where everything grew imprecise and misty, because that was how Harry wanted it. He knew Kerry had spoken to Melissa with a view to recruiting her as a grass: hadn't he laid on the meeting? But his knowledge was not official, hardly knowledge at all. Or this is how he would regard it. And, in a way, it could be reasonable, almost accurate, because Melissa had remained in that undefined area between being approached to grass and actually

149

taking it on. She had never been payrolled. Harry said: 'The fact is, you spoke to her after the shoplifting. There's always liable to be gossip, Kerry. Leaks. That's why I detest the whole slippery business of informing.'

'The Home Secretary recommends it, sir. Grassing is New Labour.'

Bell did not stop. 'Kid informing above all. To work, it has to be sealed, contained, seepage-proof – and can't be. One sighting of a conversation between an officer and a tipster and it's everywhere. Even bringing her into the nick that day. It could be spotted. A lot of the other pupils have all-seeing eyes and corny respect for *omerta*, the silence cult. This would be especially true of senior kids old enough to get libertarian ideas. And some staff, probably. They want to do us down and do down anyone who helps us.' Bell spoke without rancour as if this was normality. 'And so Titch has a word with somebody like Gill, desperate to make progress in the firm before he's into the sere and yellow of thirty-two. Titch tells him this girl child could destroy the lot. It's a sort of invitation to Gill to do something about it for him. Even a coded instruction.'

'Gill's got an ordinary pick and shovel job, sir. He seemed to be sticking at it, last I heard.'

'Of course he does,' Bell said. 'I don't say he's stupid, and Titch certainly isn't. Nice disguise. Anyway, how long is it since you did hear about him? I say again, he could be changing.'

Kerry did not answer, as though unsure when she last learned anything about Jason.

Bell said: 'Or Gill might have an idea Titch did the girl himself. Or . . . many "ors" . . . or then again, the Titch sidekick mentioned by another child in your and Viki's report from the school interviews, Gaston Devereux. He did it? Either way Gill would not want Lester suggesting to you and Viki there's a tie-up between Melissa and Titch or Titch's firm.'

'I can't believe Titch would do it either, sir,' Kerry said.

'Devereux?'

'Devereux I don't know much about.'

'There are tales about him – some London disappearance,

possible killings, Hackney, Islington?' Bell replied. 'Nothing proved, though.'

'Devereux should be watched, sir, I agree. But can I speak about the Regis for a second? It might be a tangent, but an important one. There was a man in this incident who carried a knife, produced a knife, and made a specific threat.'

So, her silence was selective. Naturally. She knew she could never trace the dark-haired man and his chum without the full police apparatus, particularly if they were from what Florence called 'away'.

'Threat?' Bell said. At least he had lifted his head from the dossier. 'To?'

'To one of Melissa Slater's friends.'

That did not grab him and he resumed turning the pages on the desk. *Of course* it did not grab him. Harry at his rank thought systems, brotherhoods, firms. He craved a vast, across-the-board victory against organised evil and would resist any notion that the girl's murder was only a bit of sex play. He saw network links. He saw a route in her death that might carry him to confrontation direct with Titch and his soiled empire – might at last ensure its destruction. You waited for a comparatively small error and then you drove your tanks through the gap. 'For now I'd like to stick with Melissa herself, Kerry. The danger in this kind of inquiry is over-diversification. I've seen it happen. The offender slips between two or three various half-hatched efforts. That's Ripper policing. You see, whichever scenario we pick, Gill would not want his woman's kid pointing a finger at Titch or Titch's outfit. He'd also be very scared. After all he's unofficial dad to a laddie who's virtually accusing Titch in the presence of two police officers. Gill would be afraid the child might say more later. So, he beats him tongue-tied. And it's effective. Lester hides his wounds. They're between him and his mum and dad. If he hadn't done the miracle nobody would have known. Mum would send a sickness note to excuse him stripping off for PE and the weals would not be seen. Perhaps we talk to all of them, Kerry – Mrs Ferguson, Jason, Lester, Devereux and Titch. Take it gently, except maybe with Jason. He's better when terrified. And visit Mr and Mrs

Slater, would you? Doug Quinn and I saw them at the time of Melissa's death, naturally. But there's this possible new material around now. See if any of the names register with them. Melissa might have mentioned something.' He sat back and put on a superintendent look. 'Kerry, these are inquiries well above your rank, but I give them to you because you're our expert on kids and this is kids.'

'I – '

'You'll need help. Viki again?'

'Could I have the other Vic – Othen?'

'I heard you can and do. Right.' He was suddenly so deadpan he could have got a burial certificate. Then he relaxed a bit again. 'Look, Kerry, I don't ignore what you say about the cinema. You've got an instinct and only a fool looks down on instinct when it's yours. Describe the threat.'

'This was to Florence Cass. We spoke to her at the school and she's come to see me since. One of the men flashes a knife at her because she wouldn't tell them where Melissa and the other girl were. Or *couldn't* tell them. They'd done a runner.'

He mulled this. 'Kerry, do you mean that one or both of these men came back later – days afterwards – and attacked Melissa because she and her pal dodged out of a sex session with them? A revenger? That's straining likelihood a bit, wouldn't you say?'

Was it? Did she tout the cinema possibilities so that her secrecy over Melissa and Titch in the Saab would cease to matter? Then there might be no hazard to her career, and she could postpone and postpone any bust-up with Mark. Was that bit of it pathetic? Hadn't she decided not long ago that a bust-up with Mark was almost inevitable and for the best? Yes, *almost* inevitable. She said: 'The cinema man comes back because he wants her, really fancied her, but she still won't have it, so he forces her, and then has to kill her. That could be well this side of madness.'

'Sure it could.'

'Rape followed by murder – it's classic.'

Bell nodded: 'It happens. She's so desirable? Well, we'd better find them if the other inquiries don't produce. My God, what's happened to children? How do they get into all this? How? We're talking about a thirteen-year-old, aren't we?' He roared the question and sounded agonised. 'For now I'd like to stick with where the beaten boy might lead. We prioritise Gill. But have we got identification for the cinema man?'

'There are two, sir.'

'Identifications then?'

'Descriptions. Melissa's other friend might have names.'

'Can we ask her?'

'She's in Portugal. I'm not sure she knows Melissa's dead.'

'Ah, looking for an excursion, are we? Would you want to take Vic on that, too?'

Harry Bell had a sprightly, insolent mind in there behind the good nature, no question. She saw it was weird to be foregrounding the cinema incident to him so she could keep things as they were at home, while simultaneously thinking of a liberty trip abroad to investigate the same incident with Vic.

31

To: Avril Grant
From: Melissa Slater
Subject: Find out

Saturday

Well, I do not think you should write so many e-mail things about my d. even in the code. The screen is in the workshop shed in the garden. He does not go there much but sometimes. I go there a lot in case you have sent something and then I wipe it as soon as I have read it. I always get up first to see if you have sent something in the night like we agreed to do so it would not be found. I expect that is how you do it over there. I heard that in America they did get e-mail back even if it had been wiped off and this is what they did to get some of the

153

letters to President Clintons dick dame. Give the girl a lolli-pop!!!!! But it was what is known as the FBI which means REALLY clever police who got them e-mails back out of the machine.

I hope my d. would never try to see what is in my e-mail post box. But he might so I go early and a lot. Or he might come in when I am reading the screen and look past my shoulder if he got up early. This might be espechally if he thought it was from you. I did not know anything about all that and it made me upset. I would not like him to find your address for e-mail. That got to be over. I heard about a book which is about how they saw through codes in the war. So you better not let your mother and father read that book or they can see through OUR code. This book is called *Enema* which is a bit rude really.

One day I might say about all that to my d. Av. I would be scared. I did not like it when you said he would never touch me. I do not think you said it because you wanted to hurt me but it did. Do you think my d. loves you more than he loves me? That is what it sounded like. I think people only touch people they love. O, I know Poison Breath does not love people just because he touches them. He just touches them because he loves touching them if they are on the way to lovely woman-hood. But usually. I do not believe my d. loves you better just because you are defnately better at school and spelling and had more clothes. But if you are so great why did that mloC at the cinema want me more than he wanted you????? O yes he did. I can tell you what he said he said my profile.

mloC still comes to near the school with his m-bike waiting for me. The other day when he said again come for a ride I said no first again and then all right. He was REALLY pleased. I think he knew I would say all right one day. We did not go very far because he did not have much money for petrol and he had to keep some so he could get home. I said where do you live but all he said was it was far away. I tried to feel if he had a efink in his pocket when I was sitting behind him and holding him but I could not tell. I do not think so. I did not want to go feeling around too much because you know what they are like.

There was no REAL behaviour. We did not go to woods or anything like that only a park. He wears leathers and boots. It

154

makes them walk funny like clumpy. I did not want to go a long way on the m-bike because my m. and d. would want to know why was I late. They would want to know where and where was the seat in the park and was there trees and who he is and all that. If my d. went on at me like that I could say what about you and your tricks?

mloC did not take me right back to the house. They would go mad if I came home on a m-bike. I did not want him to know where I live. I said just go back to Barn Square and I could walk and say the school bus was late. He knows the school but I do not want him to know where I live. He might come around there like that other one notsaG.

mloC said he would come another day and he might have some money so we could go to the sea even though it is winter. I said I did not think so. He said why but he did not get nasty only his eyes. They are brown. Sometimes they are brown but also a bit black. I said it would take too long even if we went fast on the m-bike. He goes very fast, it is great. He said maybe bunk school one afternoon so my m. and d. would not even know I went to the sea. I said how can you go for rides in the afternoon what about work? He said shifts in a factory. I said what kind of factory? He said making things. I said that is what factories do I know that but he did not say anything else. He does not want things to get known about him I dont know why. I said I did not bunk school any more because of getting qualefications for what is known as later life, such as a vet or a hair stilist.

He said why did we do a runner at the cinema. I said it was you thought of it because you are not here now and he cannot do nothing to you. I said you were famus for jokes and setting fire to houses and painting cats and things like climbing out of toilets. He said was we scared then and I did a REALLY big laugh then and said what would we be scared of???? Of course we WAS scared but it is best not to tell people. He said he liked looking at my face from the side what is called my profile he said. He said he liked this very much and he noticed this profile as soon as he saw us at the cinema even though he went with you. He said he did like you but he REALLY liked my profile. I do not want to be boasty.

155

I have decided that if I see notsaG I will just turn around at
once and walk the other way. I will not even look at him. He
still comes. I do not want him staring at me. I would be scared
in case he followed me and I did not see him and he saw me
talking to Kerry. I keep watching.

I think this should be a letter really to be private but I cant
be bothered.

Dont let them turn you Portuguese Av,
love Melissa

32

Kerry thought she should make a show of doing some of the
interviews Harry Bell wanted, although most of them she had
already covered, of course. Vic Othen went to talk to the
Maitland household again – Lester, his mother and Jason Gill.
She considered it useless, so would not handle the revisits
herself and sent Vic. That was what delegation meant. You
gave out the dud stuff. Generally she was on the other end of
the process.

Her own ideas still centred on the cinema visit. But it
troubled her that some bits of how Harry Bell read the Melissa
case might be half right. Or more. Bell had a whole career's
experience and a lot of polished instinct. Although by now he
was battered and prissy and dismally cautious, he saw plenty
– for instance, saw almost before Kerry formulated it in her
mind that she would love a love jaunt abroad with Vic. Did he
also see that perhaps she had come to feel love jaunts were the
limit of what she could contemplate with Vic? It would not be
beyond Bell's sleepless radar. Harry could look relaxed, even
indifferent, but never was. Kerry must be alert to his thinking,
his sensing. The headmaster? Devereux? God, it could still be
Titch, of course.

She had two points to counter this. One was her belief that
two-way rape lay for ever outside Titch's professional style.
Second came her terror that, if it *was* Titch, she stood hideously

guilty for putting Melissa on his plate. Of these two arguments, the first she recognised as rot. Was she a psychologist, for Christ's sake? Did she know Titch so well? And the second amounted to no argument at all. It was a sick, self-comforting refusal to look at the likelihoods, a cringe not a knock-down.

Harry Bell's speculations went beyond Titch, the headmaster and Devereux. Harry could even be correct about Jason Gill. Had he developed into an ambitious, more ruthless Jason, possibly hired by Titch to take out the apprentice grass who might endanger himself and a main aide, Devereux? This sort of thing happened in Titch's trade – people wanting a job were required first to show what violence they could handle. She thought she might talk to Devereux one-to-one herself, eventually. Something there? And she would call on Melissa's parents soon. She did not consider she could get anything further from Titch, backed by Wally Yapp. That is, if there had ever been anything to get from Titch. She still wanted to discount this. She believed in clean crookedness.

But she stuck to her own priorities. They took her to the Regis. She showed Melissa pictures to the manager. After all those movies he could do the patois of compassion: 'Ah, yes, this is the dear murdered little child,' he murmured.

'She was here one night for *Trainspotting*.'

'Much too young.'

'Of course. A couple of men bought the tickets. She and her pal met them for the first time in the foyer on the night.'

'That couldn't happen – the tickets.'

'It did. They were done up to look older.'

'Even so.'

'It's the two men I'm interested in.'

'There are crowds of people under twenty-five for *Trainspotting*. It's that kind of picture. Senior citizens not so many.'

'One with a lot of dark hair. The other close-cropped, fatter. Not local accents. Twenty to twenty-two.'

'That's what I mean – crowds of men around that age. Impossible.'

'There might have been a disturbance of some kind at the end. Or even before that.'

'Disturbance?'

The training said that when people slowed a question session by querying words they were worried. Kerry said: 'The girls had a fright. They made a run for it, perhaps through a window in the Ladies.'

He was tall, plump-faced, most of the time cheery-looking behind heavy spectacles. His body seemed to jump slightly when she mentioned the window, but he kept the nice, mine-host smile. She felt he had suddenly realised he knew something, but was going to sit on it and guard the Regis from unhelpful publicity. It could have been *very* unhelpful. Might yet be. Two under-age girls had watched *Trainspotting* with two men, picked up on the premises, who looked for at least a foreplay grope in the stalls. Then, later, one girl was abused and murdered. Perhaps he had made the connections with events at the Regis even before she mentioned the window, and decided on silence. She knew about deciding on silence. This might happen very swiftly. Careers could hang on it.

'Possibly some molesting, attempted molesting, while they watched the film, scaring them,' Kerry said. 'Perhaps they resisted – caused some distraction to other customers. Maybe you or one of your staff was called.'

'We do get incidents,' he said. 'We sort them out. It's not usually necessary to put the house lights on. Hence it would be difficult to identify, supposing they really were here and some unpleasantness was caused.'

'Did you have an incident like this in May?'

'We don't log every bit of trouble. If you've got a cinema full of youngish folk there will often be incidents, especially in such an unbridled film.'

'Yes, it *is* that.'

'Nothing serious I can recall.'

Kerry asked him to show her the window and they waited outside until the Ladies was empty. 'High, you see,' he said, pointing. 'We need a ladder to open and close it. Frankly, I'd doubt whether girls of that age could cope.'

'I hear kids use the window to get in,' Kerry replied.

'Very determined, nimble boys might manage, I suppose,' he said.

'Frankly, some girls can be very determined and nimble.

Could I have a look at the window?' The manager brought a stepladder and she began to climb. He ostentatiously did not look up her skirt. 'One girl could make a back for the other and then give a hand if her pal got a start on the basin.' She tried the window but it would open only a few inches.

'It's been adjusted,' he said. 'That's as far as it goes now.'

'Why?'

'Sorry?'

'Why have you had it fixed?'

'Obviously, because of the boys getting in.'

'The nimble boys *did* manage it, then,' Kerry said. 'And did the nimble girls damage it getting out, drawing attention to poor security? Was there other damage?'

'Damage?'

'These men would have been waiting for Melissa and friend to come from the Ladies. When they didn't they might have gone in to look. This could have caused a rumpus if there were other women inside.'

'Nothing like that.'

'Then they went out into the street and talked to a schoolgirl opposite, near the bus shelter, for a while, threatening her.' Kerry almost mentioned the knife, but stopped in time. The weapon would make the manager even less inclined to remember and talk. It would suggest a very rough type of pick-up at the Regis.

'Ah, this schoolgirl's your informant?' he asked.

'Did you notice them, say when you were going home?'

'As I told you, so many young men here for *Trainspotting*. One can't remember any particular pair. I don't know how you can be so certain any of them really *were* present, the girls or the men. Frankly.'

'I am. Frankly.'

'Based on the word of a scared schoolkid?' he replied.

'Scared schoolkids see pretty well. If you had an incident like that in the auditorium I suppose you'd speak to the people and they might talk back. You don't remember any out-of-town accents from the men, something you could place for me, narrow the range?'

'That kind of situation, there would be very little talk. We

159

don't want to spoil the film for other patrons. People usually quieten down quickly if they're warned.'

'But you don't recall such an incident, anyway?'

'Because they are almost always so brief.'

They left the lavatory together and went into the foyer. She loved the garishness of the décor, the rich striplight glow and pink striped uniforms and fine hats of stall girls doing snacks and ice cream. The thick blue carpet with its loud pattern was a bonny shot at luxuriousness. Life had been organised for cheapish pleasure here, and she longed to get some of it. The manager must have spotted that and bought each of them a carton of popcorn. They sat eating it on beige straight-backed chairs bolted to the wall under colour portraits of Jack Nicholson and Sharon Stone. For a few seconds Kerry could feel the excitement youngsters might get in this bright, hard milieu humanised by burger fumes. It was a venue garnished for romantic encounters, and nostaligia tugged at her mind. How it used to thrill her to be welcomed by the cinema darkness with someone she did not know. Occasionally, like Melissa and Avril, she would have second thoughts once they were seated, and there could be trouble. In those times you were likely to get flung out. Melissa and Avril and the boys who were men must have been lucky or everything was more relaxed now. Naturally they were or films like *Trainspotting* could not get to Main Street. 'How would you hear of such an incident in the auditorium, if there were one? An usherette?' she asked. Usherettes with their indiscreet torches could be a drag.

'Probably.'

'And would she accompany you when you went to warn them?'

'I doubt it. Occasionally these incidents will turn difficult.'

'She wouldn't have anything either that would help towards identification?'

'Unlikely. I could ask her when she comes in this evening. I'll give you a ring if she has.'

'You will?'

*

'In an inquiry of this kind information arrives from all directions, I'm glad to say, and one of the main tasks is to co-ordinate it into definite lines for investigation,' Kerry told them. She wanted to sound consoling and hopeful but thought it came out whitewash.

'Sometimes I despair,' Eve Slater replied.

'No, you mustn't,' Kerry said.

'It's not a craving for revenge, but for a kind of completion. I could rest if I knew who did it and he was punished.' She seemed to replay this in her head. Kerry could see her listening to it. Then Mrs Slater said: 'Gobbledegook. It means I *do* crave revenge, doesn't it? Yes, perhaps I do. Why not?' Her voice rasped the question and no answer was expected.

Kerry thought that in most families the *I* of these statements would have been *we*. Mr and Mrs Slater sat close together on a fine green leather chesterfield under two big framed abstract prints in vying colours, but he and she seemed utterly separate from each other, apart. Grief could do that. Sometimes, yes, it would bind people together through common sorrow, but it was also liable to fling mourners into private pits of misery. 'The investigation is on-going,' Kerry said with front-office brightness. She had found during other harsh cases that people took solace from formula terms like on-going. These were phrases familiar from safer areas of life like politics or commerce. 'On-going and intensive, as intensive as on the first day or more so. I've come to see whether you've recalled anything that might be of use to us now that the first terrible shock is past – matters you could have overlooked in the stresses of that time.'

Like, did Melissa ever say anything about Titch Raybould or Gaston or Jason Gill or boys who were men, first encountered at the Regis and who might still be around and ratty over getting ditched? Or about her empathic headmaster? Or about me and the grassing game? Help us. Show us the way.

'Well, you know, Sergeant Lake, I don't think we have, have we, Eve?' Graham Slater said. It was a voice that wanted to say, Get lost, cop.

'Girls of that age, they do cherish their secrets,' Kerry replied.

161

'What kind of secrets?' Mrs Slater asked.

'I'm thinking of child adventures apparently unimportant at the time,' Kerry replied. 'Any contacts made through these.'

'Contacts?' Mrs Slater asked. She was broad-faced, fair and, to take her word, desperate-looking, pale skin over-tight across the cheekbones and nose, perhaps from non-eating and non-sleeping, her eyes on the prowl and seemingly certain they would find nothing to bring her ease. She was about thirty-six, probably forthcoming and warm before things turned so bad.

'I expect when Sergeant Lake says contacts she means names.'

'Names, descriptions,' Kerry said. 'An account of any incidents.'

'What kind of incidents?' Mrs Slater asked.

You tell me. Kerry would not feed them. *Dig. Remember. You want your child's killer caught. Point us, for fuck's sake. Didn't she ever speak to you about tricky matters – people or events that frightened her or pleased her? Didn't you ever try to find out about the shadowed bits in her life?*

'We've always encouraged Melissa to be very open,' Slater said. Kerry wondered if, like his daughter, he had done drugs at some time. There was a flatness in his tone and a steady, terse method to the sentences which she'd met previously in people who broke a drugs habit. They were proud of their return to ordered thinking and wanted to proclaim it.

'I'd say that's the best – openness,' Kerry replied.

'She had her peer loyalties, of course,' Slater said. 'I don't suppose we knew *everything*. Girls of that age are making their first real approaches to womanhood. It is wonderful to watch. They're entitled to certain privacies. At least, that is my view.'

'I remember it – but not well from so far off,' Kerry replied. 'She was lucky to have such sympathetic parents.'

'To some degree you have to give girls of that age their, as it were, head,' Slater said. 'This is how I regard it.'

Kerry saw Mrs Slater stare at him for a second or less. He did not seem to notice, or did not show he noticed. What in God's name went on here? She would not have asked him. She might have asked Mrs Slater. She did not ask at all.

Slater said: 'My own feeling is that Melissa would probably

162

have told us anything of real significance involving herself and friends.'

'I gather her main friend, Avril Grant, went to live in Portugal,' Kerry replied.

'Melissa was quite upset,' Slater said.

'Her father's job?' Kerry asked.

'That's right,' Eve Slater said. 'That's right, that's right.' The repetition was like a chant, like something rehearsed. Kerry struggled to sort out its meaning under the meaning.

'Business opportunity. EC subsidies are lavish over there,' Slater replied. He was, say, forty, also fair, stocky, small-featured, self-consciously calm – possibly another aspect of that control he had rebuilt lately. He wore what looked to Kerry like very expensive jeans and a tan striped open-necked shirt, probably silk. If he once had a habit it obviously did not interfere with his earning power, unless he or she had inherited. The house said decent money, too. It was detached, four- or five-bedroomed, kitted as far as she could see with a happy blend of Edwardian and modern furniture, and hotel quality, mild-toned carpeting.

'Oh, I believe Melissa and her friends had deliberately hidden aspects to their lives,' Eve Slater replied.

'But your husband thinks Melissa was very open with you,' Kerry said.

'I believe they had deliberately hidden aspects to their lives,' Eve Slater replied. She seemed to need repetitions as some people needed Valium.

33

To: Melissa Slater
From: Avril Grant
Subject: Trouble

Well my old Mel how goes it on the back of the m-bike and all that it sounds great!!!??? I do not mind you going out with him

163

because it would be stupid to mind and be jealous when I am so far away these days but you better be careful. They think you belong to them if you are on the back of their m-bike like in the old days when a sheikh would throw a lady across the saddle of his Arabian mare but in front of him and carry her off in a swoon to his tents.

Here things suck but REALLY suck kiddo. I do not tell a lie. One day I was talking to Theo when school finished and my d. arrived to pick me up. He did not say he would be coming but he was passing on a buisness journey. This was only talking to Theo about school things and right out in the open but in the car on the way home my d. goes ape shit. Theo is not a bit like Poison Breath. Theo just talks. I hope there is nothing wrong with him and he never even mentions about moving towards lovely womanhood. Here comes some code, kid. My d. said am I turning into a real trat with older men such as teachers and the fathers of people? This is the only sort of thing my d. can think about these days. It is like being ill. He did not say your d. but that is what he meant I knew it. He was going mad. I said Theo talked to many kids in the school not just to me. Some were syob and some were slrig and some were Brit and some US. There are a lot of US kids in the school and they say suck and kiddo and I do not lie. But he would not listen he just kept on about what sort of a trat was I these days in Portugal or Britain it did not matter. He said he would go down the school and ask the principal there what sort of teacher Theo was if he was getting among young slrig. I said it was a lie. I said Theo taught us about the best books such as *Jane Eyre* but he said what else does he teach you about? I do not think Theo knows very much about all that anyway but I did not say that to my d. He would say what do YOU know about it meaning ME. Sometimes my d. is not too bad and he has NEVER tried anything with me or my sister although she is eighteen at university. I asked her.

This *Jane Eyre* is quite a nice book but it is older than *Trainspotting* and it is not so funny. There is no xes because it is what is known as a classic. Or I expect there IS xes because it IS a love story but the book does not tell us about getting into bed or the xes or size of their kcid like *Trainspotting*.

In *Jane Eyre* she gets a message from Mr Rochester to go back to him. But they did not have e-mail or even telephones then so the message is like magic and she can hear him calling although he is far far away. Theo said it was because their souls are so linked to each other that she can hear him. Theo sort of acts it. It is so sad and sweet and of course because it is acting Theo waves his lovely hands a bit.

I never hear your d. calling to me like that so you do not have to worry, Mel. It is like you said it is over. It is over for me but it still gets my d. mad, I mean MAD and he says how would your d. like it if something like that happened to you, Mel.

Well, I hope he does not go down the school and make a big rattiness about Theo or he might get the sack. Theo is one who would be easy to scare. Men with lovely hands like that might be a bit weak. I think sheikhs had hard hands because of holding the reins but still tender when with ladies.

Ta-ta then good old Mel

Avril

34

In the street Kerry had the feeling at once that she was being followed. It was evening and almost dark. She wanted corned beef, chillis, bread and lager from the minimarket at the corner for a quick hash dinner with Mark. She liked teaching him about the downside of catering. As soon as she stepped from the front door of the apartment building she noticed someone leave the shadows at the edge of her vision and move with her about ten feet behind. She tried not to turn her head for a better view. That was training. Get a better view and you might scare off the stalker before identification. This was someone quite burly but agile and quick, young, probably. The training said, lead on, playing unaware. You must find a spot where you had a chance of reversing things, and could suddenly get so you were tailing the tail, in control, and able to take time over your squint. She thought the small private car park of a solicitor's office might do. There were half a dozen vehicles in it, people working late or parking illicitly. She could turn into there, as if about to pick up her car, and get some cover as she slipped back towards the street and a useful position. About twenty yards. She found it frightening, the pretended ignorance. The training did warn you of that, but not enough. The training said stay causal. Oh, yea? Wasn't it mad to invite someone like this to get closer and closer? Her legs shook a bit but kept her going all right. Would they manage the quick and crafty return to the street?

It was not necessary. Before Kerry reached the entrance to the car park she heard trotting footsteps right behind. Someone grabbed her wrist. Oh, Christ! She tugged her hand away and was surprised how easily she broke the hold. Her other hand and arm she raised to protect her head.

Lois said: 'I've been waiting ages, Kerry.' She gasped a bit. 'I was going to give up. I've got to get back tonight.'

'Back where?'

'We're in a different house for a while, my mother and I.'

'Where? I was worried. Your place, blacked out.'

'I know. Titch wanted us to move.'

'He supplied the new house?'

'Until things are quieter.'

'Where?'

'Titch says not to tell the address. Like a safe house? But only if it's secret. My mother said do what he tells us. I'll go back on the last train. But I wanted to come and say . . . well, warn you, really . . . if I'm not too late. I could have done it on the phone, but there's all the tracing these days. I did not want to ring your doorbell. I don't know who's in the flat with you. Titch would do his nut if he knew I came.' Her big, heavy face was agonised. Although she would be still only sixteen, her shoulders slumped like someone middle-aged knocked about by non-stop failures. Kerry remembered her eyes as green but in the dark they seemed dull and played out.

'You thought Titch might be at my place?'

'I don't know who might be. I don't know what arrangements there are.'

'Arrangements?'

Kerry was doing it now – picking up words to slow things and give her time to think.

'Arrangements between police and . . . and trade people.'

'What trade?'

'You know.'

'Warn me?'

'He knows I told you about him and Melissa in the car on the day. I think you were keeping it secret that you knew already, anyway. I don't know why you would not say. Maybe to do with *arrangements*. I don't understand. I could tell he was surprised when I said you knew. It was wrong, to tell him. Has he been to see you about it? He has? Him and Wally? I expect so. But I wanted to tell you myself, all the same. You were paying me, I was your grass, and it was wrong to tell them. Dirty. A betrayal. So I came to say sorry.'

At sixteen she had already decided that nothing in her world would really be as it seemed to be, or as it should be. All the time you allowed for drift. 'They offered more, did they?' Kerry asked.

'They could get nasty. I knew they could get nasty, Titch and that Wally Yapp. You know, talking about my mother out by herself. They did not hurt me.' She pushed her face towards Kerry so she could see under the street lights that there were no scars. 'I suppose they could hurt people but they said it was not their style. *Not their style.*' She repeated this as though she wanted to believe it, or as though she did not believe it at all and was doing irony.

They were still near the entrance to the car park. 'I've got to shop,' Kerry said. 'Wait for me here. We'll go back to the flat and I can give you a meal as you've been travelling. Far?'

'You're fishing.'

'Only my partner in the flat. No *arrangements*. Then I'll drive you back to wherever.'

'You can't. He doesn't want you to know where it is, in case you try to get him for it and want to use my evidence. I mustn't even take you near there. You might be able to work it out.'

'You're not evidence. You'd only be hearsay, Lois. And

hearsay that's not needed, anyway. No good for a court. Besides, I know Titch couldn't have done it. Not his style.'

'I don't mean Titch when I said get *him*,' she replied.

'What? Who?'

'He's worried you'll go for Gaston Devereux.'

'Gaston?'

'Titch and Wally Yapp are shit scared that if you or your chiefs – your chiefs, especially – if you know about Melissa in the car and start digging into his firm, all his people, you'll find something about Gaston. They look after the members of the firm. It's loyalty. And I expect because they're afraid people like Gaston would talk about all sorts if you and your friends really went at them.'

'Find what about Gaston?'

'They wanted to know if I told you he was like stalking her. I didn't even know he was, but they told me a bit of it when they were asking me, so I would know what they were talking about. Something stupid happened with Melissa and Gaston and a girl called Liz. I don't know what it was, but that's what they said.'

'I know about it.'

'And Gaston went sort of crazy with rage because of it. He thought he had lost respect and so he wanted to scare her, getting his own back. You know about respect? He was frightened to do anything else because she knew Titch. Or they *thought* he was frightened to – they thought he was just staring at her and so on, just being where she was. But it might not be like that. This is what they're afraid of, I think. In case he did her. Or even if it *is* like that, only that daft stalking, they're afraid you could make it *look* like Gaston did it and fix him up because you and your chiefs have got to get someone for it.'

'Just wait here,' Kerry said.

'It's 21 Baker Place, Collam,' Lois replied. 'I was your grass. You paid me, Kerry. I've got to tell you things.'

'Right. Five minutes.'

But when Kerry returned with the supplies plus some extra to feed Lois she had gone.

35

To: Avril Grant
From: Melissa Slater
Subject: Rides

Saturday of course

Sometimes I go for a ride in the Saab and sometimes I go for a ride on the back of the m-bike. Well, I like the m-bike best because it is fun and the other ride is just a sort of work. When I go on the m-bike sometimes and we are talking afterwards when we have stopped he says why do I go in the Saab???? I have told him about going in it. I thought it was better in case he found out anyway you know how the tales spread Av. That is not ALL about it but just that it is a bit of work. He did not like it. He is like your d. He thinks everything where there is a girl and a man is about xes such as you and Theo. He did not understand about busniss. Maybe this is because he is thinking so much about xes himself. I said it is stupid to be jelus of somebody like hctiT because he is so titchy and he walks like a dog on ice. But at first he said to stop going in the Saab. I said I could not because of busniss. He said what busniss but I could not tell him that. He said busniss is what strat call it when they go with a man in a car. I said thank you very much it is not that and I would never. I said how do you know anyway????? I think you are right Av. I think he carries a efink. One day afterwards when we were talking about Mr T. R. he was getting ratty and I thought he was going to bring out this efink from his jacket on the ground. But he did not. I think he only thought about it because he wanted to scare me and stop me going to see Mr T. R. But I kept on saying it was only busniss and at last I think he did believe me and it was OK.

Sometimes I think Mr T. R. only wants to see me because he is afraid that other one notsaG the stupid staring and angry

169

one might do something REALLY bad. He will not do anything REALLY bad now because he knows I am with Mr T. R. sometimes and T. R. is his chief. I think T. R. is scared that if notsaG did something REALLY bad to me it would be REALLY bad for busniss because there would be REAL trouble and ecilop asking a lot of questions about everything that way they do with notebooks if there is REAL trouble and they have to find out who did it for the court. I do not tell T. R. very much because I do not know very much. I said to him it is a waste of petrol in his Saab taking me for rides because I do not tell him anything and he said that is all right for now. I do not know what for now means.

I told Kerry about this and she said it was all right. She will not give me any money yet. She said the money is not her own money. I said of course it was not, I knew. This money has to come from the ecilop force and not just from one person in the ecilop force or the person would not have enough for food. She said her chiefs looked after the money and they would only let her pay some when she could tell them that I REALLY gave her great info. I am not REALLY a ssarg yet. I am only learning to be one. I do not care about Daisy who used to be Jessica and who is Jessica again now.

I do not think I will say to my d. about all that. I know I said I would say something to him one day and I might one day but not now. I do not know if my m. knows about it but if she does not and if I said about it she might get to know and then she would be upset. I think she does know about it but I am not sure. I think that was bad if that happened but you are still my best pal Av and xes is very hard to understand. I hope your d. does not come over here because you made him sound scary the way he talked about me.

The book we are doing in school is not the one you said about calling the girl from far far off or Trainspotting. It is a book called Lord of the Flies and it is all about boys and the way they are bad even when they are only young stamping on the glasses of a kid called Piggy. It is great. I think it would be great to go on the horse of a shiehk with him. We would be able to smoke stuff there because they all did it was the usual in them countrys like bread and butter.

I miss you Av,
Your best pal Melissa.

36

They found Gaston Devereux as expected in the Wonders of the World disco bar of the students' union. This was his beat on Friday nights, selling a bit, collecting a bit if he had given credit last week, dancing a bit, perhaps doing a line with a student, girl or boy according to the moon phase. There was a glamour to him – a natural aristocratic blankness to his face and two brilliantly emphatic, very dark, thin eyebrows. Kerry might have come to talk to him on her own, but Vic had also collected pointers to Gaston on his visit to Ann Maitland and Jason Gill.

Vic had rung Kerry at home to say so. Mark picked up the telephone. She found it painful to observe the conversation, even such basics. When Kerry took the receiver Vic said: 'Apparently Gaston Devereux stalked Melissa.'

'Yes.'

'You knew?' He sounded disbelieving. This was a lover but the tone did not sound like that now. It was career stuff. Perhaps there would always be that mix with Vic, if things went on. He obviously thought she could not admit he might be ahead of her. He was waiting for Kerry to tell him how she knew.

So she said: 'How do you know?'

'Gill told me. He's seen him.'

'I've spoken to Gill.'

'Yes, he told me that, too.'

'Why didn't he let me know about Gaston?' Kerry replied.

'You should ask him.' It could mean Jason did not talk to women cops, only pirouetted in front of them and tried to chat them up. It could mean Vic from all his fine rough past knew how to screw someone like Jason and make him cough. It could mean that because Vic went so far back he and Jason had one of those cop-villain relationships which were half hunter-and-hunted and half old chums. 'Don't feel ashamed,' he said. 'You got the information your own way, Kerry.'

This was another request to know how and she realised she ought to tell him or he would scent bullshit. 'Lois turned up,' she said.

'Ah. The wondrous kid network.'

'We'd better see Gaston.'

'How does that fit the silence quid pro quo with Titch?'

'Fuck Titch. *And* Wally.'

When the call finished Mark had said: 'He just asks for "Kerry" when he comes on the line, not Detective Sergeant Lake.'

'Vic's like that. He's been around so long. He'd probably ask for Harry if he rang Superintendent Bell at home.'

'And the cursing with him. Mates. I feel like an outsider.'

'Mark, love,' she said, 'how crazy!' and pulled him to her. She kissed him gently and long on the lips. It alarmed her to find she missed the ciggy stink.

'I do realise you have to work very closely with colleagues sometimes, Kerry.'

'Especially now. We're not doing things quite straight.'

'He's helping you? Why?'

'He sees the sense. It's a consolation – he's so sharp and experienced.'

'How much of a consolation?' Mark said.

'A consolation.' She had kissed him once more, on the chin this time, and then left to meet Vic. She wondered how she had become so slippery.

They took Gaston to a corner of the bar. Kerry liked it here almost as much as the Regis, though as bars and dance floors went, and as student unions went, the standards were a bit down on what she had been used to. At Oxford there was all that genuine wood, the warm, dull glow of a great history. You looked for F. E. Smith's carved initials. Perhaps this was what Kingsley Amis had in mind when he said about universities, 'more means worse': the bars and other off-duty spots would be dumps. Things were garish, extensive and plastic, but not garish, extensive and plastic enough to match the Regis's brilliantly dud class. Cinemas had been around longer than this university, with time to work out an ambience. What sounded to Kerry like something from the Rae and Christian *Northern Sulphuric Soul* album was hip hopping it in the disco and sounded rich. She felt nostalgia hook her hard again. Kerry would like to have been doing something bold and derivative out on the dance floor. Why was she sitting here with a lovely silver-haired relic and a lance-corporal crook? 'Gaston,' she said, 'we heard Titch is really concerned about you. About your liberty.'

'I gather you two are a true couple now,' he replied. 'Well, on certain nights. Congrats, indeed. I think it's delightful.'

'Titch is a boy with vision,' Kerry said. 'Dwarfish but acute. Titch can see implications. He knows you're too stupid to worry for yourself so he worries for you. You're indispensable to his operation, Gaston, and yet he might have to dispense with you.'

'We feel we're doing him a kindness talking to you like this on a private basis,' Vic replied. 'We can give a sort of pre-look at what's against you, Gaston, so you can gird your busy loins and get your stories ready.'

'I see it's going to be Madam Hard and Monsieur Soft,' Gaston replied. 'Gender bending.'

'You're our guru on that,' Kerry said. 'Vivid all-round tastes.'

Vic bought some beers. Did they look cop, she and Vic? If not, what *did* they look like? She might have been a mature student, possibly, and Vic a *very* mature student. In her day, undergraduates would not have liked a couple of detectives crashing their den to work on someone, especially someone who sold them trips, ease, and mild, temporary hopes, if necessary on tick. And they would have made their hostility obvious. Nobody seemed to notice her and Vic here, though. It must be true what she heard and students had turned unbolshy, pummelled into line by New Labour tuition fees. Perhaps that loud, tall girl at Fortune School would get them stirring again nationwide next year.

'What will the Police and Criminal Evidence Act people say about a chat like this?' Gaston asked in a big satiric yelp. 'No tapes, no lawyer.'

'Informality is my second name,' Kerry replied. 'We're only here for the music. Luckily, we've bumped into dear Gaston, a confrère. One thing we're probably not going to do is search you. We know that in your innocent way you'd be scared of a plant. *You're* here for the music, too. That's our understanding. At present.' The music had moved on to *God Give Me Strength*. A chirpy girl of about twenty in a long grey-beige woollen dress seemed about to approach Gaston. He glanced at her, gave no signal that Kerry saw, but the girl suddenly swerved fifteen degrees and walked on to the bar, not looking at him. She bought a Coke. There seemed no commitment in the act. Kerry said: 'This can be quite quick if you let it, Gaston, *mon cher*. We know you've got a living to make and a sales target to hit.'

'I'm ready to leave, as a matter of fact,' Devereux said.

'No, you're not,' Kerry replied.

'Stalking Melissa,' Othen said.

'Somebody must have been, yes,' Devereux replied.

'We've got witnesses,' Othen said.

'You boys always say that. And you girls,' Devereux answered. 'The old bluffs are the best, except when they don't work. They don't work.'

'At least two witnesses,' Othen replied.

'Kerry's kids, I expect,' Devereux said. 'Young imaginations, always game to create something. Or get led into something for a little fee. They'll see whatever you want them to see, Kerry. You're magic.'

'A resident,' Othen replied.

'Where?' Devereux said.

'On the Page estate,' Othen said. 'Perhaps around her house, too. We'll have to do some asking there.'

'On the Page?' Devereux replied. 'Like Jason Gill, that sudden son of the fucking soil?'

'A resident,' Othen said.

'Gill aims to destroy me,' Devereux said. 'He's looking for work with Titch. Jason knows I'd be against. He wants me gone. Are you helping him?'

'You know he spotted you, do you?' Othen said.

'It *was* Gill?' Devereux asked.

'A resident,' Othen said.

'Had you fallen for her?' Kerry asked. 'You were genuinely after Melissa – in one of your happy paedo hetero spells? Or was it just malice, because of the Liz Quant incident?'

'The what?'

'She'd got up your nose, had she?' Kerry asked. 'Not a customary access with you but the tighter for being less used.'

'Nobody gets up my nose,' Devereux replied. 'I stay cool.'

'Oh, Christ, we're into the Pusher's Phrase Book,' Kerry said.

'I don't have to take this,' Devereux said, wagging a ferocious shoulder.

'Of course you don't,' Kerry replied. 'Of course you fucking do.'

'Don't you feel any pity for Titch?' Othen asked. 'So anxious for you?'

'I didn't even know you were into youngsters,' Kerry said. 'But then again, those vivid all-round tastes. All round.'

There was a disco interval. The bar filled. Devereux looked grateful and took a big pull of beer. Students greeted him but still did not interrupt. He was slim, pretty, dark-haired, heavy-lipped, a bit elegant, a bit remote, a bit slow-moving so as not to get himself sweaty and undesirable. The Frenchness of his names was probably authentic. His mother might have told him as a child to act up to this and he would often sit or stand not moving for half a minute or more in a gorgeous pose. He would be under thirty but always dressed formally in one of his double-breasted dark suits, black lace-up shoes and a white shirt and decent tie. Overall he looked frail but likely to continue. Women would go for the smartness and delicate nose.

'So, what was it all about, Gaston?' Kerry said. The question sounded like nothing much but she had worked on it. This was not what you would ask if you really thought he had done Melissa. This was a question with ignorance up front. It suggested there was some other explanation for his behaviour and one she yearned to believe. It offered an escape. It required him to admit the stalking and show it as innocent.

Devereux twitched the plump lips. 'She was a little interfering bitch – though, obviously, not to speak ill of a dead kid.'

'Right,' Kerry replied.

'And not simply dead,' Devereux said.

'Right,' Kerry replied.

'She might have put it around she made a fucking fool of me,' Devereux said, 'and then where am I? Where?' He seemed sure of their sympathy.

'Right,' Kerry replied.

'I have to keep an image.'

'Certainly,' Kerry said.

'With kids it's vital,' Devereux said.

'With all customers, I should think,' Kerry replied.

'Especially kids. They look up to me,' Devereux said.

'I can understand it,' Kerry replied.

'Fuck off, Kerry,' Devereux said, 'you taking the piss?'

'Image can be crucial,' she replied.

He seemed to decide she was serious. 'There's a senior girl in that school, the Fortune School, who really thinks I'm interesting. This is not some dim little nobody kid who could have a pash on anyone, all new tits and gasping. This girl has a *mind*. Everyone says. Mind is something I admire.'

'It's the French side of you,' Kerry replied. 'They go for intellect. Think of Maurice Chevalier.'

'This girl is a woman already and she can sum up things.'

'I know her,' Kerry replied. 'An asset to any school.'

'It's important what she thinks of me,' Devereux said. 'I didn't want that sniffy little cow talking me down and down. You've got to do something about a sniffy little cow like that, haven't you?'

'Like shut her up?' Othen asked.

'Like let her feel your presence now and then,' Devereux said. 'That would be enough as long as you've *got* a presence and can really put it over.'

The disco picked up again with what sounded like Krust and the bar began to empty. 'All this presence – you might have seen something one day,' Othen said.

'Something you wouldn't have spoken to us about before because it would have told us you were stalking, and on that basis we might have lined you up for the death. Well, we know about the stalking, anyway. Nothing to lose.'

176

'Then we could leave you to your customers and conquests, Gaston. The night moves on.'

Devereux drank again and gave Kerry some of his beauty for a time. 'Fee?' he asked. 'This would be information, yes?'

'Possibly information,' Kerry replied. 'Possibly a fee.'

'You're in touch with the money, aren't you?' Devereux asked. 'For the kid grasses.'

'There's a fund,' Kerry replied. 'I don't run it. You know the system, Gaston.'

'But you can put a word?'

'I can put a word,' Kerry said. 'Sometimes the word is listened to.'

Devereux leaned forward. His suit jacket showed no strain. It must have been tailored for him, and sweetly tailored. Gaston's bold body language had been allowed for. There were costs in being Gaston. 'Once, I see her start a motorbike ride,' he said. 'Picked up on the Page. She'd been before.'

'You said *once*,' Othen replied.

'No argument or anything like that, she just got on the back. You could tell it was something she was used to. I'm too far off to see the registration. I didn't want to get close, anyway. It could have made me look stupid, if she knew I saw her. She would just roar away and I'd be nowhere, left behind like bacon rind on a plate, no real presence.'

'A man driving?' Kerry asked.

'Twenties, early. He's in leathers. He had his helmet off when they met. A lot of dark hair, curly, probably. About five ten. The way he stood, holding the bike – like he owned everything – it, her, everything. But they do, don't they, when they're in leathers?' He touched his lips with three fingers, perhaps excited by the memory.

'The bike?' Othen said.

'I don't know about these things. Biggish, though.'

'If we showed you some pictures?' Kerry said.

'Him, or the bike?'

'A range of bike pictures, for an identification of make,' Kerry replied.

'It's possible.'

'And then there might be something on file about him – a

177

man who takes young girls on bikes. People work to a pattern. Did you get a good enough look to recognise him as well as the bike from pictures?'

'It's possible,' Devereux said. 'Clearly, this is worth money.'

'It's possible,' Kerry said.

37

To: Melissa Slater
From: Avril Grant
Subject: d.

Sábado

My d. went down the school but I do not think the principal believed him because Theo is still working there and it is all right he is still teaching us about *Jane Eyre*. He said do not forget about the mad woman in the attic. It is Mr Rochester's mad wife. He said sometimes the women get the worst of it even though Jane got Mr Rochester. I am glad the principal did not believe my d. about Theo but I am not glad if the principal thinks it was my fault with Theo. It is true the women sometimes get the worst of it. If that principal thinks it was my fault he might think all sorts and he might start getting like Poison Breath. I will know if he is getting like Poison Breath if he starts telling me I am getting towards lovely womanhood and all that.

My d. hates it here now I know it. It is not just because of Theo. I think he hates everything in Portugal. I do not think he likes going to work here and he does not like the people. He keeps on about them. He thinks they are all trying to cheat him. He keeps on about them to my m. and to me. My m. is getting fed up with it. I think she has decided she likes the man who has a restaurant we go to here sometimes. He is not too short and I do not think he smells of cod, or not much. I think my d. has noticed she likes this man and my d. said we would not be going there to eat any more because of her behaviour. He said we are all the same. He means women and girls. It makes him REALLY ratty. I think he is a turd.

All the time he is asking me about things that happened. You know what I mean. Before he never asked me at all. But now he is asking all the time. It is like he cannot leave it alone. I say that it is all over and private. That makes him even more ratty. There are five things that make him REALLY ratty. They are

1. Portugal
2. His work
3. The man in the restaurant
4. Theo
5. What he thinks happened when we were still over there.

This is REALLY a lot of rattyness. He is going mad. I said it before. He is. I think my m. thinks he is going mad. This is why she likes the restaurant man. I do not blame her much. The restaurant man has not got those terrible gold teeth like some of them and he does not smile all the time like some of them do to get on your right side. My d. says why is your d. still over there and all right and why was it him had to come to this bloody country which is a tip. He keeps saying why are you all right Mel? He says you are all right but I am over here putting out for a teacher twice as old because this is what I am used to. This is how my d. talks such as PUTTING OUT. It is a lie. I think he might come over there Mel. He is so ratty and mad. If he came there you would be able to see how ratty and mad he is. It would be best to watch out. He could say to my m. a London trip for buisness or to see a head doctor. That is what he OUGHT to say. She would believe it I think. He does know people in London from buisness from before. But maybe he would not stay all the time in London he might come there. Perhaps you would not be around anyway. Perhaps you would be away on the back of the m-bike. I think that would be best even if he has got a efink and even if he is always wanting it.

The principal did not kick Theo out but Theo said the principal told him he should be careful. I said what does that mean, does he think I am after Theo like my d. said? Theo said he did not know but I think this principal might be thinking about himself. You know how they can be. This is to get Theo

179

out of the way maybe. The principal is not too old but he is very jerky when he walks like changing the guard and an arse like the back of an ambulance.

I have been learning quite a bit of the lingo and when I am down the clothes shops I can say No thank you very much that is like Queen Victoria used to wear. Queen Victoria is someone they have heard about. If he comes over there and starts shouting at you in the street or something like that just go away or tell him not to be such a turd. I do not know what sort of a car he would have for you to look out for in case. I expect he would hire it in London. Buisness people often hire cars, it is their way. Theo said my eyes are always full of warmth and fun and I said he has the best hands I ever saw.

Cheers then Mel

Avril

38

Kerry and Vic Othen flew to Oporto and had a walk along the river bank near the port wine warehouses. She held his arm. It was like a holiday. Was it like a honeymoon? Now and then Vic would touch her softly on the neck or cheek or wrist, possessive, deeply tentative, almost apologetic contacts. He seemed happy. His smoking would be only at the norm level here. They paused and leaned over railings near a yellow-brown arc of outfall in the Douro and watched it constantly freshed up by new, long vigorous spurts from sluices in the bank. Encompassing the arc was a bigger, shimmering one as a million silver-grey fish eagerly nudged and skirmished for feed.

In the late afternoon, when they hoped Avril would be home from school, they took a taxi for the forty-minute motorway drive north to Guimaraes, where the girl and her parents had a flat, and where Brian Grant's softwear factory was situated. Guimaraes was apparently once Portugal's capital and still had a big, bold, handsome castle from those big bold days. They booked two rooms in an hotel in a narrow cobbled street near the centre but would sleep in one. It was a token security measure. They would need to put the hotel bill in to back their expenses claim, and there was no need to proclaim in writing what Harry Bell already assumed, that the trip was more than a work trip. They arrived at the Grants' flat without forewarning. This was Vic's idea and probably a good one. Avril was not at home yet. Her mother took them into the lounge.

'We're trying to identify a man with a motorbike that Avril and Melissa might have met at the cinema, Mrs Grant,' Kerry said. 'We've had no luck tracing him. It's a bit of a long shot. The description we have for the motorcyclist does match one we've been given by a friend of Avril and Melissa who was with them for a while at the cinema. Perhaps Avril remembers something about him that would help. We don't think he was local. That makes tracing very difficult.'

Mrs Grant was tall, virtually statuesque, her hair blonde and cut in an Eton crop, her face lively, large-featured, almost beautiful, almost friendly, intelligently suspicious. She would be very striking in this country of short-legged, dark people. 'Avril is still terribly upset about Melissa's death and so on,' she replied. 'In a sense it was made worse – I mean from Avril's point of view made worse – because she sent Melissa an e-mail the day after she died.'

'The girls kept in touch by the Internet?' Kerry asked.

'Oh, yes.'

'Did Avril print the letters from the screen, I wonder?' Othen asked. 'They might have some information.'

'Unfortunately, all wiped, except the last one, not from Melissa but from her parents informing us of the death – this sad, sad reply to Avril's last. Avril was devastated. Occasionally they wrote by mail for some reason. But I don't think any of these letters survive, either. We are having to be very supportive. My husband tries to pick Avril up from school at Oporto most days. They'll be here very soon.'

Emma Grant brought coffee and sweet cakes. They sat in easy chairs in the large first-floor room full of uncoordinated bits of mostly heavy furniture. It overlooked a driveway and small flower garden where tall purple autumn flowers Kerry could not identify clustered around a small fountain. It produced no water now.

'We'll be very brief, very careful,' Kerry replied. 'It is only to do with the motorcyclist.'

'Why? You think he might be involved? Someone they met at the cinema?'

'We need to know more about him,' Kerry replied.

'Avril has never mentioned anyone they met at the cinema,' Mrs Grant said. 'Which cinema? Which film? I might recall when she and Avril went to see it. I'd be able to think more clearly whether she has mentioned anyone.'

'Oh, you know what children of that age are,' Othen said.

'What?' Mrs Grant asked. She smiled continuously but there was a doggedness to her voice. Kerry felt something of the unease she had experienced with the Slaters.

'They forget,' Othen replied.

'A man, you say – old enough to drive a motorcycle?' Mrs Grant asked.

'It's possible,' Kerry replied. 'That's really what we want to check. There might be two quite different men.'

'But *men* – not boys?' She clapped her hands sharply. Enough of this roundabout stuff. 'Are we talking about Avril and Melissa being picked up at the cinema by a couple of men?'

'We're not really clear *what* happened,' Kerry replied.

'But you say another of their friends was with them.'

'Not all of the time,' Kerry replied.

'I expect this would be Florence Cass, would it? A sweet child but timid. Melissa and Avril went off with the men? Is that what you're telling me? My God.'

'We're not really clear *what* happened,' Kerry replied.

'Which cinema? What was the film? I might remember whether Avril said anything.'

'This, too, we're not clear about,' Kerry said.

'But Florence – couldn't she tell you that? If she saw the man you're interested in she must have seen where Avril and Melissa met him.'

'We're not sure he's the man we're interested in, you see, Mrs Grant,' Othen replied. Kerry saw her gaze at him as if aware they meant to block her from some of the stuff they knew. Much of the already doubtful friendliness had slipped from her face. She was not smiling now.

'So the suggestion is that one of these men wanted a relationship with Melissa,' Mrs Grant asked, 'and came back to see her?'

'Conceivably,' Othen replied.

'And raped, buggered and killed her?'

'We have many possibilities,' Kerry replied. 'We work by eliminating all but the right one. Well, by trying to.'

Kerry saw a small green Fiat stop on the driveway.

'There's absolutely no reason for Avril to know about the sexual violations,' Kerry replied.

'Thank you,' she said.

'Mr and Mrs Slater told you about the abuse as well as the death?' Othen asked.

'Oh, no, no indeed,' Mrs Grant said. 'Theirs was a simple tragic message to say only that Melissa had been murdered. We knew already. My husband was in London on business at the time of her death and read of it in the Press. He telephoned us, of course. Or telephoned me. I broke it to Avril – broke it that Melissa had been killed. No more than that.'

'Of course not,' Kerry said.

Avril was out of the car. She did not look much more than thirteen or fourteen now, but Kerry could see that with some work on her hair and in the right clothes she would. She wore baggy sand-coloured trousers and a black T-shirt with some kind of astrological motif on it. The Oporto English school must be relaxed about clothes. She carried an open holdall in which Kerry could see books and folders. Avril waited for her father who seemed to be gathering things from the back seat of the Fiat. In a moment he joined her. Kerry saw tallness, thinness, creeping baldness front and back, fairish to mousy hair, bony pale to sallow face. He had a briefcase in his left hand and a carrier bag containing what might be food in the other. He disappeared with Avril presumably into a doorway below. Emma Grant went from the room and out on to the landing to let them know there were visitors. When the three entered she made the introductions. Brian Grant shook hands with Kerry

183

and Vic and seemed to her affable and interested. Perhaps selling came into his work and he might be able to switch on the pleasantness. Avril stayed back, as if wanting to be ignored. She was fair to blonde like her mother, pale-skinned, longish-faced, again like her mother, but with more delicate features and a greater shapeliness to mouth and chin, though this might just be one of the pluses of youthfulness.

She did not know anything about a motorcyclist. She and Melissa had met no men at the cinema. Florence Cass was a nice girl but she got things wrong, made up things, she was a dreamer, it was well known. She would see something and then build up all kinds of tales from it. Avril would never go anywhere with someone so much older than herself, and especially not to the cinema. She did not think Melissa would either. Their parents had told them over and over to be careful when they were out in the town.

'That's certainly true,' Brian Grant said, 'and I'm really pleased it sank in, Av.'

Kerry decided, fuck this. 'We're talking about the Regis, Avril,' she said. 'Do you remember the Regis back home? And the film was *Trainspotting*.'

'We would never get in to see *Trainspotting*,' Avril replied.

'This is that film about drugs and all sorts of things, isn't it?' Emma Grant asked.

'Florence couldn't get in there, but one of the men bought the tickets for the four of you, so the girl at the box wouldn't see how young you were,' Kerry said.

'Not a chance,' Avril replied. 'They know that trick. They watch.'

'I wondered if you got scared and did a runner,' Kerry said.

'Scared?'

'Of the men.'

'I would be scared if I was with them. So would Mel.'

'A runner?' Emma Grant said.

'Got clear,' Kerry replied.

'But how would this man know how to find Melissa if that were so?' Emma Grant asked.

'Florence.'

'It's rubbish,' Avril replied.

'I think we'd better leave this, don't you?' Brian Grant asked. 'A mix-up by the sound of it.'

Vic Othen said: 'You didn't call on the Slaters while you were over there on your business trip, did you – old friends? When you read of Melissa's death, for instance.'

'I was flying back that day,' Grant said. 'I tried to telephone them from a Heathrow booth to say how sorry I was but could get no reply. Perhaps they were out. Perhaps they were not answering. That would be understandable. We have e-mailed sympathy from here.'

'Ah, e-mail,' Othen replied.

Kerry's bed at the hotel was double and they used that. They did not bother to disturb Vic's. It was Harry Bell they had to fool – or try to fool – not the hotel. 'It's only one night, but not a one-night stand,' she whispered to him when he was in her and lovingly taking his time in her.

'Of course not. A way of life.'

'And not just a job thing,' she said.

39

There was another call for Kerry to go up and see Harry Bell. She had already told him they learned nothing much in Portugal so it would not be about that. She did not rate the engulfing sense of edginess in the presence of Brian and Emma Grant as anything worth talking about to Harry, and he would not have rated it either. God, this time he might have those damned delicatessen people with him, all mouth and nosiness.

But he was alone in his office. It *was* to do with the delicatessen, though. Bell said: 'Kerry, we've been in touch with a Mr and Mrs Conti who run a business down in the centre. George Ince and Hilary were looking in at some more shops with pictures of Melissa – oh, I've asked George to drop the headmaster inquiries: nothing there beyond natural unpleasantness. Mr and Mrs Conti told George and Hilary they had not seen the girl but that they did, *of course*, have one of George's and

Hilary's colleagues upstairs above their shop watching something on the day. George asked which colleague, what "of course"? They had assumed George and Hilary knew about it. *None* of us knew about it but we worked out from the description that it must have been you. Was there something I should know about?' Harry asked.

'Not really,' Kerry replied at once, her voice good, she thought. 'I wanted to keep one of our informants under surveillance. This is the girl code-named Cheryl. Lois Fauld.'

'Ah,' Bell replied. 'Cheryl, yes. I expect so. Apparently Mr and Mrs Conti mentioned to one of their customers on the day that they had a detective upstairs. They realise this was gossipy of them but they were intrigued and were good enough to admit it to George and Hilary. Only one customer. George and Hilary traced her, just in case. She said that when she came out of the shop she looked around to see if she could find what it was you were watching. Curious, you know. A Saab was pulling away with she thinks two people in it. She could only see it from behind. But what interested her was a man who seemed to have been watching the Saab from further down the street and who now ran back to a Laguna that was parked on double yellows, jumped in and appeared to tail the Saab. I expect the man and the Laguna were out of your vision. She was so interested she took the number of the Laguna on the back of a chequebook. She waited a minute or two outside the shop in case you appeared and also followed the Saab. She could have given you the Laguna number. But you didn't – not while she waited, anyway – and she came to the conclusion that none of this was what occupied you, so she went home. But she was able to find the registration number for George and Hilary.'

'Oh, yes?' Kerry said.

'Titch has a Saab, hasn't he?'

'I think he has.'

'Was Cheryl-Lois meeting Titch?'

'Oh, no.'

'Of course, there are a lot of Saabs.'

'Yes,' Kerry replied.

'The Laguna was from a London car hire fleet.'

And, Christ, oh, Christ, on the day, the right day, the hirer was Brian Grant, wasn't it, wasn't it? The intuition swooped on her, stuck its beak hard and savage into her thinking.

'The car was hired for several days by a Brian Grant, whose address was given as the Mayfield Hotel, Earls Court. I think Melissa's little friend Avril is called Grant, isn't she?'

'Is there a description of the running man?' Kerry replied.

Bell looked at a note. 'Tall, lean, fairish, thinning hair, sallow skin.'

'That's her father.'

'What would he be doing here? He works in Portugal now, doesn't he?'

'He was in Britain on business.'

'We *know* that?' Harry asked, his round, friendly face intent.

'We do.'

'So what goes on, Kerry?'

Yes, what went on? She thought of the chill in the Slater household when anything to do with the Grants was mentioned. God, something between Slater and Avril and hence the withdrawal to Portugal? Did the resentment stick with Brian Grant, to a point when he sneaks back and takes vengeance on Slater's child? Perhaps when Melissa turned around on the estate it was because she had spotted him, not Gaston, and knew there might be trouble. How? She might have retreated and possibly met the motorcycle man again. He could have taken her down to see Titch, Grant following. Melissa must have persuaded motorcycle man that the meetings with Titch were only business, no cause for jealousy. Grant would observe the meeting with Titch, then tail the Saab until Titch put Melissa down. Perhaps he picked her up then – forcibly, maybe. Grant could have been back in London before Melissa's death was reported by the media. The motorcycle man would never come forward and explain what happened for fear of being involved as one of the last people with her. Thank God for the hire car. Grant would have had to provide proof of identity for that: documentation, his real, easily traceable name.

'I can't make it out, sir,' she replied.

'You saw Grant in Portugal?'

'Yes.'

'Did he say he had been down this way?'

'He specifically said he hadn't.'

'Why would he do that? Something wrong between these two families?' Bell asked.

'It's possible,' Kerry said. But the Slaters would not suspect Grant. They could not know he was in Britain at the time, because Grant's booth phone call from Heathrow failed to reach them – if there really was a booth phone call. Wouldn't Grant have been mad to risk that? Perhaps he *was* mad, but revenge mad, not careless mad. He would not have appeared on any paedophile list. This was a one-off act for him, a vengeance act, not a way of life.

Of course, buried in Harry Bell's question, and not buried very deeply, lay the assumption that it was Melissa in the Saab and that Kerry knew it was Melissa in the Saab but could not say she knew it was Melissa in the Saab. He would let it lie? He knew what detectives were like, especially fast-track detectives. He knew the routes towards a provable case were often devious, and he would accept them.

'Is there any way of finding whether some sort of hatred existed, some kind of hellishness between the Slaters and Grants?' Bell asked.

'The two girls were in touch by e-mail,' Kerry said.

'Wiped?'

'But bits of such stuff are sometimes recoverable. They brought a few wiped letters out of the machine in the Clinton-Lewinski case.'

'Recover what you can,' he said, 'here and in Portugal. Stir Interpol if necessary.'

She stood up.

He stood, too, and smiled. 'Kerry, you did damn well to be at that spot above the deli, didn't you? Fast-track skills on show. We'd have no registration number otherwise, no lead to Grant.'

'Thank you, sir.'

'Regardless of what you were there for, regardless of why you delayed.'

40

Only a disjointed spatter of fragments from three erased e-mails between the two girls could be salvaged, like snippets of a torn-up letter blown in the wind: perhaps the technology was more advanced in the States, and, of course, they would have used their very best retrieval people when it involved dogging the President. All the same, these garbled scraps of the Melissa-Avril correspondence were just about enough: enough with his lies to justify an application for Brian Grant's extradition – 'sextradition', as Vic called it. DNA would do the rest. Kerry and Vic returned to Portugal to bring him back.

On the night before the court hearing she and Vic again booked two rooms and used one, this time in Oporto at a flashier hotel not far from the jail. They were thinking about sleep when Kerry said: 'Vic, I hung about above that bloody delicatessen, debating whether to follow Melissa. If I hadn't, I might at least have been given the car registration by the woman customer. Yes, at least.'

Vic was lying on his stomach in bed having what might be the day's last cigarette. He gave his frame another fat parcel of sucked-in smoke before answering. The words emerged sharp and clouded: 'Oh, God, not another self-scourge session. Don't, Kerry. It's still out of character. You hung about because you thought Melissa was safe. She *was*, from Titch. The hire car number would not have meant anything to you then. Or not in time. Melissa would have died, just the same. Grant would still have been determined to do his pay-back.'

'Yes. We could have got him sooner, though.'

'So? We've got him. That will do. Policing is about making the best of a dud hand, like most jobs. Stop craving forgiveness. You don't need it.'

Kerry had a copy of the e-mail material with her. She wanted Grant to hear it, wanted him to know his daughter had more or less rumbled him. On the plane back, Vic released the handcuffs which locked Grant and him together, and Kerry, sitting on Brian Grant's other side, indicated and read out quietly bits of the letters that in their incomplete, struggling way foresaw Melissa's destruction. It did not please Kerry to be close alongside him, nor to have to get even nearer when she explained the extracts. Was there a stink from Grant? No, she knew there wasn't but longed to think there was. She could have put it down to shame, couldn't she? Or fright. On the whole she would have hoped fright. He wore a very good dark suit – almost as good as one of Gaston Devereux's – and looked flimsy and lost, but exceptionally svelte. He must be planning to appear like a wholesome non-murderous non-raping non-sodomiser to a jury when it came to that, and it would.

At one or two spots she had written in translations of the code. 'Here, you see,' she said, and pushed her finger slowly along one fractured almost opaque statement: '... *seem better with each other now but she looked* REALLY *ratty on Tuesday when he said to me did I ever hear about you these days and so I pretended I* ... This one is from Melissa, Mr Grant. My view is it would have started, *My mother and father seem better*, and so on. How it ended – what she pretended – it's hard to guess. Pretended not to hear? Could be. Her father was still interested in Avril, perhaps?'

'I wouldn't be surprised,' Grant replied. He sounded sickened by the idea and crushed, and looked away from the paper. There was a tiny, momentary flash of pink-to-red on those yellowy cheeks. Perhaps rage lingered in him even now, despite what he had done to expend it all on Melissa, and despite his present-seeming collapse into defeat.

Give the bugger – yes, that – a bit more. 'And this,' she said, pointing again: '... *going mad. I said it before. He is.* Meaning you?'

Grant glanced at the paper, then turned away again towards Vic and the window and did not reply.

'Meaning you?' Vic asked. 'But definitely not mad in the diminished responsibility sense that might get you off.'

Grant stayed silent.

'Of course meaning you,' Vic said.

Kerry read from another sheet: '... *bloody country which is a tip. He keeps saying why are you all right Mel. He says you are all right but I am over here putting out for a teacher twice as old because this is what I am used to. This is how my d. (dad) talks such as* PUTTING OUT. *It is a lie. I think he might come over there Mel. He is so ratty and mad.'*

'Undoubtedly you,' Vic told him. 'You hate Portugal, poor dear?'

'She's a sharp kid, your Avril,' Kerry said. 'Look: . . . *maybe he would not stay all the time in London he might come there. Perhaps you . . .* Perhaps you what? It didn't save her, whatever it was.'

Avril and her mother had arrived at Oporto airport in the Fiat to see Grant off. Vic unmanacled him then, too, and the family talked privately for ten minutes in a room in the airport police building, Kerry and Vic waiting outside. Afterwards, Grant's wife and child had waved through a window as he, Kerry and Vic were driven in a police car out to the aircraft from the lounge: waved once then immediately turned away and disappeared. 'They've got some thinking to do, I expect,' Vic had told him. 'They must decide whether they'll ever want to fly over to visit you in jail.'